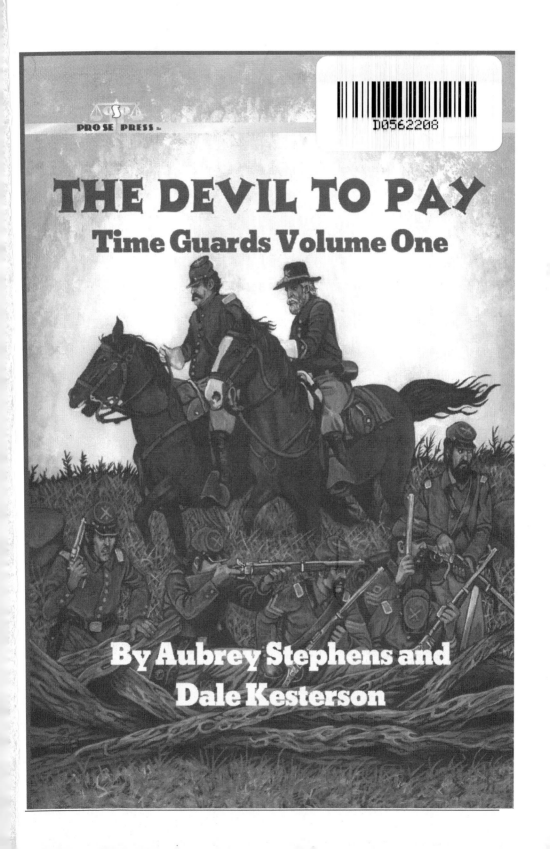

PRO SE PRESS ™

THE DEVIL TO PAY
Time Guards Volume One

By Aubrey Stephens and Dale Kesterson

The Devil to Pay

TIME GUARDS VOLUME ONE

Aubrey Stephens & Dale Kesterson

Pro Se Press

Aubrey Stephens & Dale Kesterson /Pro Se Press Publication
www.prosepress.com

Book Layout © 2016 BookDesignTemplates.com

The Devil to Pay: Time Guards Volume One/ Aubrey Stephens & Dale Kesterson. -- 1st ed.
ISBN 979-8-6313149-9-3

CONTENTS

CHAPTER ONE

Part One: The Setting

The hot June sun beat down on the dusty road. The troops in blue were wearing a thin dusting over their exposed skin, and the blue cloth took on a slightly brown cast from the fine particles. Their faces were as distinctive as terrain maps, cut by rivulets where sweat had coursed through the heavy coat of dust. The men were tired, but there was a surge of palpable energy throughout the ranks as they took their position on the slight hill just beyond the town of Gettysburg.

Looking down on his troops from the steeple of the seminary, a very determined, almost sinister-looking man carefully considered the scene before him. Concentration etched his face as he gazed beyond his own blue-clad troops to those in grey belonging to the Army of Northern Virginia. He knew well enough that where a small representation of Lee's army was visible, the main force would not be far behind. Today, in this quiet Pennsylvania town, the only thing available to stop the unbeaten Confederates was his brigade of cavalry. The relief he had requested had not yet arrived. The idea of his cavalry, holding alone against the Rebels for an undetermined length of time reminded him too much of another field of battle.

John Buford turned to his aide. "If the Rebels gain this ground they will control the entire fight, and then we'll have the devil to pay." His voice was soft but deep, forceful, and slightly bitter.

As Buford spoke, several horsemen rode up to the foot of the building. Buford leaned forward to determine who had arrived at his command. It was with a feeling of relief, more overwhelming than he would or could admit to those around him, that he saw the riders were General Reynolds and his senior staff.

Seeing Buford in the tower, Reynolds hailed him with a jaunty, "John! What is happening?"

"There's the devil to pay," shouted Buford in reply, with his face settling into a slight frown. "We have run into Rebels and they appear to be gathering in force to advance on this position."

"My troops are at least four hours behind me, but they are going to be coming up fast." Reynolds fixed the other officer with a hard stare. "John, can you hold?"

Buford, realizing that fate was putting the whole mess in his hands, thought briefly before replying, "I reckon we can. We'll hold until you come." As these words were spoken aloud, his thoughts raced. *By heaven, we'd better hold, or Bobby Lee is going to kick the Army of the Potomac in the teeth again. And if he does it this time, the only thing between him and Washington would be the crowd of Rebel sympathizers cheering him as his army marches down Pennsylvania Avenue to the White House.*

Buford turned to climb down the ladder, his defense plans formulating in his head. He was hoping to avoid another Thoroughfare Gap, but that depended in part upon Reynolds and his force.

The battle began with the rattle of gunfire, which could have been early Fourth of July fireworks, but wasn't. All through the long, hot, dusty afternoon day the already-weary Union soldiers skirmished against the butternut and grey-clad figures in front of them. The Rebels' relentless pressure began to tell, until finally, as the afternoon waned, the boys in blue began to give way. Pulling back their lines, the union troops reluctantly retreated, heading back towards the town they were trying to defend.

"That's a wrap!" The assistants relayed the message to the troops after receiving the word from the director.

It was Saturday, the 27th of June, 2015, just outside of Gettysburg, Pennsylvania.

A cheer went up from the Confederates as Buford's troops left their lines. Dust-streaked and just as reluctantly leaving their lines, the Rebels were treated to a returned cheer, a salute from their Union counterparts.

Soon both armies intermingled, as the now-genuinely weary re-enactors returned to their camp and began the ages-old ritual of swapping stories of the day's fight, ready to enjoy the luxury of finishing up before four o'clock.

This gathering was a bit different, even for the "veteran" living historians, because there were a few extra items on the battlefield and a new roster of orders in addition to the usual military ones. This time cameras, directors, and call sheets were evidence of a documentary in progress.

As he made his way to the medical tent, John Andrews noted that the layout of the camp was more elaborate—as if the re-enactors were trying to convince the filmmakers that this was not a totally primitive location. He also noted that some of his fellow veterans were grousing about having to do some of the skirmishes over. Smiling to himself, he decided that it would all work out in the end. Camera angles and battle angles would eventually converge.

His smile faded somewhat as he approached the first aid tent, and he stopped outside to listen.

"I'm sorry but if the past four hours are anything to go by, a half a dozen elastic bandages aren't going to last," a familiar feminine voice stated evenly. "I agreed to run this first aid unit, but I can't do it without supplies."

Mary Catherine Howell was up to form, John decided as he made his entrance. He stood just inside to watch as she confronted both the re-enactment coordinator and the documentary's associate producer.

Cathy, all five feet and ninety-five pounds of her, was staring up at the towering coordinator. Her whole posture enforced her demands, which John suspected were entirely within reason. A doctor used to running a major emergency room wouldn't back down through intimidation, which is what they were trying to do. As she switched her gaze to the associate producer, John smiled to himself. *Facing Cathy wasn't easy, even if she did look like a thirteen-year-old boy in her current outfit.* The loose blouse and slightly baggy trousers didn't disguise her professionalism.

"Mr. Steiner, unless you want your extras limping *into* battle tomorrow, I'll need additional items, supplies," Cathy said simply. "Any drug store will have the necessary items."

"Dr. Howell," John Andrews interrupted, "I told you that we can't have twenty-first-century Band-Aids showing during a nineteenth-century fight."

"Dr. Andrews," she replied, too sweetly, "Does *your* ankle-wrap show?"

"Ah, John," the relieved coordinator greeted him, "How did the last skirmish go?"

"Fairly well, Randy, at least from my viewpoint," Andrews responded. "I have been hearing grumbles about having to do things twice or three times, but still, it's not bad for the first day."

"I understand," Randall Thomas nodded. "And in spite of the current dispute, I do want to thank you for bringing us Dr. Howell." The tall, barrel-chested coordinator smiled at the petite doctor.

"Glad to help out, Mr. Thomas," Cathy said, also smiling, which took taking some of the sting out of her words. "It reminds me of home."

"Home, Dr. Howell?" David Steiner asked, puzzled.

"Dr. Howell runs the emergency department at our university hospital," Andrews explained. "She's used to chaos."

"So for your vacation, you came here," Randy Thomas wondered aloud, scratching his head.

"I figured it had to be easier than a major medical center over a summer weekend," she admitted. "So far I've been right. But I would like to ask a question, if I may."

"Fire away," the coordinator said with a slight bow.

"What idiot decided to shoot this film in the high heat of late June?"

"Cathy, the battle took place at this time of the year," Andrews reminded her.

"Then it's up to you fellows to make sure all your men have full canteens and make use of them, or we'll lose more people to heatstroke than sprained ankles." Cathy smiled; this time it wasn't sweet.

"We are after a realistic re-enactment," Steiner said defensively.

"I doubt that a constant supply of water will show any more than the elastic bandages will," she returned. "I also doubt that the Civil War combatants were used to air conditioning and driving everywhere. You may be recreating a battle that took place over a hundred and fifty years ago, but you're populating it with men who are used to modern comforts."

John Andrews barely smothered a chuckle at the producer's expression. To further cover his reaction, he added, "She has a point."

"Thank you, er, Dr. Andrews. Are you a member of her staff?" Steiner shifted his glance between the slender man in the dusty Union captain's uniform and the small physician in her period outfit. John had selected it with care after asking Cathy if she wanted to appear feminine. Her answer ("I need to be *comfortable*, not pretty!") had not surprised him. Hence her clothes.

"No, I don't qualify."

"John holds a doctorate in civil engineering, not medicine," Cathy supplied. "He teaches at the University of Missouri."

"John Andrews, at your service," he added, extending his hand. "I head up the Third Missouri dismounted cavalry, and we are honored to be here."

"John, was there a specific reason you came in? Do I need to readjust the strapping?" Cathy's question held genuine concern as well as being to the point.

"No, it's fine. I just wanted to make sure you stopped long enough for supper. Besides, I have a present for you."

"Dr. Howell, if you will make out a list of the articles you need, I will make sure you get your supplies," David Steiner told her. "When can you have one ready?"

"Now." She tore a sheet of paper from the wooden clipboard John recognized as the one he had given her when she graduated from medical school and handed the list to the producer. "It's as reasonable as I can make it. Most of it is to replenish supplies we have used today."

He scanned the list quickly. "This is first-aid stuff. don't you need medicine?"

"Mr. Steiner, I assure you all I am going to do here is basic treatment. If anything trickier arises, it'll go to a fully equipped facility. From what I have seen today, we'll get more sprains and abrasions than anything else. I'm only requesting the casting materials in case I have to immobilize a limb or two."

"Are you sure that's it?"

"I have my own field kit, if anything unexpected comes up." She lifted up a large back-pack. "I can perform minor surgeries, if necessary. I plan to be mobile, but in constant touch with the base here."

"How?"

"One of the major advantages we have over our nineteenth-century counterparts is technology," Randy Thomas answered. "We provide all department coordinators with portable communications."

Steiner noticed the small holster seated around Cathy Howell's waist for the first time as she drew and brandished a two-way radio. Thomas had one as well.

The associate producer nodded satisfied with the arrangements. "I'll have the supplies to you within the hour." He gave orders to his assistant as they left the tent.

"Dr. Howell, forgive me for underestimating you." Randy Thomas gave a sweeping cavalier's bow. The re-enactment coordinator had rarely been more gallant, Andrews noted wryly, in spite of the fact that she was dressed in something their drummer boy could wear, right down to her shoes.

"Please, the name is Cathy. Didn't John warn you about me when he volunteered me?"

"Mary Catherine, may I also present my compliments?" John Andrews grinned, his dark brown eyes twinkling. He knew, from long experience, how susceptible - not - she would be to the flattery.

"Only if you quit calling me Mary," she responded, "But what did I do now?"

"My dear girl, you have single-handedly cowed the presence of an egotistical producer."

"I haven't been your 'dear girl' since high school," she noted dryly, "He's an associate producer, and his ego wasn't any worse than your average surgeon's. You mentioned something about supper. It's early, isn't it? I want to wait until the supplies come in."

Randy spoke up. "I can have the supplies delivered to your tent, Cathy. Why don't you take a break while you can?"

"What a novel concept – a break in a work day. John, give me a minute and I'll be right with you."

John and Randy watched her as she gave instructions to the medical team with whom she would be working for the weekend, leaving Gail Collins, the registered nurse, in charge for the rest of the shift. She also stowed some more materials into her backpack, making it a fully equipped field kit.

"That's quite a lady," Randy commented as he watched her. "Are you two, er, an item?"

John Andrews threw back his head and laughed heartily. "Randy, trust me. She's more than you can handle."

"And you can?" Thomas was frowning slightly. "You didn't answer my question."

"I've known her long enough to know that Cathy only looks like a small, defenseless sprite," Andrews replied vaguely. "Have no doubts, Randy. That is one dedicated and efficient lady who puts her career first."

"Where will she be sleeping?"

"You don't give up, do you?" The professor returned question for question. "In case you need her, she'll be in my tent."

"Your tent? You? The hermit of the Union Army? She'll be with you?" Thomas' skepticism was evident in his chuckle.

"I'm all set, John, at least for now," Cathy commented as she rejoined the two men. She hoisted her large backpack. "Did I miss something?"

"Randy was concerned about your sleeping arrangements," Andrews replied.

"I'm with you, aren't I?" Cathy frowned. "I mean, that's okay, isn't it?"

"It's fine," Randy responded. "It's just a little unusual – especially for John. Most of us call him 'the Hermit of the Union Army.'

"The hermit?" She looked up at her friend with a slight smile, always pleased with what she saw in the strong, intelligent face framed with dark, almost black, wavy hair. "I guess that fits."

John Andrews relieved her of the back-pack and offered his arm. "Shall we go?"

"I'd like the chance to change clothes. – and by the time we get to supper, I'll probably be starved!" She grinned. "You told me I don't have to dress like this all the time." She looked up at Randy Thomas. "He insisted that I wear period clothes even for the medical tent."

"Well, it wasn't absolutely necessary but it does help," the tall man replied. "We like to have everyone on-site blend in, especially if the documentary people start wandering around with cameras."

"I can understand that – John gave me the choice of wearing a long skirt or trousers. I wanted freedom of movement, so we went this route."

"Cathy, our first stop is my tent. I have a present for you." Andrews winked at Thomas. "Randy, we'll catch up with you at the mess tent."

"I'm looking forward to seeing you later, Cathy," Randy said, smiling as he gave her another bow.

Cathy insisted on checking the delivery of first aid supplies the producer's assistant brought to their tent before doing anything else. John saw she was pleased as she packed a second field kit and stashed it with the first one in her huge duffle bag. He then gave her the large box he had shipped as a surprise for her to Randy, who lived in the area of the re-enactment.

A little over an hour later, John had the satisfaction of seeing his comrades gape, open-mouthed, at the sight he and Cathy made as they entered the mess tent. With all the regal bearing of a queen, Mary Catherine made the outfit he had commissioned for her as much a part of her as she did the Tudor dress she wore for Society of Creative Anachronism events. This was a much simpler camp day dress, designed for day wear with a petticoat (no hoops). He had chosen a dark green skirt and shoulder shawl to set off her dark auburn hair and green eyes, with a light green blouse for contrast. Her hair, swept up into a graceful bun, almost looked like a reddish-gold crown. He had washed and changed into a clean uniform, and his smile reflected his enjoyment of the moment. He wore the standard dress of a cavalry officer, although he had a complete civilian outfit in his gear, complete with vest. To Cathy's eyes, he presented the appearance of a chivalrous nineteenth-century officer. John Andrews, although not 'Hollywood handsome,' was well above the baseline for attractive. He wore his outfit like a true uniform, rather than a costume.

The overall effect of their appearance brought his group to their feet, mostly out of shock. This was the first time any of his friends had seen him with a date, and he was basking in the fun of it. As dinner progressed, Cathy was pleased to see John was relaxed, especially when she saw the glint of humor in his dark brown eyes. Playing her part, which they had discussed on the drive, she graciously turned aside other suggestive advances from the men who were still a bit skeptical. John was asking them to accept that she was both his good friend and a capable physician as well. The first they would just have to take on his word and her actions; the second she would amply demonstrate.

After dinner, John offered to walk her around the camp, which was near part of the actual battlefield. As they strolled, he became her tour guide, explaining in generalities what had taken place.

"I have always paid more attention to the Red and White Roses than I have the Blue and Grey," she admitted, "But this is fascinating. It's a shame that we still have to listen to traffic noises and jets overhead. Otherwise, it would be possible to imagine we are back in the 1860s."

"You're not sorry you came?"

"Not at all," she smiled at him, "even though you did buffalo me into it."

"The last three times we've had the chance to talk, you've sounded like you needed a break," John told her honestly. "Plus, we needed a doctor up here. A vacation isn't going to kill either one of us."

"You know me too well." Her expression changed. Frowning slightly, she slipped her arm through his. "Maybe in this place, with so much gallantry around, one of us will be able to answer the question which has plagued anyone who knows us."

John Andrews nodded. At five feet seven inches he wasn't tall, but he seemed to tower over his small companion. Looking down at her, he smiled. Friends since early childhood, closer than most of the married couples he knew, and totally comfortable in each other's company, their relationship had puzzled many, including their parents. "I know. We have known each other most of our lives, and I've always felt closer to you than other person."

"I agree. We always enjoy being together, yet we've never crossed the line to a more romantic relationship. Haven't you wondered why?"

"Wondered? Yes, and often. Been actively bothered by it? No. We've both been busy, too. Besides," he grinned, "We have time. Meanwhile, let's go back and join the gang. It's time for some serious story-swapping." John formally gave her his arm and led her back to camp.

The rest of the evening became a bit of a blur with stories and songs around the campfire, accented with beer and wine. Cathy enjoyed watching John have fun. Her title of physician tended to intimidate the other girlfriends present; she was used to that. John kept an eye on her and saw that she expertly turned more than one pass aside. He also wryly noted that as the alcohol flowed, the passes were more frequent and less genteel. *Oh well, she could handle that, and a lot more.*

When they retired to their tent, Cathy was amused to see that John was embarrassed by the antics of his fellows. She also saw that he was a little the worse for the wine. The night air was chillier than Cathy had imagined it would be, so she gratefully sought the double bedroll John had borrowed for the occasion.

"Cathy?" John slightly slurred her name. "I hope you don't mind..." His voice trailed off uncertainly.

"What?"

"The guys, sharing the tent, you know..." He was sleepy but wanted to make sure she wasn't offended. "I'm sorry."

"Don't be, John," she replied, smiling to herself. "Go to sleep."

"I'm glad you came, Cathy. G'night."

*****

John Andrews' eyes snapped open as if something had jarred him to consciousness. He propped himself on his elbow, and let his eyes adjust to the soft illumination which came through the white canvas of the tent. A noise was coming from Cathy's communication unit, and he turned it off. It seemed to him that the moon was especially bright - bright enough to give a silvery blue tint to the light filtering into the tent. It looked as if someone had turned on a major strobe, using an odd rotating filter to cast weird shadows; it was a familiar pattern, but his mind was too fogged with sleep and alcohol to put a name to it. He knew the studio's lights were removed each night, so that wasn't it. According to the watch he pulled from the pocket on his uniform, it was a minute past midnight.

While wondering what woke him, he noticed a warm bundle snuggled up to his back. He shifted slightly surprised he could see Cathy so clearly. The flickering light and the soundness of her sleep made her look much younger than her thirty-five years and far too young to head (and sometimes terrify) a staff of doctors. He brushed a strand of hair from her cheek and eased back down next to her, without disturbing her. He knew, from experience, that the five a.m. call would come much too soon. He dropped back to sleep.

CHAPTER TWO

Sunday

When he next opened his eyes, it was daylight and much later than it should have been. John recognized that he was more than likely being set up for a massive practical joke because he knew his unit was finding great humor in him having company. It was a form of initiation he could easily do without. Still, it wouldn't do to delay the production. Quickly pulling on his daily uniform pants, John stuck his head out of the tent flap in hopes of getting the big laugh over with before Cathy woke up. Forcing the sleep out of his eyes, he stared at the sight in front of him, too startled to move or speak.

It was overcast, threatening rain at any minute, instead of the sunny weather which had been predicted. That wasn't the problem. The problem was the view.

Where there had been row upon row of white canvas tents the night before, there were only the trees and undergrowth normally found in a forest. The clearing, which had been crammed with men and tents, was now totally empty. A look of worry appeared on his normally calm face. His engineer's mind, trained in logical cause and effect progressions, strained to find an explanation. None came.

At that moment Cathy awoke and called his name.

"Catie," he replied with a trace of tension in his voice, "I think you should see something."

"All right," she mumbled, wondering why he used her childhood nickname. "What's the problem?"

"I need you to see this," he persisted. "Please."

"Why? Is something wrong?" She struggled to extricate herself from the sleeping roll. She noticed the high spirits which had been bubbling in his voice the evening before had vanished.

"I need to know that you see it too." His voice was strangely flat. "It's important to me."

"Okay, I'll look, but I'm still foggy," she warned as she joined him at the tent's opening. She looked out, saw the now-empty clearing and noted the absence of the other tents and men. As they both stared, trying to make sense out it, they realized that the noises from the hundreds of men and women involved with the war re-enactment were also missing. The only sounds they could hear were the chirping of birds and distant rain.

The silence became eerie.

"Johnny," Cathy began slowly, unable to bear the silence any longer, "Where is everyone?" She used his childhood name as he had used hers, perhaps reaching for a more secure time in their lives.

"Catie, if only my company was missing, I'd say we were the victims of a practical joke." John found it hard to swallow.

"Johnny, they're *all* missing. That's some joke." She pulled her head back in and started to get dressed.

"I know." He crawled out of the tent and stood.

A quick survey of the area revealed no signs that there had ever been a tent bivouac. Although the living history units were good about packing out garbage and leaving sites as clean as possible, there was always *some* sign of the camp, even if it was just matted grass. In his short stroll, he saw no sign that there had ever been a tent city in the vicinity.

Cathy emerged from their tent wearing her drummer boy out-fit as he was kneeling to examine the area where Randy Thomas' tent had last been seen.

"Well?"

He looked up, bewildered. "I can't even find the holes from the tent pegs. If you were to go by the signs, or lack of them, it would be impossible to prove there had ever been a bunch of tents here. It also rained last night, apparently hard."

"But it was perfectly clear when we went to bed. Johnny, this is insane. There *has* to be an explanation."

"I'll be damned if I can see what it is. There is no way to hide this many guys. A company or two, maybe, but not the whole damned army." John rose shaking his head. "Catie, I'm stumped. If the whole unit moved, the noise alone should have awakened us. If we were moved, we should have awakened."

"Okay, I have an idea."

"I'm open to suggestions..."

"Do we have the supplies to make some coffee? We both function better with caffeine."

"Right." John rummaged in the tent and set up an area for a small fire. He stopped when he realized he needed water. No support trucks, no water.

"I have a better idea," he countered. "Let's pack up, grab the car, and go out for breakfast."

"Sounds fine to me," Cathy replied. "Why don't you go for the car while I pack?"

She had finished loading their packs when John returned. He was walking slowly, looking very dazed, almost in shock.

"Johnny, what's wrong?"

"Catie, we don't seem to have a car anymore."

"WHAT?" She dropped the large duffle bag she was zipping and stared at him. "It's been stolen? That's a rental!"

"There is no car parked where I left it." He raised his hand to stop her. "Wait, it gets better. The parking lot is gone, and so is the road."

Cathy's mouth fell open. Too much was going through her mind. She sank to her knees, swallowed, took three deep breaths, and looked up at her life-long friend. Her first attempt at speech failed. She swallowed again.

"Coffee?" She tried to smile.

He nodded. "There's a stream nearby."

"Maybe if we boil some water from the stream we won't die by parasite or waste ingestion. We need something normal and hot coffee is it." She was trying to become the logical practitioner in spite of their circumstances.

"You wouldn't happen to have any water purifying tablets, would you?"

"Of course I do, but there's something I want to try first. With luck, I even might be able to tell if it's toxic or not."

While John tried to find dry wood for a fire, Cathy went to the stream and drew a bucket. When she got it back to their tent, she dug into her backpack for what looked like a pool testing kit.

As he wrestled with the fire, John watched as she made a few tests, but before she said anything he knew Cathy was pleased.

"Clean?" he prompted.

"Remarkably," she responded with a grin. "According to this, I don't even have to add the tablets. I still think we should boil it, but it looks cleaner than I had a right to expect."

"Why the test kit?" John inquired as he put a pot on the fire. "We use tap water in the water buffalos."

"You know me. I'm a bit of a freak on clean water, so I got a field testing kit from the Ag department. I thought it would be interesting to take a few samples in the Pennsylvania wilderness. I never dreamed it would be necessary."

"That's my--" He broke off at her look. "Okay, the coffee is being made. Now what?"

"We decide what happened," she replied. "Remember, when all probable explanations fail, whatever is left, however improbable, must be the truth."

"Fine, sound like Sherlock Holmes. See if I care." He took the edge off his words with a smile. "Do you have a theory?"

She started humming a familiar theme from an old TV show.

"That's a hell of an answer," John said with a slight grimace. "Shall we wait until a man comes out from behind a rock or a tree and tells us that we've crossed the boundary?"

"He's late." Cathy yawned and stretched.

"All right, Mr. Serling loses. How about UFO kidnappings?"

"Without taking us? The nerve of some aliens," Cathy snorted. "Let's we save that until we're totally desperate. When it sounds like a good theory, we'll know we're going over the edge."

"Sounds reasonable," John murmured and winced at the pun. "Sorry, it just came out."

"Let's start with last night," Cathy said, generously skipping over it, "And see where we lost about fifteen hundred people."

"Right. We went to dinner, took a stroll, sat around the camp-fires swapping stories, were escorted to our tent, and went to sleep."

"Amidst a considerable amount of 'wink, wink, nudge, nudge' which I could have lived without," Cathy recalled, wrinkling her nose. "You didn't tell me I was coming to summer camp."

"I didn't think it was going to be that bad," John replied. "I did apologize."

"So you did. Then we got up this morning," Cathy continued, "And you…"

"Wait a minute," John interrupted. "Something woke me up during the night – I don't remember what - and there was a full moon. I thought it was odd because it was as bright as if someone had turned on a strobe light. I saw something else, but I was too sleepy to make it out."

"You saw a full moon last night?"

"Well, something woke me up and the interior of our tent was lit."

"Did you see the moon, or are you assuming light came from the moon?"

"I guess I assumed it was the moon."

"Uh, Johnny, I hate to be the bearer of bad news..."

"But?"

"There wasn't a full moon last night." Cathy watched his face as he digested her words.

"There was no full moon last night? You're sure?" John was hesitant.

"My head nurse keeps me well posted on these things," Cathy explained, "Whether I want to be or not. Trust me – he's good at this. There was no full moon last night. If I remember right, Gerry said the full moon was going to be on the first, which is still a few days off. There wouldn't have been enough light to illuminate much."

"If there was no full moon, then what the hell woke me up at midnight? Light did, but if it wasn't the moon, what was it?"

"How should I know? I was asleep."

"And cute, too." He ducked as she grabbed a handful of grass and threw it at him.

"Seriously, Johnny, what did you see? Think about it, without assuming moonlight."

"I saw light filtering through the canvas of the tent. We were nowhere near the big movie lights, and I couldn't think of anything else it could be, so I presumed it was a very bright moon."

"It was a logical, if erroneous, assumption. We assume what is familiar, like someone from New York feeling an earth tremor would assume a subway was nearby," she admitted. "How bright was the light? And how long did it last?"

"I'm not sure how long it lasted, but it was bright enough for me to see you clearly at midnight inside the tent," John confirmed. "That's how I know you're cute when you're asleep."

She grabbed another handful of grass but didn't throw it. Cathy stared at it. "I thought all the bivouac area was supposed to be mowed before we got here."

"It always has been, mostly to minimize the damage our activities would cause. Why?"

"This grass has never been cut."

"What? How can you tell?"

It was Cathy's turn to be on hands and knees to examine the ground. She crawled around a bit, then sat back and accepted a cup of coffee. She sipped at it for a moment, collecting her thoughts.

"I give no iron-clad guarantees, but I'm willing to bet that this grass may have been gnawed on by an occasional animal, and hacked by some sort of scythe, but not a power mower. Those blades leave a clean cut." Cathy moved back to the fire, suddenly chilled. "Johnny, it's also longer than it was yesterday."

John gave her a sharp look and did some examining himself.

"You're right." John took a sip of his coffee, trying to keep his hands from shaking. "Maybe we slept through the war."

"A full two days? I doubt that. How long could we have slept? I only had one beer, and unless someone spiked it, that's not enough to put me under for more than eight hours." Cathy looked at John, mischief in her eyes. "You, on the other hand, were downright tipsy."

"You weren't supposed to notice," John grimaced. "However, I don't think we can accept the Rip Van Winkle theory."

Cathy thought about it and nodded "I agree. Your beard isn't more than normal next-day stubble." She chuckled when he checked.

"What have we got so far?"

"A bright light at night, but no full moon. Assorted personnel missing, not to mention horses and equipment. A car gone, along with a parking lot, and a road. Grass that has grown overnight by at least an inch and a half. A beard which hasn't grown more than normal. A rain-drenched campsite when it hasn't rained. And two rather confused people." Cathy ticked the items off on her fingers.

"Something else is missing, you know," John said, looking up and around.

"Such as?"

"Jet contrails. The traffic noises we heard from this spot yesterday."

"Okay, so everything has vanished, leaving us here." Cathy tried to state it as fact, but her voice trembled.

"The opposite, that we have been somehow moved without any of those around us, could be equally true."

"Johnny, I have heard better choices."

"Well, it's simple enough. Either we have been moved, or they have been moved. Logic dictates that it would be easier to move us than the multitude."

"That sounds like two sides to the alien theory."

"Can you think of anything else?" John poured another cup of coffee.

"Don't ask reasonable questions in such unreasonable circumstances," she retorted. "And, no, I can't. Wait a minute. Yes, I can. My walkie-talkie unit."

She dug into her pack, pulled it out, and clicked the on button. Static sounded.

"Nothing."

"That's what woke me up! I heard this weird, whiney noise, and reached over to turn the radio off."

"You could see it?"

"I told you – the tent was lit up."

"I think this is where we came in. So now what?"

"When we finish here, we pack up, and we start walking."

"Do we have a destination?"

"Gettysburg." John pronounced the town's name with a certainty he was not sure he felt.

"Why Gettysburg?"

"It's there. It's been there for a long time."

"And if it's not there?"

"Catie, if the town of Gettysburg has vanished, then I will personally invite Mr. Serling into our camp."

"I hope he can make better coffee," was Cathy's reply as she picked up her backpack and duffle. "But if I see a huge, round rock with a hole in it, don't be surprised if I ask it a question."

John laughed. "If it responds by saying, 'A question...I have long waited for a question,' don't be surprised if all you can see is my dust."

Cathy's laughter echoed his, a little edgy. "Sounds fair to me."

John struck the tent, packed it, and they set off. He tried to remember to keep his strides short enough for Cathy to keep up, while he sought to find a familiar road. He found a road, but it was dirt.

John knew where the roads into town were with respect to the camping area. The main road from the park to the town wasn't there. There was a field where he thought a building should have been, and no sign of any asphalt, although there should have been an access road. He decided not to mention this to Cathy.

Cathy decided to ignore the mystery of their situation for the moment in favor of taking in the countryside. Even with the onset of a light misting rain, it was beautifully unspoiled, far more untouched than she imagined it would be. Somehow the dirt road fit the nostalgia of the area. She also found the air, like the stream, to be incredibly clean and free of pollutants.

"This is lovely! So natural..." She broke off as she noticed a man staring at her from a side road intersection ahead of them.

The man was dressed like a farmer from by-gone days, not even wearing blue jeans. Cathy thought he might be part of the general citizenry of the re-enactment. He was staring mostly, she felt, at her rather than John.

"Johnny?" Her voice dropped to a whisper. "That man is star-ing at me."

"At us, you mean," was his reply, also whispered. "It's prob-ably my uniform."

"I don't think so. I'm going to wave." Cathy flashed her brightest smile and waved at the man, adding a cheery "Good morning!"

As they approached him, the farmer slowly removed his hat but did not return the greeting.

"Good morning," John echoed.

The man nodded. "Captain, I feel I ought to warn you. The Rebels are here."

"What?" Cathy really didn't mean to say anything.

The farmer looked at her, taking in the pants, the shirt loosely tucked into them, and the hair pulled into a ponytail at the nape of her neck. "I'm sorry, boy, if I startled you but as a loyal Union man, I want to make sure that the Captain knew that Jubal Early and his men were in town a few days ago."

"My thanks, sir," John replied, tipping his hat. "I have been separated from my company for some time, and I have no current information."

"The Rebs are looking for food and shoes."

"That does tally with the general rumors I have heard." John looked at Cathy, who was standing next to him. "General Early's troops come up from the north through Chambersburg," he explained.

"Can we whup them?"

"I assure you, we shall certainly try," John replied, trying to sound authoritative, and repressing a smile.

"What unit are you with?"

"The Third Missouri Cavalry," John replied promptly.

"Cavalry, eh? Heard tell of a bunch of Union cavalry on the move towards these parts. Up from Emmitsburg. That's why I've been wondering if the Rebs are really coming back here." The farmer reached up to wipe his forehead with a handkerchief. "I had hoped that General Lee's boys wouldn't venture up this-a-way again after being here a while back. But they showed up in town last Friday and moved out again the day before yesterday. Preacher this morning told how our boys in blue are moving north to stay between the Rebs and Old Abe's house in Washington."

"Oh?" John smiled slightly. "I hope you townspeople aren't getting carried away."

"Excuse me," Cathy said politely to the farmer as she tugged at John's sleeve. "Cap'n, may I have a word with you, sir?"

"You, too?" John mumbled. He gave her a sharp look but followed her a short way from the farmer. "What gives?"

"John, that man may not be role-playing. I think he means every word he is saying. And today should be Sunday, June 28th, right?"

John nodded. "So?"

"According to him, today is Sunday."

"Well, it *is* Sunday. There are times that the townspeople, seeing the re-enactment and especially movie cameras, get carried away. I just thought he was a bit of a crackpot overdoing it. I know we're both nervous, but let's try…"

"I'm trying very hard not to be paranoid," Cathy insisted, "But if I know anything about human nature, that man is as practical and rational as they come."

"We need to know what day it is, John murmured.

"Just be careful how you put things to him," Cathy whispered as they rejoined their new acquaintance.

"Why don't you do the talking?" John suggested.

"Sir, if you will forgive me my ignorance, may I ask a question?" Cathy approached the farmer with a small smile.

"Of course, boy," the farmer returned the smile. "What do you need to know?"

"How far are we from town?"

"'Bout two miles, on this here road."

"This road?"

"Yes, this here is the Hagerstown road. If you take the left fork, it goes straight into Chambersburg Street."

"In Gettysburg?" Cathy tried to look friendly but dull.

"Of course Gettysburg," the farmer replied, not unkindly. "Youngster, it's plain that you are a stranger here. Have you got kin around these parts?"

"No, sir," Cathy replied, thinking fast. "I'm trying to get to some in the west." She looked down and kicked the dirt. "Could you tell me what day it is? I've been walking for a long time, and I've lost track of the days..." She let her voice trail off. She saw that John was staring at her. *I hope Johnny doesn't think I've totally lost my mind.*

"I reckon that it's Sunday, June 28th." The farmer looked at John. "You're helping the boy?"

"As much as I can, sir. He's been helping me, too," John added and smiled. "We'd best be on our way. Thank you for the directions."

As John and Cathy resumed their walk, they heard the farmer call out to them:

"God go with you, Captain! You have the prayers of the loyal Union behind you!"

*****

They continued until they were out of sight and earshot. Then John grabbed Cathy's arm and pulled her into a wooded area on the shoulder of the road.

"Catie, this can't be!"

"What do you mean?"

"If that farmer is right, and this is Sunday, the 28th of June, just outside of Gettysburg, we've been transported in time."

"Now who's getting carried away?" Cathy asked, pleading with him. "Today *IS* Sunday, the 28th of June, you know."

"Wait a minute – the days haven't changed?"

"Nope. Yesterday was Saturday, the 27th of June."

"Yes, 2015. You said that man wasn't role-playing. Are you taking that back?"

Cathy sighed. "No, I stand by that, Johnny. His sense of time, place, and person were intact."

"You are sure?"

"Everything he told us tallies within its own framework. The time references work with the day he quoted to us, and there were no contradictions. Also, there was no hesitation in anything that he said. It was all given freely and forthright." Cathy frowned slightly; John was once again reminded that his companion was a highly observant professional. "This is nuts."

"Okay, let's see. That man took my uniform in stride. He gave me a warning about enemy soldiers. If he is correct, and to-day is Sunday, the 28th of June, and we are just outside of Gettysburg, Pennsylvania, and the Confederate army has already passed by here, then we are in the year 1863. Maybe the years match, days and all."

"If that's true, it means - " Cathy's mind reeled with the implications.

"It means that one of the bloodiest battles in the history of humanity is going to take place in three days, and it is going to happen here."

Cathy sat down, hard, as if her legs would no longer hold her. The damp ground matched her spirits.

"Johnny, do you know what you're saying?" It was a whisper.

"Unfortunately, yes." John Andrews joined her on the ground.

"We've traveled back to the time of the battle? The actual time and place of the actual battle of Gettysburg? The real thing?" She was incredulous, and John didn't blame her.

"I'm having just as much trouble with this idea as you are," he told her gently. "Maybe more so. I'm wearing a uniform which could make me an active participant in the whole thing."

"This can't be real, this can't be happening," moaned Cathy. "It's crazy."

"I agree, but can you think of any other explanation which covers it?"

"Would you mind if we did some more checking before I have to talk myself into accepting this irrevocably?"

John realized that Cathy was begging him for an out.

"No problem. We should do a lot more checking, but if it turns out that we are in the past, we have a huge dilemma."

She pulled out her cell phone and turned it on. "We can check one thing – fast. This should tell us for sure."

"That's a great idea. I left mine in the rental car."

"Johnny?" She sounded like a lost little girl as she held her phone out to him. "No signal. And there was a signal here yesterday, even at the site."

"Catie, we have a major problem."

"What?"

"We know how this is supposed to unfold, but we can't do anything to alter it."

"Oh my God!" Cathy winced. "All those lives?"

"Slightly upwards of 50,000 casualties, and we can't do a thing." John watched her carefully. "Get used to it. We may have to deal with it."

She nodded. "Can I say now that I won't like it?"

"Sure. You can even say that you hate it. Meanwhile, we have a hike to town." He rose and turned to pick up his pack. If the farmer was right, he needed to change out of his uniform. He settled for taking off the military jacket and putting on his civilian vest and coat. His shirt and pants were plain.

"Johnny, should I be a boy or a woman?" Cathy's voice held mischief, and he whirled She was standing there, grinning. "No, I haven't gone over the edge. I want your opinion."

"What?" He was cautious.

"Shall I change clothes and become a female, or should I remain as I am and be taken for a boy? That farmer assumed I was a boy." She regarded her feet. "You said this outfit is period."

"Why don't you stay comfortable for the walk? You can always morph later." He grinned as he thought of the very feminine doctor masquerading as a young boy of about thirteen. Her slight stature and slim build would not be enough to give her away.

"Thank you! I'll be faster in these shoes than in a full skirt and my other shoes." She reached down for some dirt and rubbed her cheeks. He watched, glad he had chosen dark green for her pants, as khaki would have been too close to Confederate butternut.

"Need help?"

She shot him a look as she wiped her hands on her cheeks. "I think I'm ready."

"You do look appropriately scruffy," he admitted. "What shall we call you in this guise?"

"I think any variation of Mary Catherine is out," she agreed. "Name me."

"How about Mike?"

"It's as good as any other name. Mike," she said, mulling it over. "Let's go."

CHAPTER THREE

Sunday, 28th June 1863

Gettysburg was ahead of them, and unless some major film producer had recreated the entire town of the nineteenth century as a set, John figured that they had indeed jumped backward in time.

They were on a slight rise. The place that John knew as a city, with all the trappings of a historical tourist site, was spread out in front of him. It was a thriving town, but there were no power lines, asphalt roads, interstate interchanges, or even traffic lights. He knew that from where he was standing he also ought to be able to see the tall observation tower which overlooked the entire area, and it wasn't there. The film "Gettysburg" had had to shoot around it, but now there was no sign of it.

It still misting, but it wasn't a cold rain. Apparently, the century change had affected daily time by an hour. John's pocket watch read ten minutes past one o'clock. According to one man on horseback, it was shortly after twelve. John had stopped the man as asked as both a time check and an appearance check. The few people they had encountered had accepted their appearance as a man and a scruffy boy.

"Now how did I gain an hour of time?" John wondered aloud, looking at his watch. "This watch is accurate, and it's still ticking."

"An hour? Exactly an hour? Your watch shows one hour ahead of what we were told?"

"Yeah – strange."

"Maybe not. Cripes, it adds to the idea that we are in 1863."

"I'm lost. Again. Or is it 'still'?"

"Your watch was set to Eastern Daylight Savings Time."

"Of course!" he exclaimed. "Since there's no such thing as DST in 1863, local time is an hour off."

"Umm, Cap'n?"

"Yes, Mike?" John unsuccessfully tried to smother the smile which told Cathy that he was taking some healthy amusement from the circumstances.

"I'm hungry. When do we eat?"

"A better question would probably be 'how." John frowned slightly. "I have some money, but if we can scrounge, I'd prefer to save it."

"You have money that will work here and now?"

"Uh-huh."

"Not plastic? Real period cash money?"

"Catie, I doubt that a credit card would be of much help. Yes, I have some greenbacks and a few coins authentic to the era."

"Funny, you never were a boy scout..." She laughed at the look he gave her. "Okay, how do we scrounge? Barter?"

"If possible."

"Johnny, if we really are stuck in the nineteenth century, I may be able to trade some medical skills for food."

"We may have to do that, but you're going to have to be very careful about saving someone who should die to keep the time-line correct."

"Ugh. Why do I get the feeling that nothing is going to be simple for a while?"

"Because nothing is going to be simple for more than a while."

"You're a big help," she told him tartly.

"We're here."

He felt Cathy's hand steal inside his own.

"Johnny?" Her voice was hushed, and the question hesitant. "We're really in 1863? Really there?"

"It looks like it, Catie. You can see for yourself: no cars, no street lights, and no highways as we know them. We drove through this town Friday. Recognize it?"

"No." She sighed. "Johnny?"

"Yes?"

"If I have to be stuck, I'm glad I'm stuck with you."

It took him a moment, then he started to chuckle. Cathy sounded so small and lost, and the statement was so odd, he had to.

She looked up, and a smile started to sneak across her face. "At least we can still laugh. What's next?"

"We need a base of operations." John put down his pack and began to rummage through it. "I have a map in here somewhere."

"I had one, but I left it in the rental car," she murmured.

"No, I have a now-contemporary one," he told her absently. "I hope it's as accurate as it's supposed to be."

"Amen to that." Then she giggled.

John's head snapped up at the sound, which wasn't typical of her. "Are you all right?"

"Yes, fine. I'm sorry, but the thought just hit me that if the map isn't accurate, when we get back you can complain and demand your money back."

"Yeah. Catie, you are not a well person."

"I know, but it's part of my charm. You've said so yourself." Cathy's face became solemn. "We will get back, won't we?"

"I hope so," John mumbled, still digging in the bag.

"Yep." Cathy was silent. "I don't suppose now is the time to ask how we can do that."

"Definitely not, especially since we have no idea how we got here in the first place." He straightened up. "Got it."

Cathy tried looking over his shoulder, then under his arm. John, realizing her problem, got down on his knees and made room for her. Orienting the map to the direction they faced, he pointed.

"That's where we are now. I think." He pointed.

"I think you're thinking is right," Cathy echoed.

"I appreciate the confidence." John allowed himself a smile. If Cathy was happy to be stuck with him, he was just as grateful to be stuck with her. As he had told Randy last night - one hundred and fifty-two years from now - Cathy may look like a helpless sprite, but she was very resourceful.

"What we need is a place we can live, far enough away from the rest of the town to be able to hide our modern gear while we keep it available," he told her.

"If we are in the middle of the Civil War, there should be some hope of finding an abandoned cabin or barn we could use," Cathy replied. "But where would we look?"

"We have an advantage," John mused. "We know where the battle will take place."

"Yep, Gettysburg."

"No, I mean we know where around the town the actual fighting will happen."

"We do?"

"Well, I do."

"Oh, I see what you mean." Cathy stared at the map for a moment. "Well, don't stick us in the middle of an attack or anything. Okay?"

"I'll do my best," he promised. "Any other specifications?"

"A stream for running water would be nice, and somewhere I could plant a garden would be helpful if we are going to be here for a while."

"A garden?" He stared at her. "As in growing your own veggies?"

"Uh-huh. My summers on my grandmother's farm may just pay off." She grinned. "I even have some seeds."

"Oh yeah, what you bought for her at the roadside stand outside Bedford." He returned the grin. "Doctor, you may come in handy."

"Just see to it that you don't force me to practice major surgery. I'd have a hard time explaining my actions."

"Which brings us back to a location. Why don't we try looking in this area?" He indicated a section on the map just east and slightly north of the town.

"You would pick an area on the far side from where we are at the moment." Cathy studied the map and pointed to an area south of their position. "Why not here?"

"Uh, that would land us smack in the middle of what is called Pickett's charge, scheduled to take place on Friday." He grimaced and took a deep breath. "Trust me. No."

"Oh." She drew a deep breath of her own and let it out slowly. "I'm sorry. I don't know much about this. I bow to your expertise. The other side of town it is."

John carefully folded the map and tucked it safely in a pocket. "Maybe we'll pass an apple orchard on the way," he said as he hoisted his pack.

"We can hope."

*****

As they entered the town, each took notes on what was considered appropriate and what would not fit. John's goal was to cover the town as quickly as possible, drawing little attention, if any. Whatever had happened over the past four days had left the citizens of Gettysburg with less-than-average curiosity. Then he remembered that the Confederates had already passed through once, which would make them more cautious. The knowledge of what was yet to come weighed on him heavily and he was reluctant to begin making friends with the town's citizens.

Cathy was busy studying the children, especially the boys. John saw that her walking style changed a bit as they progressed along Chambersburg Street to the center of town and made a note to tease her about it. The mist was still with them as they crossed West Street, approaching Franklin Street. John was beginning to relax about their progress when a woman approached them.

"Sir?" The woman was slightly older than he was, hatless, but with a determined and self-confident air. "Forgive me for being forward, sir, but we don't get many strangers in town – unless they are in uniform. Are you lost?"

"Ma'am," John replied, bowing slightly, "I would say we are more displaced than lost. However, 'lost' will suffice."

"Union?"

"Yes, ma'am." He took a breath, deciding to risk it. "Captain John Andrews, Third Missouri Cavalry, currently detached, at your service." He noticed the woman staring at Cathy. "This is a young friend of mine, Mike. I realize I am out of uniform. I made the decision for safety's sake since I'm not traveling alone."

"Captain, I don't wish to appear too forward, but I would like to ask you if you have any information to offer about the location of the Union forces."

"Mrs.?" He hoped it wasn't too presumptuous.

"Oh, do please pardon my lack of manners," the woman sighed. "Blame it on the times. I'm Mary McAllister, Miss, not Mrs. I run a general store."

"Miss McAllister, I'm afraid I have little information to give. I've been - " He stopped abruptly, not sure of what to say.

"The Captain here has been on medical leave, ma'am," Cathy put in quickly. "He's ashamed of it, and hates telling." *Boy, oh boy, I'll catch it later for that one.*

"Now, Captain, there's no reason to be ashamed of being sick or wounded. Are you here to rejoin your company?"

"No, ma'am, the 3rd is in the West, but I do hope to offer my services to the general in charge of the cavalry I've heard is heading this way."

"Ah, so you are aware that there is cavalry coming here."

"So I have been told. I suspect that if your town has seen the Rebels already, the idea of a battle in this area is not totally far-fetched." *Talk about hedging the truth.*

"So I thought myself, Captain Andrews." Miss McAllister brushed her hair. "This misting has been most annoying. Would you both care to join me for a hot cup of coffee?"

"That would be very hospitable of you, Miss McAllister," John began. He had full intentions of politely refusing the invitation when he heard Cathy cough. She caught his eye and glared. "We would be honored and delighted. We've been walking all morning."

They followed Mary McAllister to a house further down Chambersburg Street.

"I live here with my sister Martha and her husband John Scott," their hostess explained. "We've been more than a mite nervous the past few days especially after the rebels came through."

"I can understand that," murmured Cathy.

Martha came to the door. She didn't seem surprised that Mary had shown up with company, nor did she seem to mind.

'Mike' asked if he could wash, and Cathy washed her hands and face in the kitchen, using the pump. The coffee was good and, after discovering their visitors had not had a mid-day meal Martha Scott served some warm bread with honey. It was very welcome, and John said so. Cathy was doing her best to keep to her guise as a scruffy boy, thought she was doing well, but the illusion was abruptly shattered.

"Captain Andrews," began Mary McAllister, "Why on earth is your lady companion dressed like a boy?"

John choked a bit on his coffee, turning red as much from embarrassment as from choking.

"Oh well," Cathy mumbled to him, "At least we've had a cup of coffee. Johnny, are you all right? Can you breathe?"

He nodded, his color returning to normal.

"You'll have to forgive me, as I haven't acted the tomboy in quite a while," Cathy told her hostesses. "I certainly meant no disrespect, Mrs. Scott, Miss McAllister," she said, nodding to each in turn, "And I sincerely apologize for the deception. For my own knowledge, may I ask what gave me away?"

"You don't hold a cup the way a young boy would," Mary informed her with a smile. "Other than that, the way you sit is too cautious. A boy wouldn't be as careful of the furniture."

"I assure you the secret is safe with us," added Martha. "May we assume there is a reason for it?"

"We decided it would be safer for her travel this way than openly as a woman," John explained. "Times are strange, and we did not want to risk counting on normal kindness."

"A wise tactic, to be sure," replied Mary. "However, Mike, if you would like to wash off some more of the dirt, please do so."

"As much as I would love to rid myself of the disguise, I don't think it would be wise," Cathy replied, smiling. "If someone has seen me enter as I am, and then was to see a woman leave in my stead..." Cathy let her sentence hang on its own. "I do thank you for the thought."

John noticed that Cathy was reverting to a language with more flourishes than colloquial English of the twenty-first century. He blessed her experiences with the SCA, which is what enabled her to do this; he was relying on both his SCA and living history lessons for his.

"Mrs. Scott, Miss McAllister, may I present Mary Catherine Howell?" John had risen and performed the ritual with a slight bow. *Crap! Last names don't match – think fast!* "Miss Howell is my step-sister. She came to attend me while I was on medical leave, for which I was most grateful. I was hoping to secure a railroad ticket for her so she could return home, but that plan looks rather vague now."

"Now, sir, you know I won't leave you if there's a chance you might be going back into battle. What if you are injured?" Cathy's indignation was real. *Step-siblings! Great idea - clever, Johnny!*

"You see, ladies, my dilemma," John said, turning to them with a rueful smile as he sat down again.

"In truth, Captain, you surely do not wish to rid yourself of my company," Cathy smiled at him, seeming to press her point because he couldn't argue. "I am far too good a nurse to be so dismissed. My father is a doctor, and I assisted in his practice," she added to the sisters. "My brother knows full well that I would take better care of him than most should the need arise."

The sisters laughed at this display of sibling chivalry.

"Miss Howell," Mary McAllister began, "If you are skilled at nursing, perhaps it would be in the best interests of the Union troops to delay your departure from our fair city."

"If my dear brother is going to volunteer his services, I should truly wish to remain in the vicinity," Cathy stated simply. "Sir, perhaps our new acquaintances would know of a small house which we might inhabit for a time?"

"Mrs. Scott, Miss McAllister, you would do us a tremendous service if you could guide us to some humble dwelling. If I am to see action, I would at least like the comfort of knowing my sister has a roof to protect her." John was serious.

Their hostesses exchanged glances.

"I'm not aware of any home in town which would be available. You might perhaps be able to rent a room," Martha mused.

"My circumstances are such that I must watch every penny I spend," Cathy told her. "As convenient as it would be to get a room here in town, I doubt I could afford the luxury."

"I understand, Miss Howell," Mary McAllister quickly assured her. "Times are hard, and you are a long way from your home."

"I enjoy the exercise of walking, and distance does not bother me," Cathy stated. "Perhaps there is an old barn or cabin on the outskirts of town? If it has a small plot of ground with it, I would be able to grow some of my own food."

"Martha, what about the grandfather's cabin?" Mary McAllister asked her sister.

"You can't mean the old cabin in the woods north of the York Pike! Surely that poor old structure has fallen down by now," her sister replied.

"It was still standing last fall," her sister stated.

"Is this cabin your grandfather's?" John asked the question he saw in Cathy's eyes.

"No, Captain Andrews, it is referred to as being 'the grandfather's cabin' because no one is quite sure who built it or how old it is," Martha Scott said by way of explanation. "As far as I know, no one has lived there for at least five years. You might try that."

"How would we find this cabin?" John asked. "Would we be trespassing if we occupied it?"

"Captain," replied Mary McAllister, "I'm not at all certain we would be doing you and your sister a service, much less a favor, by giving you directions to it. It is a poor thing at best, not fit for a gentlewoman."

"I would consider it a genuine disservice, Mary," Martha Scott stated flatly. "It's a rough structure; if the roof is intact, it would only shelter you from the wind and rain."

"None-the-less," John replied, "We are in need of shelter, and as we have little means to pay for it, I am certain we can make it habitable."

"Please," Cathy begged their hostesses, "It would be either the cabin, rough as it may be, or my brother's canvas tent. I assure you, I shall prefer the cabin."

The sisters exchanged glances. Martha shrugged.

"Your point is well taken, Miss Howell," Mary said. "I doubt the cabin is inhabited or will likely be recalled to most minds. The pathway leading to it is overgrown, so your best course would be to follow York Street to where it branches off to the northeast, and follow that over Rock Creek. The Hunterstown Road branches off to the north, and you will need to walk almost mile along it until a dirt road forks slightly to the south. Follow this road to a small creek, and about a half a mile further on the right fork of the creek is the cabin. It sits at the edge of a wood."

"How far away is it?"

"From the point where the York Pike branches north, the cabin is a little over two miles." Mary McAllister smiled broadly. "There used to be a shortcut, as I mentioned, that would render the walk to about a mile, but it is overgrown. I've walked the route I have described at a leisurely pace and it takes me less than an hour."

"Mary McAllister!" Martha sounded a bit shocked.

"Martha, I'm the only woman in Gettysburg to own and run a business. I also enjoy exercise."

"So that's how you know the cabin is still standing?" Martha Scott was obviously disturbed at the way her sister ignored certain proprieties.

"Oh, do stop pretending that you are scandalized by my behavior," Mary teased. "You washed your hands of my carryings-on a long time ago."

"Captain, I think we should take our leave," Cathy said, standing. "Mrs. Scott, Miss McAllister, you have our profound thanks for both your hospitality and assistance."

John rose and bowed to the two Gettysburg ladies. "I add my thanks to those expressed by my sister. I hope we can find some way to repay your kindness."

Martha Scott stood. "Captain, you and your sister must come and dine with us."

"That would please us both, I assure you. Perhaps Mary Catherine may call upon you tomorrow? It would ease my mind considerably to know she has some friends, should anything untoward happen to me." John bowed again.

"She must indeed call, Captain, especially should she be in need of any assistance," Mary McAllister stated firmly.

"I only hope you will be able to recognize me, Miss McAllister," Cathy added with a smile. She glanced down at herself. "I hope that when I am properly attired, I do not in the least resemble my current form."

All three ladies laughed.

"We are in your debt," he told them, meaning it.

They left the Scott home only after Martha Scott furnished them with a loaf of bread and a small crock of molasses. In return, Cathy promised to call the following day and bring the sisters up to date on the state of the cabin.

"Wow," she commented as they crossed the town square, called the Diamond. "We got lucky. Damned lucky."

"We got considerably more than lucky, Catie. We have been downright blessed."

"You were going to refuse the invitation, weren't you? Why?"

"I was debating the wisdom of getting to know any of the locals, that's all. Thanks for the prod."

"No problem." Cathy grinned. "I told you I was hungry. I thought we were dead meat when they tripped to the fact that I'm not a dirty boy."

"Yeah, so did I." He reflected on their visit with the two sisters. "They took it rather well, all things considered."

"I will never again make fun of using flowery speech," she mumbled. "Somehow, I've always felt awkward using it at SCA events, but boy! It came in handy. By the way, the step-siblings idea is brilliant."

"It just came to me as I was introducing you. Inspiration through panic."

They walked along Hunterstown Road, each lost in thought.

Cathy broke the silence. "Johnny, are you really going to offer your services to the cavalry?"

"General John Buford arrives in the area Tuesday. He's one of my heroes, and I guess I've always wanted to meet him. This is my chance."

"Have you considered that this is going to seem odd?"

"How?"

"Johnny, you can't just walk up to a general, introduce yourself, and start fighting."

"Oh yes, I can." John grinned. "Cathy, this is not the age of communication. A man who is wounded and separated from his unit is expected to report to any unit he can find when he has healed."

"Don't they keep records?"

"Not good ones. They didn't use replacements the way a modern army would so when ranks were decimated in battle, any commander would happily accept able-bodied men." John shrugged. "Not only am I able-bodied, I'm an officer."

"You're also out of your mind," Cathy retorted forcefully. "If you do this, there seems to be a good chance you are going to get yourself killed. I wouldn't appreciate that. Not even a little bit."

"Catie, can we postpone this discussion until we get to the cabin?"

"If you insist."

Rock Creek flowed and was slightly swollen from the rain. Mary McAllister's directions proved very accurate, and they had no trouble following either the roads or the creek bank, although the creek was acting more like a brook.

The cabin stood in the middle of the clearing, where the stream forked. Weeds had grown up around the small structure but had not yet succeeded in overtaking it completely.

John was pleased to see that the building looked sound and not nearly as rough as the sisters had made it out to be. It even had an overhang over a small porch. He also noted that it had taken them less than forty-five minutes to make the trek.

"It looks sort of quaint, don't you think?" Cathy was contemplating it with her hands on her slim hips.

"Shall we?" John bowed formally as the rain started to fall in earnest. He instantly abandoned his pose, shouting, "The last one in is a rotten egg!"

They raced to the porch, getting drenched in the process.

The door to the wooden structure was not bolted. Once inside, they dropped their packs and surveyed the interior.

It was a small log cabin, with one inside room partitioned off on the far side of the main room. They noted a stove, a dry sink with a metal basin, a long table, two chairs, and a set of cupboards on either side of a sideboard. Inside the smaller room was an iron bedstead with sagging mattress and a small chest of drawers. Although the interior was dusty, the roof didn't leak and everything was neatly arranged. There were two windows in the main room and one in the bedroom, and they also appeared watertight.

Cathy looked at John. "I think this is where we find out if our luck is holding," she told him.

"Meaning?"

"Say a little prayer that we have enough basics here so we don't have to go out and buy stuff." She walked over to the cupboards nearest the table and pulled it open. "Eureka…."

She was staring at plates, cups, and even some pots and another basin. John came over to inspect the array.

"Utilitarian."

"You said it," she agreed. "No pump for water."

"You have your choice of streams outside."

"No toilet."

"You have your choice of bushes outside."

"Hmmm. A one-holer would have been nice."

"May I offer my compliments on your acceptance of the situation?"

"Damn it," she retorted, "I have to use the flowery stuff with the natives, but not inside these walls! But yes, you may offer your compliments."

"On the 'beggars can't be choosers' theory, let's see what else we've got."

They went back into the bedroom. John pulled open the drawers of the chest. Cathy was more than relieved to see some sheets and other linens in the bottom drawer.

"Okay, let's get to it. When we've unpacked, we'll see where the gaps are," John commented.

A half-hour later, with most of their gear stowed and an inventory in hand of what they found inside the cabin added to what they carried, they conferred. Sitting at the table in the main room, Cathy regarded her companion.

"I think this is where we congratulate ourselves," she commented. "It's almost as if this place had been set up for two way-wards to stay." She had investigated the other cupboards and found most of the essentials of life, including some food staples and an oil lamp with fluid. "No frills, but we can manage," she said, wrinkling her nose.

"I thought I saw a chamber pot in the bedroom. At least we have a bed."

"True," she agreed, thinking of the bedstead with its sagging mattress, "But I still say that a one-holer would have been nice."

"Would help if I add that I found a woodpile outside under a small lean-to?"

"Probably." Cathy shifted in her chair. She stood up suddenly, dug into her jeans pocket and held out her cell phone. "Oops – forgot I tucked it in this morning. Habit." She turned it off. "Too bad it's useless," she added as she sat down again, holding it as if it was a lifeline.

There was an awkward pause.

"You're the living historian, Johnny," Cathy said gently. "What's next?"

"We're not too badly off. We have shelter, some food, a source of heat, and water. We're okay, at least for a while," John summarized.

"Oh, I forgot – I do have a decent supply of protein energy bars in the bottom of the second bag of first-aid supplies," Cathy added. "Plus the field medical kit."

"Stashed?"

"On the bed for the moment. I'm going to try to condense it down into one bag so we can use the duffel to cart things."

"Good idea."

"I have a list of stuff we'll need if we are going to be here for any longer than a couple of days," Cathy said, pushing her clipboard towards him. "Which brings up a question. Johnny, are we preparing to spend a few days or weeks or months or years?"

He sighed. "I wish I knew. I don't, and I really wish I did." He saw the first item on her list and smiled. "I should have figured on this first one."

"Well, I refuse to have to spend all my evenings in the dark," she said with a grin. "Candles would help. The lamp is great but limited. So is my solar flashlight. I want something so I can read or write after sunset. Since you found that woodpile, I figured we have all the essentials covered, and we could move from absolute needs to strong wants."

"Okay, I suppose we can handle that. Just don't go crazy."

"I'm going to ignore that," she said, sniffing, "On the theory that we may already have gone nuts."

"Catie, I didn't mean it that way," John began, "And I know-"

They both froze as a knock sounded on the door. As they exchanged stares, a woman's voice called out.

"Captain? Mike?" The voice came from just outside the cabin.

Cathy grabbed her clipboard, her phone, and her open backpack, and bolted for the bedroom. John strode to the cabin's door, opening it once he was sure Cathy had their 21st-century gear out of sight.

Mary McAllister was standing on the porch with an umbrella, looking worried. She brightened when she saw John in the doorway.

"Forgive the intrusion, Captain, but my sister and I were concerned that the cabin might not be habitable." She offered him the small bundle she was carrying. "We also thought you might find this of use."

"Johnny, please invite Miss McAllister in," called Cathy from inside. "We wouldn't want our benefactress catching sick."

John opened the door and let their visitor enter. John took her umbrella, closed it, and put it in the corner behind the door as he handed the bundle to Cathy. It proved to be a small blanket around a supply of candle tapers, two holders, and matches.

"Oh, Miss McAllister, how very thoughtful of you! I was telling John only a few moments ago that the one thing we didn't have was candles. This is wonderful." Cathy smiled at the older woman. "I did find a lamp, however, there are two rooms here. Thank you, most sincerely."

"As grateful as we are, however, I would urge you not to put yourself out by coming all the way out here on your own again, with all the activity that will undoubtedly be occurring shortly," added John.

"That, Captain, is the other reason for my visit. The Rebels do seem to be outside of town to the east, and I fear for your sister's safety." She looked around. "I must admit that the cabin is better appointed than I had supposed it would be. How are you fixed for food supplies?"

"We consider ourselves quite fortunate," Cathy agreed. "I found basic utensils and some canned goods, which are most welcome. My situation is such that I cannot afford much beyond staples for supplies. John is determined to volunteer his services to the first Union commander he locates, so I shall accompany him to town. May I ask the location of your store?"

"Miss Howell, I have given considerable thought to your situation, and I discussed an idea I had with my sister, who is an uncommon judge of character. With the war on, I am having great difficulties keeping help at the store. If it wouldn't bother you to do so, I would like to offer you a position assisting me. I would not be able to afford much in the way of wages, yet I would be open to giving you some stock in the way of a trade." Mary McAllister smiled at the pair in front of her. "That is, of course, with your permission, Captain."

John looked at Cathy, noting the tears of relief that filled her eyes. "Miss McAllister, I would forever be grateful in these uncertain times to know that not only would my sister have good friends in such a new place but a means of living as well. I would welcome such an opportunity on her behalf."

"Miss McAllister," Cathy added, "I accept with all my heart although I know I can never repay such kindness. I have never worked in a shop, yet I have worked as a nurse in my father's practice, and once helped out in a small tea shop. I can only assure you that I will do my utmost not to let you down."

"Then that is settled. You may think I am doing you a favor, Miss Howell, but you are doing me one just as great." She turned to pick up her umbrella. "We shall expect you for supper this evening, Captain. If you and your sister will come to the house, I will take you to the store. You can choose what you will need for the immediate future. Consider it an advance on Miss Howell's wages."

"It will be our pleasure, Miss McAllister. We shall follow you shortly. I'm certain my sister would like to clean up and change." He bowed as she left the cabin.

Cathy collapsed on a chair, her eyes still teary. "God above, Johnny, this is amazing. Luck doesn't even begin to cover it."

"I agree."

"It's almost as if she knows we're not from this time," Cathy murmured. "Geez – there's a thought. It would be lovely if there was someone local who would understand all this." She shuddered. "Oh well, I'd best morph into a female. Maybe I can barter for some material to make a skirt and blouse. I don't want to wreck your present stocking shelves."

"We can't have that," he chuckled. "By the way, when did you work in a small tea shop? I thought you were a waitress in a four-star restaurant during college."

"Well, I had to say something – a tea shop sounded genteel. Let's finish stowing the modern gear – I stashed my duffel under the bed in a hurry. I'll empty it into the field pack so we can take it with us. Then if you'll get a bucket from the stream, I'll wash and change. It wouldn't do to be late for supper."

"We'll have to find a small strongbox or trunk of some kind to store the electronics – I don't want to think about trying to explain a phone or computer," he mused as he picked up the bucket next to the cupboard. "I'll work on that while you wash and change. For now, I'll use the back of a drawer."

"Okay – and while you are playing with the electronics, take the battery out of my cell phone. That may help save it."

*****

The early supper was light, but compared to what she would have concocted on her own, it was a feast. Before they left, the duffel bag was filled with things from Martha Scott's storage cellar. Mary had explained that most of the food stuffs had been moved out of the store to avoid having the Confederates take it; she insisted that they take as much as they could carry. John Scott, looking ill to Cathy's trained eye, proved to be an entertaining host, and the men exchanged views on the war situation while the three women cleaned up the supper dishes. When it was time to leave, Cathy promised her new employer she would return to the house in the morning so she could start her duties.

"After all," she said smiling, "I have to earn this advance on my wages."

The walk to the cabin was already becoming familiar. As the sun went down, Cathy set out the oil lamp, topped it off from the jar Mary McAllister had sent with them, lit it, and sank gratefully into one of the chairs.

"Are you going to be all right?" John asked as he sat in the other chair.

"Oh sure – I'm used to clocking five to ten miles a day on a shift. I was going to ask about you – you spend most of your time at a desk," she teased. "I will admit, though, to be tired."

John nodded. "How about calling it an early night?"

"In a bit." She took a deep breath. "Is there any way I can talk you out of volunteering to fight? From everything I know about the battles around Gettysburg, the one fact that keeps jumping out is the casualty rate. If you are wounded, I don't know if I can save you, and if you die I'll be stuck here alone. You seem to be enjoying this, and it's too serious a situation to simply run out to get killed."

"Catie, I am taking this very seriously. There must be a reason we have been thrown back in time, even if we don't know what it is. You know I don't believe in coincidences, and even though this is eerie, we are here. I promise I will do my best to stay in one piece." John pulled out his map of the area. "I know where General Buford will be on Tuesday. I will find him and see if he'll accept me. He's got two brigades, one under Colonel Devin, and one under Colonel Gamble.

"I'll come with you – if you get hurt, I damn well want someone to know that I will be the one to take care of you. The last thing you would need would be a military surgeon."

"Okay, that's fair."

"Tomorrow, I want all details on you medically – blood type, meds, allergies, etc. Just think about it for now. If I have to administer an antibiotic, I want to be sure I won't kill you in the process of curing an infection."

"Relax – I don't have any drug allergies and I can take penicillin. My blood type is O-positive. But where would you get an antibiotic? They don't exist yet."

"For a brilliant engineer, you do have blind spots. If I need it, I can reinvent penicillin – exactly the way it was discovered. It's been a staple science fair experiment for decades: basic bread mold. It is possible to grow it with cheese as well, but I think I'll use bread – a small piece is all I'll need. I'll set it up tonight before I go to bed." Cathy laughed at the look on his face. "So, now that you know how I will counteract an infected wound, you can make sure you don't get shot, right?"

"I'm not planning on getting shot, honest. What are you going to do when the shooting starts?"

"Will there be shooting in town?"

"Yes, there will be some. Buford's troops pull back through town the first day and it turned into a bit of a running battle. As far as I know, there is only one civilian death, but there were some casualties. Both armies did their best to keep civilians out of it, but bullets go wide." John's dark brown eyes held her green ones. "You are to keep indoors with your head down when you hear firing. Promise?"

"Yes, I promise. I wish I could get you to do the same. Will you at least try to stay to the rear, or at least not get carried away and assume a place in the front line?"

"I will do my best, I promise." He yawned. "We have tomorrow and Tuesday to get organized. The actual fighting doesn't begin until Wednesday."

"Good. I like the Scotts, and Mary McAllister is someone I can relate to." She stretched. "I'm concerned about John Scott, though. He didn't look good this evening. I hope he's not getting sick."

"Why?"

"Because I'll have to do something about it."

"Cripes."

"Every bit of that," she said as she yawned. "Let me get my culture started and then maybe it is time to go to bed. I don't think we could get much done tonight, and we'll probably be up with the sun."

CHAPTER FOUR

Monday, 29 June 1863

Morning brought with it one major disappointment: they were still in the cabin in 1863. Cathy could tell by the lack of noise outside. She rolled over to look at John, to find he was also awake.

"Okay, I admit I was hoping to hear traffic or plane noises," she said, sitting up. "By the way, where would this be in our time?"

"This?"

"The cabin. If we woke up in our own time, where would we be?"

"To be honest, I'm not exactly sure. I'll let you know if I work it out. Without signposts, it's tricky." John swung his legs out of the covers. "Let's get going – I want to make sure we have everything as settled as possible before I find the general on Tuesday. His headquarters will be at the Eagle Hotel, in Gettysburg."

"Okay, I'll bite – what don't you know about Buford?"

"How to save him – he died, er, dies, in December of pneumonia or typhus or typhoid fever."

On their way in, carrying the once-more empty duffel, Cathy wondered aloud if there was a shorter route between the cabin and town.

"Mary McAllister mentioned a pathway was overgrown. I wonder if we could find it." She sighed. "I like walking, but it would be nice to find a route that's only a mile or so instead of over two. Maybe I can ask her – if we can find a shorter route, it would save time."

"Yeah, this could get to be a really long walk."

*****

They went to the Scott home, and Mary McAllister took them to her store, which turned out to be across the street from the house. John noted the streets were quiet. *Too quiet, as if this truly was the calm before the storm.* John helped the women reorganize some of the merchandise. The three of them also conferred on what should be moved to the Scott home for easy access. The duffel was filled with items to go back to the cabin, amid protests that their hostess was giving them too much. Mary McAllister stopped that discussion before it gained momentum.

"Captain, I'd rather give it to someone I know than have an army simply take it."

On their mid-day break at the Scott home, John asked about a shorter route to the cabin. While he and Mary McAllister went over directions, Martha Scott pulled Cathy to one side.

"Miss Howell, I don't wish to offend, so forgive me for asking, but do you have any other dresses with you?"

"Mrs. Scott, I couldn't possibly be offended by anything you or your sister ask or suggest," Cathy replied, "And no, I have no other garments with me. When I received word that my brother needed my assistance, I left in considerable haste." *What the hell, what's one more white lie to keep the story straight?* "I was going to ask Miss McAllister if there was any material at hand to make another skirt and blouse. A change of clothes – other than those I was wearing when we first entered this house – would be most welcome."

"Miss Howell, I am certain we will be able to find clothes for you." Martha Scott smiled at the younger woman.

"I cannot tell you how blessed my brother and I feel about the friendship your family has offered us. The war has torn so much apart. John is determined to do his duty, and while I cannot find fault with this, I do feel it places me at a disadvantage being so far from home. Yet, as I said yesterday, I dare not leave for fear of his being wounded."

"I understand, and I know Mary does." Martha paused. "I have some skirts that I no longer wear. Perhaps we can find one to fit you. I believe that Mary may have a blouse she no longer uses, as well."

"I know it's a small detail when compared to everything else that is going on, but it would be a pleasure to have something else to wear," Cathy said, smiling. "Except for my 'young boy' clothes, this is the only outfit I have. Only another woman would understand, Mrs. Scott, truly."

Martha Scott chuckled, nodding. "Something else I under-stand entirely. Let me go through what I have in my chest upstairs, and I'll ask Mary if she has something she can spare." She left the room.

Mary McAllister looked up as Cathy joined her and John as they were consulting over John's map.

"Did I hear my name mentioned?"

"I'm afraid you did, Miss McAllister," Cathy replied. "I be-lieve your sister is going to volunteer you to donate a blouse to go with a skirt she is offering to loan me. I did assume it will be with your permission, of course."

"Well, now, it's not often that Martha takes action before I have a chance to do it first," her hostess stated, "However it does happen. Of course, we shall find you a blouse. Meanwhile, I think it's time you call me by my Christian name. I realize this might be considered a mite too informal for such a short acquaintance, but I've never cared overmuch for some proprieties."

"I was going to suggest 'Miss Mary', but I will abide by whatever you suggest, as long as you call me Cathy."

"Cathy?"

"My full name is Mary Catherine, but most of my family and friends call me Cathy. You may hear John call me Catie, I suspect simply to be different; however, I would be honored if you and your family use Cathy."

"Mary," called Martha from the foot of the stairs, "John is sick." She looked worried as she came into the room. "He isn't making sense when he answers me."

"Has this been coming on?" John asked, remembering Cathy's words the night before.

"He said he was feeling tired and poorly last evening after you left," Martha admitted.

"Perhaps Cathy can be of help?" John said, turning to Cathy. "She's the best nurse our town ever had."

"With your permission, Mrs. Scott, I'd be happy to see if there's anything I can do."

"I'd be most grateful."

Cathy disappeared up the stairs, returning after about ten minutes.

"Mary, I believe I can help, but I need a word with my brother first." Cathy pulled John into the hallway. "Johnny, I need to know something. Mr. Scott has a high fever, but only mildly swollen glands, and he's complaining about aches. His breathing, from what I can tell, is getting labored but not raspy. I'm not absolutely certain if it's bacterial or viral – it's probably viral - but either way he needs some intervention. How much can I do?"

"Cripes – what would you need?"

"Aspirin would be a good start. It's a general antipyretic, analgesic, and mild anti-inflammatory. Acetaminophen and ibuprofen would be the other choices, but I'd like to start with aspirin. I have all three in my bag at the cabin, but I wanted to clear any actions with you. He also needs fluids, which I can start now."

"Is he in any serious danger?"

"Maybe, but even if it's not fatal, he's in for a long haul if I don't get the fever broken. I am going to suggest bathing his face and torso, which should also help." She looked up at John. "Can you get my large backpack? We owe these people a lot."

"Catie." His tone was a warning.

"Johnny, I won't go nuts, I promise."

John nudged her as he looked past her shoulder.

"Pardon the intrusion," Mary said, coming to join the pair. "You seem to be debating about something."

"Cathy needs what she calls her medical bag, which is back at the cabin."

"Why don't you and I see if we can clear the shorter pathway we have been discussing. We can then retrieve the bag."

"An admirable suggestion," John said. "You can manage here until we return?" he asked Cathy.

"Of course. What about the store?"

"It's locked and closed," Mary told her. "Anyone local needing something would come here and Martha can take care of that."

In the two hours it took for John and Mary to return, Cathy instructed Martha on some of the basics of non-medical interventions. The two women talked as they worked, which Cathy found awkward. She tried to be open, keeping the white lies to a minimum. Bathing Mr. Scott with lukewarm water did seem to start bringing the fever down, without sending him into chills.

"Martha! We're back." Mary's voice sounded from the kitchen.

Cathy flew down the stairs, grabbed her bag from John and deposited it on the nearest table. Mary went to check on her sister.

"Anything to report?" Cathy asked without looking up.

"We have a short cut to the cabin, and I almost blew our cover. I think I managed to bluff past the blunder, but Mary is probably getting suspicious. The field kit has a zipper, you know, and they don't exist yet. Small detail, but it got sticky for a minute." He nodded to the stairs. "How about here?"

"I'm almost sure what I'm fighting is viral – which is good because it means I don't have to figure out how to administer penicillin – but he is going to need support. He's more lucid so we're making progress. Other than that, I've had to get a tad creative about answering questions about our family, but I would imagine you have, too. Hopefully, our improvisations match. Just so you'll know your mother is now married to my father the doctor." She straightened up, holding a bottle. "Eureka. Since I can't show the damned bottle, I need a saucer or small cup."

He turned to the sink and grabbed a saucer, into which she put nine tablets.

"Aspirin?"

"Yep – two reasons. First, these tablets aren't stamped. Second, I'm saving the acetaminophen for you; if memory serves, you don't tolerate ASA well. I will hold the ibuprofen in reserve. I saw a carafe of water and a glass in the room, so all I'll need is a spoon."

Cathy picked up the saucer and John handed her a spoon. Upstairs, she showed Martha – and Mary – how to crush and dissolve a tablet in a glass of water, then administer the medicine, one tablet every eight hours.

"Make sure he finishes the whole glass. It's going to taste bitter," she warned John Scott, "But this will help break your fever. My father makes these himself, and it works wonders. Drink it all down," she encouraged her patient as she helped him sit up enough to drink the glassful. She smiled as he grimaced. "Father always jokes that the worse the medicine tastes, the better it works. You might want to drink another glass of water to get the taste out of your mouth."

John Scott nodded. Martha poured a glassful from the bedside carafe and he drank it down.

"Now we shall leave you to rest." Cathy left the sick room and started down the stairs, but Mary called her to the other bedroom.

"Before you go downstairs," she said, "Martha and I have some things for you."

John Andrews, who had come up the stairs, followed Cathy into the smaller room. Her face, as she saw a blouse, a skirt, and a day dress lain out on Mary's bed, reflected the gratitude he felt. She turned to him and tried to smile, but her eyes filled with tears and he drew her into a hug.

"We can't tell you how much all this means to us," he said to the sisters, and then gave Cathy a nudge. "Try on your new clothes."

"We'll go downstairs," said Martha, "And leave you to it. Come, Captain."

When Cathy appeared in the drawing-room some time later, John grinned as he stood. She was wearing the new blouse with her old skirt, carrying the other garments.

"Oh good, it fits," said Mary, smiling. "I was afraid the blouse would be a bit big. The day dress is a bit heavy for this heat, so you may want to wait for cooler weather to wear it."

"The top of the day dress is loose, yet a small alteration will put that to rights. I do have a sewing kit with me so it won't be a problem," Cathy told her. "The skirt is perfect. I changed into the new blouse because my own is ready to stand up without me inside it." The comment made the two older women laugh.

"I did look in on Mr. Scott before I came downstairs," Cathy continued, looking at Martha. "He is resting comfortably, his fever is down somewhat, and his breathing has eased. I think if you keep up the medicine and get him to drink water and possibly broth, he will recover."

Martha nodded her thanks and left the room; her footsteps sounded on the stairs.

"Now, what else is there to do today?" John asked. "Miss Mary, is there anything else that can be brought over from the store? We should probably clear out as much as we can. I have a feeling that this town is going to be the center of a major dispute in a day or so."

"If you think it's a good idea, Captain, we can certainly try."

The afternoon was spent reorganizing and moving items in the store, if not to the Scott home at least to the store's cellar. On the last trip to the house, Cathy checked her patient. He was responding nicely to the aspirin, she decided. He was still weak, so she told Martha to stick to the medication regimen and push fluids, but ordered John Scott to stay in bed.

"If you try to get up too soon, sir, you will set yourself back several days. Miss Martha said you felt poorly last night. Get up too soon and you'll end up right back in bed." Cathy admonished him. "The only move I want to see you make is to the cellar, and that's only if shooting starts in town."

"Yes, ma'am," John Scott replied. "I will abide your advice."

Outside the sickroom, Martha smiled at Cathy. "There are moments when you seem more the doctor than the nurse."

"Well, in all fairness, I have seen my father with his patients far too many times to not adopt his more successful techniques," Cathy confided. "He told me he uses whatever he thinks will work, including gently bullying and threats." Both women chuckled.

Mary and John Andrews were in the kitchen.

"Your sister is remarkable," she commented. "I find her both skilled and efficient. It's surprising that she isn't married."

"In truth, Miss Mary, I think her suitors – she has had several – find her a bit too intimidating. I often think Shakespeare had her in mind when he wrote, 'And though she be but little she be fierce.' I've seen her when she was vexed, and I am always thankful her wrath is not directed towards me."

"Ah, I see my brother is quoting Shakespeare again. 'A Mid-Summer's Night's Dream'," Cathy clarified as she entered, followed closely by Martha.

"Act 3, Scene 2. I always associate that with you, my dear girl." John smiled, knowing full well she couldn't argue the term at the moment. "I was explaining why you are not yet married."

"The man I would choose to marry probably does not exist," she responded lightly. "At least I never found him while I was of marriageable age, and as I am now past it, it is of no account. In turn, I would like to point out your own reluctance to enter into the marriage state. I don't see a ring on your finger, brother *dear*." She emphasized the last word deliberately.

Mary sputtered with barely repressed laughter.

"All this sounds quite familiar," Martha observed. "Indeed, I have had this conversation with Mary many times. She, too, frightened off suitors. Our parents were a bit disappointed."

"I suspected as much. My father and step-mother gave up on us both after many years of encouragement and hoping," observed Cathy with a smile. "Mary, I would say that you and I are somewhat kindred souls," smiling as the older woman nodded in agreement.

"Are you ready to head back to the cabin?" John inquired. "There is one more task I would like to accomplish before I seek out the cavalry tomorrow. If I may presume on your hospitality for one needed item, Miss Mary, I would be much obliged."

"By all means, Captain. What do you require?"

"A small shovel or spade would be most welcome. I think it would be appropriate for me to dig a sink near the cabin."

"Martha, why don't we have an early supper before the Captain and Cathy depart?"

"I have already prepared for it. I also have broth heating on the stove for John."

Later, after they promised to return in the morning, John and Cathy headed back to the cabin with a packet of sliced ham with some bread in addition to the contents of the duffel bag and John's requested shovel. Cathy had left her field kit in the Scott's cellar with their permission. Zipper or no zipper, she knew she would need it, in town, before another forty-eight hours had passed.

*****

"Hey, this really is a shortcut," Cathy said as the cabin came into view. "Halle-bloody-frikken-luyah!"

John laughed at her out-of-period exclamation. "I'll bet you have wanted to do that all day."

"No bet. It's not as hard to remember to keep my language in line as I thought it would be – probably due to the influence of the sisters – but that seemed to be the thing to say now. Before you ask, yes, I enjoyed it."

"Yeah, I can see that. By the way, Dr. Howell, is John Scott going to make it?"

"I think so. He's been fighting with this for a day or so, according to Martha. I'm lucky it isn't typhoid fever. When he pushed himself yesterday to meet us, he screwed himself up again, which is why I hit him with the orders I did. Miss Martha did say I act more like a doctor than a nurse, but I was able to pass it off as things I have seen my father the doctor do."

As they entered the cabin, John commented, "Jim might be surprised to hear he is a doctor – he thinks he's a lawyer. Elaine might wonder, too, since she's his law partner as well as his wife."

"Yep, and now we have him married to your mother. Mom would not take that kindly." She laughed. "Come to think of it, Joyce and Keith wouldn't either. They're all good friends, but still. I think I'll skip telling them about all this."

"Catie, when we get back to our own time, we will have to skip telling ANYONE about all this. Not that anyone would believe it."

"Hell, the expressions on their faces might be worth it." She held up her hand. "I know – and *when* we get back, I'll be good. Promise. Now, while I get this stuff unpacked, you have a latrine to dig. Then I have a favor to ask you."

He emerged from the bedroom wearing jeans and a t-shirt. "I decided to be comfortable while digging. You should probably ask whatever it is now. I might be too whacked later."

"Fine. Do you have a handgun I can use while you're off fighting the rebels?"

"I'm going to need my weapons with me, including my officer's pistol."

"I'm not talking about period weapons. I want something I know how to handle in case I need it in a hurry. You didn't happen to bring your Beretta I've been coveting, did you?"

"Now that's a good thought. As a matter of fact…" He disappeared into the bedroom again and came back with a small pistol case and a box of ammunition. "I had almost forgotten about it. don't go berserk – we'd have a hard time explaining how someone got shot with a .22 hollow-point round."

"You are the one going to war with the black powder and Minie' balls. I just want to be able to defend the homestead." She took out the small handgun, making sure it wasn't loaded. "I do like this one. It doesn't tear my wrist apart when I fire it, like the 9mm you prefer."

"Okay, Annie Oakley. There's an extra magazine in the case. While you play with your new bang-bang, I'm going to dig a small latrine. If you're really lucky, I'll work out how to make a seat for it."

*****

"Well, you are definitely an engineer," Cathy said later, eyeing the new 'facility.' The hole in the ground boasted a rudimentary seat, raised up about two feet. "It's better than a bush, at least. I'll try to avoid getting splinters in odd places. Johnny, I know I'm pushing my luck, but any chance you could rig some sort of a shelter for it? It does rain here, you know."

"I'm working on it. Consider this is a decent start."

By the time the sun was setting, Cathy had the cabin organized, and was working with her sewing kit on some of the clothes. John called her outside one more time to view his handiwork. The latrine was now partially sheltered by a piece of canvas. He had anchored the ends with rocks.

"Nice. Isn't that part of the tent we shared at the re-enactment the night before last?"

"Yeah, one hundred and fifty-two years from now." He surveyed his creation, pleased with the progress. "I don't want to use any more of the tent for this – I may need it for real."

"Don't worry about it. I can check with Mary and Miss Martha to see if they have anything I can use for a front panel. It's not as if we are in the middle of town here, so I'm not really concerned about privacy. It's more for a windbreak." She smiled. "Your skills are as handy as mine, Dr. Andrews. Now it's your turn to see what I've been up to."

Cathy had been busy, and it showed. She had arranged the interior to make it as much of a home as possible with a few small touches. There was a tablecloth on the table, and curtains on the windows. The oil lamp was burning and cast light on the table. All their gear was stored out of sight.

"Wow," John exclaimed as he stopped short in the doorway, "This looks great! Where did you get the material for curtains and a tablecloth?"

"Miss Martha gave it to me. Mary apparently described the cabin to her, and she found some scraps that are too small to make any clothes. I used pins for right now – I wasn't sure they have safety pins yet, but I decided to risk it seeing as how we are not on the regular route of social calls. When I have some time, I'll sew a casing and find a wood rod. The tablecloth was another gift." Cathy paused, thoughtfully. "We are fish so far out of our own water that we might as well be living in a tree. I don't know what I'd do without the sisters. They have been amazingly generous."

"I know what you mean." He sat at the table. "Look. I don't think we were put here for me to get killed, but if the worst happens, I want you to know it means a lot to me that you're here with me. I can't think of anyone else I'd be comfortable sharing this with."

"I feel the same way, you know that," she said, setting out the small loaf of bread and some of the ham. "Let's have a light snack. Slice the bread while I get water."

She used a small pan as a ladle and filled two cups and sat down. "It's not much of a meal, but it's better than nothing."

"The ham is good, but the bread is terrific," he said, taking a bit of the ham. "Get the recipe. You'll shock them back home."

"I guess it would. I could always pass it off as something I came across on the trip. On another subject – the last thing I shoved into my backpack was my sewing kit. I took in a few seams in the day dress top and made a small alteration in my skirt."

They ate in silence for a few moments.

"Catie, I won't try to tell you I'm not scared about volunteering."

"Glad to hear it – fear can sharpen senses." She chewed a bite of bread. "I won't be able to relax until the battle is over. If you do get hit, be for damned sure you are brought to me. I'll try to be at the Scott home or the store. I told you that I want to meet at least General Buford and possibly the head of the brigade you get attached to."

"If anything does happen, I'll make sure I get to you." He looked around. "This place really does beat the hell out of living in a tent."

"Yep – and it's private enough so that if I do need to perform out-of-period, medical miracles on you, no one will be the wiser."

"Speaking of which - how's the penicillin coming along?"

"Nicely – I'd kill for some agar and petri dishes, but I think I can isolate the appropriate culture and keep it going. If I don't need it, I can toss it, but if I do, I'll be glad I have it handy."

"I'll rinse the plates while you play mad scientist. Then we can turn in."

"Mwuuaha-ha-ha...."

"Cute. Catie, you are not a well person."

"You've said that already."

CHAPTER FIVE

Part Two: The Week of the Battle and Immediate Aftermath

Tuesday, 30 June 1863

John was packing his gear appropriately for nineteenth-century duty as a dismounted cavalry officer when Cathy emerged from the bedroom. He was wearing his uniform pants and shirt, with his jacket, hat, and sword on a chair. She was carrying the dirty blouse and was wearing the one Mary had given her.

"I figured I would rinse the blouse and take it with us. I'll have to iron it before I wear it. Miss Martha said I should figure on doing that sort of thing at their home."

She grabbed the bucket and headed outside. After trying out the privy, she filled the bucket with water from the stream and rinsed out her blouse. She rolled up the wet garment in a towel, John had finished his packing and was watching her from the doorway.

"It doesn't compare with a washing machine, but it will do," she said as she edged by him. "You're going into town as military?"

"Yeah, since this is the day the cavalry shows up, I thought it would be okay."

"Will it matter to Buford that you don't have a horse?"

"Not much – they will be dismounted tomorrow anyway, and it'll be one less horse for someone to hold." John grinned suddenly. "It just occurred to me that when we get back, I will make a first-class technical advisor for our next re-enactment."

"Just don't get carried away and tell them why you know so much." She sighed. "I'm glad you keep saying 'when'."

"We have to believe that."

"I'm trying, really. In the middle of the night last night I woke up thinking that we could be here for life - neither of us has a spouse or children, so genetically we are not needed."

"You always were a joy in the morning. Not to mention being a pessimist," he teased.

"Well, optimists get all the bad surprises. Pessimists, on the other hand, only get pleasant ones."

"Seriously, Catie, we'll get back. Once we find out why we are here - and I can't help feeling there really is a reason – and we do whatever it is that needs to be done, we should end up back where we belong."

"Keep telling me that. It's frightening to realize that we're both only children and our parents live away from us - we are really isolated. About all we have *is* each other."

"Amen for that." John hoisted his rolled kit onto his shoulder. "I'm ready if you are. Will you be coming back here tonight?"

"I should come back here to tend the bread culture. It's covered with a plate and the heat should act as an incubator but; I'm trying to get a relatively clean culture. Mary and the Scotts might insist I stay in town, so I'll have to see how it goes. I can't impose forever, but since I don't know exactly where things are going to get hot, I may opt to stay if it's offered." She looked up at him. "Where will the Rebels be tonight?"

"Some will be east of town along the York Pike, some will be north of town, and there are some to the west. I was concerned about having to travel along the Pike, so I'm glad the shortcut we cleared yesterday eliminates having to walk along it." He regarded her carefully. "You have the Beretta on you, don't you?"

"Uh-huh. Just in case. I used an ACE wrap to strap the clip holster to my hip under the skirt. Thankfully the skirt has a pocket and I took the seam out so I can easily reach it if I need to. Concealed carry at its best."

"That's my clever girl." He grinned at her glare. "Okay, I know, but the compliment is genuine – take it that way."

"I'll try." She made a face as she pulled the cabin door shut. "We really can't establish any more local connections, can we?"

"Best not to – however, we have made the point that we are strangers here, that home is in Missouri, so no one will expect much for anything long-term. To change the subject – if there's a carry-bag empty, you might want to roll the blouse up and carry it that way. Your towel is too modern."

"Oops. Be right back."

*****

The walk into town was shorter. They arrived at the Scott home after less than a half-hour of brisk walking, which, as Cathy pointed out, beat the crap out of a forty-five-minute hike. Mary offered them coffee, which John accepted, but the first thing Cathy did was check on John Scott, who was improving nicely. She repeated her warnings about getting up too soon even if he felt better.

"Thank you for that," Martha said as the two women descended the stairs. "He was just saying that he felt up to it."

"I gathered, by the way, his face chastened when I had finished my piece, that it was on his mind," Cathy replied. "Two more days ought to do it, and I shall make sure you have enough tablets for the next few days."

Mary handed Cathy a cup of coffee and a slice of warm bread as she entered the kitchen. Cathy accepted the offerings while she shot John a glance as Mary turned back to the stove.

"I'm about to cook some eggs," she announced, "So please take a seat."

"Miss Mary asked if we had breakfasted," he said with a shrug. "I replied that we hadn't as we wanted to arrive as early as possible." He turned to the sisters. "Once more, we find ourselves unable to repay your friendship."

"Nonsense, Captain! We are already grateful to you both for your sister's assistance with my husband's illness, if nothing else, for without her intervention he'd be worse and trying to get up and around in spite of that. Anyone who can force common sense into John Scott's head is more than welcome in this house!"

The kitchen echoed with laughter followed quickly by a complaint.

"Now look what you've made me do, Martha McAllister Scott," said Mary. "My eggs are ruined."

Cathy popped up to see two of the yolks had broken, which undoubtedly had happened when Mary was laughing.

"Oh, simply scramble them," she suggested. "Here, allow me."

"I honestly prefer eggs scrambled," Cathy said five minutes later as she dug into her portion. "Somehow, trying to keep the yolks intact seems like too much work."

"Cathy is what my mother calls a basic cook – good food, but definitely nothing fancy," John supplied as there were more chuckles. "Would it be possible for one of you to write down the recipe for your bread?"

"Johnny is convinced that if I can return home with your bread recipe, I shall surprise everyone," Cathy stated, then sighed. "He's undoubtedly correct. Loaves I make don't turn out nearly this well."

"My mother would also be eternally grateful if you could also coax Cathy through the rigors of creating gravy that did not re-semble – how did she put it? – broth with hard beans." John looked up just in time to see the face Cathy made.

"I'm certain we can do something," Martha replied, laughing. "It's not difficult."

"It seems so for me," Cathy sighed. "I take comfort from the fact that I'm not expected to do much cooking or baking at home."

"I would think you would take more comfort from the idea that not everyone can stand the sight of blood, much less set a bone or stitch a wound," John observed.

"Talents and skills do vary from person to person," Mary McAllister added. "Martha is the cook here. I run the store."

"I do have one reasonably domestic skill I would like to demonstrate, if possible, this morning," Cathy said.

"You did just fine with the eggs," John put in. "Are you cer-tain you want to press your luck by trying something else?"

"I sincerely hope you realize how firmly I am resisting the temptation of snapping my napkin at you, brother of mine. How-ever, I find it interesting that you bring up the subject of pressing." Cathy turned to Martha. "I rinsed out my soiled blouse this morning, and it needs to be ironed."

"May I inquire if you two are like this all the time at home?" Mary asked, smiling broadly.

"I assure you, Miss Mary, we are not – we are generally much worse." John grinned.

"Those who know us well have long given up on us," Cathy added as she nodded her agreement.

"John, why don't you and Mary go over to the store and see if anything else needs to be done. In your absence, I will test Cathy's ability to handle an iron. Your presence might impel her to forcibly place it somewhere besides her blouse." Martha's face was all innocence as she collected the now-empty dishes and took them to the sink.

"I see not all the humor in the room came in with us," Cathy commented. "I'm always afraid that people will take offense at the way John and I tease each other."

"Far from it, it seems," said John. "As for the suggestion, I'm willing. As Miss Martha observed if I'm not here you can't brandish it at me. Shall we go, Miss Mary?"

"I would like you to take notice of the idea he is leaving just as there are dishes to wash," Cathy murmured to Martha.

"So is Mary," she murmured back. "I'll get the iron and put it on the stove. I don't think we'll need the sad one, so it shouldn't take long to heat up."

*****

At the store, John helped Mary rearrange some of the merchandise to make the store look less picked-over. He insisted on moving the heavier items, and once she saw that she wasn't going to be able to argue with him, Mary ceased to try. Most of the customers who entered the store questioned him about the location of the Union Cavalry.

"Be assured that they are coming, and will be here soon," was his standard reply, with what he hoped was a reassuring smile.

"How can you be certain?" one woman asked.

"Ma'am, I just am," he said, hoping he projected confidence.

Mary McAllister regarded him for a moment after the woman left.

"I would also like to know how you come by this conviction, Captain."

"Miss Mary," he said, as he consulted his watch, "It is just after eleven o'clock. Why don't you close up and let us go back to your home."

They were still on the store's side of Chambersburg Street when they heard cheering and yelling coming from further down, near Washington Street.

"Here they come, Miss Mary," John said with a grin.

"Yes, and I for one am most grateful," she replied. Turning to him, she added, "It does seem that you knew. You were certain, right down to the hour."

"It was a lucky guess about the time," he replied, "But yes, I knew they were coming. It's simple, really. They had to come."

"I believe I take your meaning, Captain."

They watched as the cavalry unit came towards them. John spotted General Buford, Colonel Gamble, and Colonel Devin in what amounted to a parade. People were cheering, women were offering bread, cakes, and some were giving flowers to the men. One group of young girls sang for them. John felt sure that the tired, dirty men appreciated their welcome.

"General Buford, sir!" John called out sharply and saluted as the dusty, tired officer crossed Franklin Street. "Captain John Andrews, Third Missouri Cavalry. May I have a moment of your time, sir?"

"Captain," Buford replied, returning the salute as he pulled to the side of the road, "last I heard, your unit was in the west."

"Yes, sir. I became detached due to illness." Taking a deep breath, John took his dive. "Sir, I would like very much to present myself for assignment, if you feel you could make use of my services."

"Captain, how long have you been here in Gettysburg?" Buford asked as his aide, Captain Myles Keogh, rode up.

"I walked in Sunday, sir, with my sister."

"Captain Keogh, this is Captain Andrews, Third Missouri Cavalry." The two junior officers shook hands as the general continued, "Captain Andrews has been here for a few days. Can you recommend a location for my headquarters?"

"Sir, the Eagle Hotel on Chambersburg Street, just a-ways ahead, would serve you well. The other hotel, the Globe is more of a tavern."

"Captain Keogh, see to the needed arrangements at the Eagle Hotel," Buford ordered.

"Yes, sir!" Keogh saluted and rode off.

"Why is your sister here with you?"

"She is a nurse, General Buford, and tended me during my illness."

"You seem to be reasonably intelligent, Captain, and hopefully not over-pampered. Come see me at my headquarters and we'll see about getting you back into this fight."

"Sir, I would ask that my sister be allowed to accompany me to the meeting."

"Is that necessary?"

"Sir, begging your pardon, it is entirely my fault, I'm afraid. I have spoken of you to her and she would like to meet you." John gave a small shrug. "My sister is the best nurse in Columbia, Missouri, and after nursing me back to health she would like to take the opportunity to meet my new commanding officer." John paused. *What the hell – there's nothing to lose.* He added, "I can assure the general that she did not pamper me. Quite the contrary, she had me back on my feet faster than most would have thought possible."

"Captain, I have little time for civilians and all of it is begrudged. However, if she is giving me an officer, I suppose I can try to be sociable." The words were gruff, but a glint of what might have been humor flashed briefly in Buford's eyes. "Before that, though, what can you tell me about the enemy's location?"

"I believe General Ewell is east of town on the York Pike. He came into town last Friday and moved out to the northeast to his present position. I have heard of some sightings of General Pettigrew's troops west of town along the Chambersburg Pike. I do apologize, sir, for not having more solid information for you."

"That will do for a start. I shall see you later at my headquarters. Shall we make it about four o'clock? You may bring your sister," he replied, ignoring the apology and pulling out his watch.

"We shall be there, sir." He saluted. "Thank you, sir."

John watched as the veteran cavalry commander rode off. He found he was shaking a bit, at least on the inside. *I hope like hell it doesn't show.* He took a deep breath.

"Captain, you are full of surprises," said Mary McAllister. "And someday I would like to know more about you and your sister."

John, still recovering from meeting John Buford, started. He had almost forgotten she was there. "Ma'am?"

"I shall not press you now, for you seem a bit unsettled at the moment, and I can't say I blame you. The General does appear formidable. However, I would like to talk more in the near future."

"Miss Mary, let us discuss this at the house."

Cathy was standing in front of the house, watching the procession. She saw a general, two colonels, and some lesser officers go by.

"You spoke with the General." She was not asking.

"Inside, you." He paused and looked down the street at the Union troops.

"Of course." As she passed him in the doorway, she murmured, "Watch the colloquialisms."

"Cripes, thanks."

Once seated in the parlor, Mary called for Martha to join them.

"Captain? I believe it is time," she stated as her sister sat on the settee.

John looked at Cathy.

"Johnny, I know I trust Mary and Miss Martha the way I would our own family at home. We are guests here, however, and we shouldn't add to the burdens that are coming." *Come on, Johnny, catch what I'm not saying – explain but not everything.*

"Cathy, Captain," began Mary, "Please understand. I have never before felt this close to any strangers as quickly as I have to both of you. Under other circumstances, I would not pry, yet my curiosity is piqued. Whatever you tell us shall be held in strictest confidence."

"Miss Martha, Miss Mary, let me begin by saying that we shall always be grateful to you and your family for taking us in the way you have. Cathy and I are quite literally on our own here. You helped us find shelter, opened your home to us, and provided us with more than we had the right to expect. You do indeed deserve more candor than we have provided."

"Be assured that my brother does speak for us both," Cathy added. "To start, we are indeed from Missouri."

"I was teaching engineering at the University in Columbia until classes were suspended due to the war. Cathy works at the medical center at the University. She is considered to be one of the best nurses there, almost a doctor."

"Captain," said Martha, smiling, "I have suspected your sister was more than an ordinary nurse. Believe me, we are all grateful for her knowledge."

"Miss Martha, I have seen more than one doctor turn to her for assistance," John stated. "She has a true gift for healing." Mentally, he shrugged. *At least that was accurate. Catie had been born to heal, no matter what century she happened to be in.*

"From her father?"

"To be honest, that is one of the things which had made me uncomfortable," Cathy said with a slight grimace. "My father is actually a lawyer. I took to the sciences early on, which was surprising considering no one in my family ever had. The explanation we offered at first was what we believed best for an introduction. When we first arrived, we were so uncertain of our circumstances we decided not to chance anything. Please forgive us?"

"In the middle of a war, it's difficult to know whom to trust," John added. "I am with the Third Missouri Cavalry, and I was separated from my unit in circumstances too lengthy to explain. I have no horse, and I was specifically looking for General Buford. I have been following his progress since the dust-up at Brandy Station."

"You haven't been sick?" Mary queried.

"No, I wasn't, thankfully. Please understand it was the best explanation we could think of to explain why I wasn't where I should be." He breathed a sigh of relief as the sisters nodded.

"After John became separated from his unit, and once he could communicate with me, I decided to join him. This does not lessen my concern now that he may now become wounded. With all due respect to local and military physicians, I far prefer to treat him myself," Cathy explained. She sat back in her chair with a sigh of relief.

"We truly do apologize for not being more forthright," John said, going to stand behind Cathy's chair, putting a hand on her shoulder.

"No apologies are necessary, and we shall honor the confidences you entrust to us." Mary moved her hand as if to wave away all that had passed. "Now then, Captain, you hailed General Buford out in the street. Do you have an appointment with him?"

"Yes," he replied with a glance down at Cathy. "I am to present myself to him this afternoon at his headquarters at four o'clock."

"Am I to accompany you?" asked Cathy.

"I specifically requested that he receive you as well, yes, and somewhat to my surprise, he agreed."

"You were surprised?" Martha asked.

"Yes, ma'am. The general has a reputation for not tolerating civilians well, I'm afraid," he responded. "Catie, we have just about enough time to go back to the cabin for you to change clothes. I should have told you to bring the day dress."

The look on her face told him how welcome that thought was, but she was saved from trying to phrase it properly when Mary intervened.

"Nonsense – I have a day dress of lighter material which would be more appropriate for this weather." She got up. "Come, Cathy. Martha, don't let lunch get scorched."

As Cathy stood up, she put her hand in her pocket, and as she passed him, he thought he heard, "You lucky bastard," but he decided not to question her. He also found himself with his Beretta in his hand. He shoved it in his pocket, wondering how she was going to explain the ACE bandage.

Upstairs, Cathy looked in on John Scott, who appeared to be better. She opened her mouth to say something, but he held up his hand.

"Cathy, ma'am, I am not planning on going for any long walks, but I would like permission to come down to lunch."

"That may be a longer walk than you are reckoning. Shall we start with something basic? First, you need to get out of bed." She was smiling as she went into the room and positioned herself at the bedside, standing close enough to assist if it became necessary. "The fever has left you weak." John Scott made a move, and she continued, "Please before you move, listen. Roll onto your side, push yourself up with your arm, and sit on the side of the bed until you aren't dizzy anymore. Once you have done that, we'll see about standing up."

"That is very sensible," Mary said as she regarded the younger woman. Cathy did know her business, and if John Scott listened, so much the better.

"It's a trick I learned the hard way after I spent three days in bed," she said by way of explanation. "It takes almost one day of going easy for every day you have been in bed." Cathy watched closely as her patient followed her instructions and sat up. "That makes it easier, does it not?" she asked as he sat there. "Now we come to the hard part. Keep your feet about this far apart," she said, holding her hands to indicate two feet, "As you stand. Use my shoulder to help you balance if you need to do so. When you are ready…."

Martha appeared in the doorway behind Mary as John stood up. Once standing, he did reach out for Cathy's shoulder, as she knew he would. He wobbled a bit but stayed on his feet.

"Now we are going to take three steps towards the door, turn around, and come back to the bed where you will sit back down.

When you turn, let go of my shoulder. I'll be behind you and I shall make sure you don't fall."

The sisters moved back to make room, and John Scott did as Cathy had instructed. As he sat back down on the edge of the bed, she smiled at him. "That did take more out of you than you thought it would, did it not?"

"I feel as weak as a newborn kitten," he admitted.

"Lay back down the way you got up, turning on your side and using your arms," Cathy said, adding encouragingly, "You did very well."

"When will I be ready to come downstairs?"

"Possibly later today or tomorrow. Whenever it is, it won't be for long." Cathy turned to Martha. "I showed Mr. Scott some hints about...."

"John, please," he interrupted.

"I showed Mr. John how to sit and stand. I think you'll find it the easiest way to do it. You, sir, are now allowed to get up and take a few steps about once an hour IF someone is in the room. You have to ease your way back into doing things. If you are fortunate, you may get to sit in a chair today."

"Cathy, you will get no arguments from me." He sank back into his pillows, obviously tired.

"Miss Martha, let's continue the medicine and make sure he drinks plenty of water. I also believe that today he can have some light food, like bread with honey to start for lunch, and later some pieces of ham and some mashed potato." Cathy noted that John was smiling with his eyes shut. "I thought you'd appreciate that!" she added, and his smile became a grin.

They left John to rest, and Mary took Cathy to her bedroom. Martha came in and closed the door.

"He is behaving himself," she said with an air of wonder.

"I hope he's afraid not to," Cathy replied. "I do believe that the worst is over, but he could still set himself back badly. I am trying to show him he needn't force himself too fast."

Mary dug into her wardrobe, pulling out a summer day dress. It was light muslin with a delicate, small floral print. The neckline was scooped but not too low, the half-sleeves were gathered at the cuffs and midway up the arms, attaching to the bodice with a slight poof. The blouse fit into the full skirt at the waistband, and the skirt had three tiers of ruffles around the hem. Mary also held out a matching button shoulder shawl, with a ruffle all the way around it, which was designed to sit over the bodice.

"Mary, this is too lovely," Cathy protested. "I can wear this skirt with the clean blouse I pressed this morning."

"Stuff and nonsense – you are making an official call on a superior officer and you have to make a good impression," Mary said firmly. "Martha, you have an extra crinoline and I think she will need it. This skirt will be too long without it."

"Mary is quite correct," Martha agreed as she nodded. "You must look your best. We can't have you meeting the general looking like a shop assistant. I shall return in a moment."

"I would lend you mine but I'm taller than you are and the skirt is a little long. We shall have to see if you need hoops," Mary added to Cathy, as Martha returned to the room carrying two petticoats. "We'll have to see which one looks better."

Cathy was relieved to see she didn't need the hoops – she wasn't used to them on a daily basis, only for a few hours at a time. The shawl overlay hid the fact that the bodice was a little large, and the skirt length was fine with the full crinoline. Before she went downstairs, Martha asked Cathy to let John see her in the dress as she had explained the upcoming meeting to him when she retrieved the petticoats.

"Young lady," he said, smiling, "If you don't impress the general, he doesn't deserve your brother!"

Laughing as she descended the staircase, she saw John waiting at the bottom. All three ladies chuckled at the sight of his mouth falling open. Cathy proceeded to the parlor and gracefully turned around.

"Mr. John approved," she said to him. "I presume by your expression, brother dear, that I pass muster?" She laughed as all he could do was nod. "I believe he's impressed," she told the sisters.

"Miss Martha? Do I smell something coming from the kitchen?" John asked, still admiring Cathy's appearance.

"Oh my goodness – my biscuits!" Martha exclaimed as she flew out of the room to make sure nothing was burning.

Cathy made sure she had a clean dishtowel covering her bodice as they ate their noon dinner, which was roasted chicken with mashed potatoes and some fresh green beans. Martha had also made some biscuits, which had not scorched. Cathy noticed that John was a bit more quiet than usual, and chose to listen to the three women chatter while he ate. Martha set out her husband's fare on a tray – with the added surprise of some beans, which Cathy felt would be good for him if he could tolerate them - and took it upstairs to sit with him while he ate. Cathy and Mary had finished cleaning up the dishes and putting the left-overs away in a stone crock to keep them cool when Martha came back downstairs, chuckling.

"Cathy, my dear, you have made the most solid impression upon my husband," she said. "He saw the green beans on his plate, and before he touched them, he asked me if I was certain you had agreed to them being there!"

"You sound surprised," John said, laughing. "Cathy has dealt with more querulous men than your husband. I sincerely hope that her restrictions hold when the shooting starts."

"There you go again, John," Cathy admonished as the two sisters abruptly stopped laughing, "Frightening everyone. I thought I was the pessimist."

"Now, Cathy, in all fairness to the Captain, there are rebel troops east of town and federal troops in town. Shooting is, at this juncture, almost inevitable, I'm afraid," said Mary.

"Unfortunately for the citizens of Gettysburg, the geography itself is disturbing in this situation. Your town sits close to the border of Maryland not far from Virginia, thus the Confederacy is close. In addition, there are several main roads which converge here. Those facts alone put you in danger," John stated. "All we can do now is hope we can push the rebels back."

"We've not done well so far," said Martha. "It seems as if the rebels have had the upper hand."

"I'm afraid that everyone now thinks that General Lee is invincible, and our own leadership has been somewhat lacking," John said glumly. "Perhaps General Meade will turn things around."

Cathy, who had listened to this hoping John would not give too much away, let out the breath she had been holding.

John rose and bowed slightly. "Ladies, if you will excuse us, I'd like a few minutes with Cathy in the parlor before she meets

General Buford. With your permission?" John rose and bowed slightly. Cathy followed him out.

They both spoke at once.

"Typical of us," John observed. "Catie, normally, I'd let you go first, but I'm dying to know: what did you do with the ACE wrap?"

"Huh? Oh – nothing. It's still in place. I have my long slip on, so I pulled it over the wrap and put the crinoline over the slip. What's Buford like?"

"Well, he didn't chew me up and spit me out, if that's what you mean. Nervous?"

"Oh, every bit of that. Is there anything you can tell me that would help?"

"He's about what I expected from what I've read about him. No-nonsense, very efficient, dry sense of humor - but it is there. Old for his age, which, by the way, is thirty-seven. I told him you nursed me back to health, so we'd better take it from there."

"Speaking of which – I'm glad we were opened up a bit here since we can't explain fully. I was afraid you were going to get carried away at the table."

"After the zipper bit, I'm trying to be more careful. Can you take the Beretta back?"

"Sure – I won't be able to draw it, but I can keep it with me." Cathy lifted up all her skirts and tucked the .22 back in the elastic bandage. "I thought these guys are in business now."

"Not with semi-auto handguns. They started in the 1500s with arquebus barrels."

"Show-off."

"I want to warn you, Catie, that after we meet with General Buford, I may not be able to do much more than escort you back here, and I may not be able to do that. Be prepared."

"No problem. I'll try not to fall apart, but I will give you a hug if that's acceptable. I'll do it even if it isn't. How's our time?"

"Not quite three o'clock."

"Good. I want to visit the privy and then make sure Mr. John enjoyed his lunch. The green beans were a test." Then, if we have time and can find one, I'd like to visit an apothecary."

"Huh?"

"I'd like to buy a small can or bottle of ether if I can."

"To go along with the bread mold, I suppose."

"Uh-huh." She brightened. "Hey – I have an idea!"

"Anything you want to do now?"

John followed her as she went back to the kitchen.

"Miss Martha, would you have a small jar or glass, a piece of bread to fit in the bottom, some meat broth, a piece of paper, and a piece of string?"

"Will this do? I used it to cut the biscuits." Martha held up the small glass she was drying. "As for broth, I believe there is a little bit of chicken broth left. I should caution you, it doesn't have any salt in it. I haven't baked bread today, though, so all I have is one left-over biscuit."

"That will be fine, in fact, the plain broth and the biscuit will be better." Cathy trimmed the biscuit, slipped it into the glass, and added enough broth to moisten it. "The paper and the string will provide enough protection for it."

"I'm curious. May I ask what this is for?"

"I want to try sprouting some seeds," Cathy replied, as she fastened the paper to the top of the glass with the string. "May I leave it here until I get back from our interview with the General?"

"Of course."

"Cathy," said Mary as she came down the stairs, "Here's a small reticule for you to carry."

"Thank you! Now I have a place to carry some money." Johnny," Cathy said as she turned to him with her hand out for some. "I truly would like to visit the apothecary before our meeting."

"I was waiting for that," John teased her, handing her some currency. "Since you wish to go shopping, we should probably leave shortly. I also imagine that you want to peek in on your patient, so while you do that I'll find out where the apothecary is."

Cathy found that Mr. John was resting. He thanked her for the green beans, which he told her had tasted good enough to be dessert. He got up and took a few steps without assistance, which she reported to the sisters back downstairs.

"This is always the dangerous time. He feels better and will be tempted to overdo, and it's going to be hard to hold him back, partly because he's not going to have much to do. If you have the time, Miss Martha, you might want to take the newspaper up and read to him."

"I shall make the time," Martha said, nodding.

"Shall we go?" John asked.

Later, when they were out on the street, John asked her how sick John Scott had been.

"For this day and age, very. It was a virus attack which he was fighting off, but the elevated temperature could have been a major problem in itself. He was showing signs of disorientation already, plus hydration was not usual thinking until the 1950s. While we think nothing of taking an aspirin or acetaminophen and pushing fluids to keep going, no one here is accustomed to it. He responded to the aspirin, but even so, if he tries to get up and do too many things, say, tomorrow, he's so weak he is probably going to collapse." She frowned. "Even in our own time, a viral infection can leave an opening for a secondary bacterial infection to take hold."

"Interesting. Here we are – let's see if you can get what you want."

John was never able to describe how she did it, mostly because what he witnessed was a medical discussion. He stood inside the shop, listening, as Cathy managed to fast-talk the apothecary out of a small can of ether 'for the good boys in blue'. She had to display clear knowledge and describe some of the surgeries she had 'assisted'. The apothecary, impressed with her, sold it at cost and threw in a supply of cotton gauze to use with it. Back on the street, she told John that she didn't have the heart to tell the man that a cone of gauze was not the most efficient way to use it.

"No?"

"Definitely not. I'll borrow a tea strainer, line it and cover it with a piece of gauze, and use that."

"Sounds like the scene in *Destination: Tokyo* where they take out the appendix."

"Exactly. That was well done – they used what they had, which is what I'm going to have to do. We don't use ether anymore, partly because inhalation agents are not as controllable as intravenous ones, but when used properly, it's still effective." She sighed. "I couldn't very well walk in and ask for a vial of propofol with an IV kit and a couple of syringes."

"No, I guess not." John nodded ahead. "Look, there's the hotel, and that's General Buford riding up."

They approached the general, who appeared to be lost in thought.

"Sir?" John wanted to make their presence known.

"Captain Andrews." Buford looked around, started to move in his saddle, and stopped.

"May we be of assistance?"

Cathy reached for the bridle as John held out his hand to the other man.

"Much obliged. My aide seems to be busy."

Buford swung down out of the saddle, Cathy noted, with great difficulty. She took in the stiffly-held frame, pained face, gnarled hands, and the overall exhaustion. *Rheumatoid arthritis so bad it was almost crippling, with pain preventing refreshing sleep.* She saw John had to steady him once he stood on the ground.

"Grey Eagle." John Andrews didn't realize that he spoke aloud as he patted the horse before Cathy handed over the reins to a young aide who came running up to take charge of the animal.

"Captain, you know my horse's name?" Buford was soft-spoken, but his voice was deep.

"Yes, sir." John recovered his manners. "General, may I present my sister, Miss Mary Catherine Howell?" Cathy bobbed a small curtsey.

"Captain, Miss Howell, let's find chairs inside. No sense making things easy for enemy shooters."

The small party found seats in the hotel lobby. Cathy again noted Buford's mobility difficulties and had to remind herself that she couldn't say or do anything. His uniform was dusty, and she decided the actor who played him in the epic film – one hundred and thirty or so years from now? – had the outfit correct. Blue corduroy pants tucked into plain boots, no frills; plain, worn shirt and a jacket with a pipe in one pocket and a tobacco pouch in the other. Yet the man's presence was amazing.

"Well, Captain?"

"Sir, I would very much like to get back into this fight if you will allow me to join your command. I have been trying to catch up with you for some time."

"Captain, how long have you been in the army?"

"General, I was teaching at the University of Missouri until classes were suspended due to the war in the spring of 1862. I joined the Third Missouri Volunteer Cavalry, and was with them until I fell ill in Arkansas."

"Where you came in, Miss Howell?"

"Yes, sir. I was a nurse and teacher at the university medical center. When John sent word he needed me, I went. He had some type of fever that would not let go."

"My sister is the best nurse in Missouri," John put in proudly. "Others had already given up on me."

"You say you have been looking for me. Me in particular?"

"Yes, sir. We traveled, mostly on foot, dodging the Confederates here and there. I wanted to report to either General Pleasanton or you, to see if I could be attached to the First Division of the Cavalry Corps."

"I will gladly take you on, Captain. I have two brigades with me, and I need officers. Bobby Lee has a lot more men. I do want to make sure you know our odds are not good, begging your pardon, Miss Howell."

"I am at your service, General, wherever you would care to place me," John stated evenly and firmly.

"General, may I speak frankly?" At Buford's nod, Cathy continued; she strove to be unemotional. "My brother is a hardheaded, stubborn man. I do not doubt that he could get a desk position somewhere in Washington, but he has decided to fight. Here. He assures me you are the best cavalry commander in the Army, and we have followed you so he could join up with you and your men. If he is to be wounded or killed, sir, I would be happier if it was with someone he respected. However, I do have one request, sir, if you will permit me to ask it."

"Ma'am?"

"My brother has informed you that I worked at the university medical center. I worked as a nurse, a nursing instructor, and also assisted physicians in their work, including surgery. With all due respect to your surgeons, if my brother, once entrusted to your command, is injured or wounded, I would, in my turn, request that he be entrusted to my care to better his chances of recovery."

"I see intelligence runs in your family, Andrews."

"Sir, Miss Howell is my step-sister. The greatest intelligence in our family was evidenced when her father married my mother. We grew up in a home that prizes individuality," John explained. "I trusted her with my life when I fell ill, and I'm here. However, yesterday I used Shakespeare's words to describe her."

"I begin to understand, Captain. 'Though she be but little, she be fierce.'" As John smiled and nodded, Buford continued, "Miss Howell, are you staying in town?"

"We have spent most of the last two days in town, sir, althhough I am living in a small cabin outside of town. We have been most fortunate to find friends who have seen to it that I have employment, and some of my things are at their home, just down the street."

"Gettysburg is most likely to be the site of a sizable dispute over the next couple of days. May I offer a piece of advice?

"You are about to tell me to stay indoors with my head down until the shooting stops." Cathy smiled at the man in front of her. She nodded towards John. "I have heard this before."

"You seem to be taking this rather calmly."

"I bow to the inevitable, General, once I see that it *is* inevitable." Cathy looked at John. "I shall not attempt to convince anyone that I am neither worried nor scared. However, the Union will be preserved."

"You believe that?" General Buford seemed genuinely curious as if her opinion mattered.

"Yes, sir, I do, with all my heart. I also believe that what happens here in the next few days will help determine that as the ultimate outcome of the war."

"Captain, can SHE ride a horse?" Buford gave Cathy one of his rare smiles.

"As a matter of record, she can indeed. When we were children, she was quite the tomboy and every bit as at home in the saddle as I was."

"Before the general gets any odd notions, let me hastily add that I gave up riding in company when Mother forced me to wear skirts and use a sidesaddle. It wasn't nearly as much fun," Cathy stated as she made a face. "I, therefore, beg to be excused from active duty, unless you need a courier to ride that magnificent mount of yours."

She had the pleasure of seeing Buford's smile widen for a moment with a chuckle, but it faded altogether as he got back to business.

"Captain Andrews, I will attach you to Colonel Devin's brigade or possibly to my staff. Miss Howell, how can we find you if you are needed?"

"I had hoped to come into town tomorrow morning, General, so I can assist in whatever needs to be done. Yet, if you think it best, I could remain at the cabin. I will abide by whatever you both think I should do." Cathy looked at John and laughed at his stunned expression on his face. "Johnny, General Buford will think I never cooperate if you keep making faces. I should like to think that I know when to obey as well as when to argue."

"Catie, I am so used to squabbling with you that reasonable thought startled me," he told her. "I have already stated I would prefer to have you stay at the cabin."

"Miss Howell, I sincerely recommend you remain out of town, safely away from stray bullets. No one can be sure of how this fight will begin or where it will wander. There will be plenty of patients to assist once the shooting stops." Buford rose painfully and pulled out a map of the area, which Cathy recognized as the same one John had. "Captain, can you show me where the cabin is located?"

"It's here, sir, near this small wooded area, situated alongside this stream."

"General, begging your pardon for my insistence, will you send word to me if John is injured?"

"Miss Howell, I shall do my best to send *him* to you if he is injured. Anyone who willingly walked across the war with her brother to help him rejoin this fight is not someone I care to displease." The barest flicker of a smile passed quickly. "Captain, will you see your sister to her friends' home? Then join me for a briefing on the situation. I have scouts out based in part on the information you gave me earlier." Buford nodded to Cathy as the captain John had met earlier came up to him. "Captain Keogh, Captain Andrews will be joining us once he sees his sister, Miss Howell, to her friends. Miss Howell, it has been a pleasure meeting you." He tipped his hat to her.

"General Buford, the honor is mine," Cathy said, curtseying as she rose.

John offered Cathy his arm as they walked down the street.

"He's a good man, John. I wish I could help him – one good night's sleep would do him worlds of good."

"You can't. I know it's frustrating but you just can't." He stopped for a moment. "On another subject - I just thought of something. There's a present for you in my stuff from the reenactment. Dig around for it and go ahead and open it. Call it a 'just cuz' gift. I hope you like it."

"I'm sure I will." They continued in silence until they reached the Scott home. "Johnny, I'm not going to say goodbye. Just be careful. Please, be very careful."

"I'll be okay, Catie. We have to believe that." He looked down at her. "I'll get word to you when I can."

"Warning: I'm about to be very undignified." She threw her arms around his neck, gave him a big hug, and kissed him on the cheek.

"I can deal with that," he said, returning the hug as he kissed her forehead. "I'll be careful, I promise."

She was standing there, watching him go down the street when the door behind her opened.

"Cathy?" Martha called to her.

"Coming." She turned and entered, stopping short when she spotted John Scott seated in the parlor. He grinned at her, and she smiled back, wagging a finger at him. She glanced at the clock and saw it was not quite four-thirty. The interview with the general had not lasted long.

"The Captain is going with General Buford?" John Scott asked.

"Yes, the general was pleased to accept his offer of service, as I suspected he would be, I'm afraid." Cathy sniffed the air. "Bread baking? It smells wonderful."

"Mary and I felt we should do something. It seemed as good an idea as any."

"I can think of something else if you are willing to sacrifice some bed linens. I have a feeling that there will be a lot of wounded men around here in the next few days. Strips and squares of cloth would be useful as bandages. Be prepared for men asking for water and the extra loaves of bread won't go to waste."

"Cathy – you are back," said Mary, coming from the kitchen. "The Captain?"

"He's going to be with General Buford's second brigade, under Colonel Devin, or possibly be attached to the General's staff." Cathy took a deep breath, letting it out slowly. "Forgive me. Johnny and I had a long journey here, and it's going to take some time for me to get used to the idea that I'm on my own." She realized what she had said, and putting her hand to her face, quickly added, "Oh dear, that didn't come out right."

"Pay it no mind – I think we all understand. Will you stay to supper and the night?" Mary asked.

"Please, we can easily put you up," echoed Martha.

"You have been wonderful, and I thank you both. I'd love to stay for supper. However, both Johnny and General Buford feel it would be best for me to return to the cabin tonight and stay there throughout the fighting. The general knows where the cabin is, and should anything happen, he has said he will get word to me." Cathy paused for a moment reflecting on the meeting. "Thankfully, the general is an honorable man."

After dinner, having promised to come back to visit once it was safe, Cathy left enough aspirin tablets for an additional six days. Armed with a few recipes, she made her way back to the cabin, toting her medical bag and her carry bag, which was packed full of what Miss Martha had called "All sorts of useful things." She made herself a cup of tea and sat lost in thought and feeling sorry for herself.

Here I am, one hundred and fifty-two years from the time I belong to, in the midst of what was historically acknowledged as one of the worst battles the world has ever known. The companion I trust the most is heading into the thick of it, and I'm alone in a cabin in the middle of nowhere. I have no way to find out what was going on, and if anything happens to Johnny I won't know about it until he shows up on the doorstep.

"As situations go, this one sucks," she said to herself out loud. "Howell, get back to work."

As the sun changed angles in the window, she lit the lamp. First order of business was the culture. She used a sterilized paper clip to transfer four small bits of the cleanest looking mold to the jar she had prepped in Martha's kitchen. She unpacked her medical bag onto the table so she could take a closer inventory of what she had, and added the ether and gauze.

Not much, but better than local stone knives and bearskins. The surgical kit included sterilized instruments, suture, and needles – she had packed it herself. The ether was a good addition. She found one bottle of antibiotic pills, which would come in handy for support but the penicillin would make a great poultice. The small first-aid kit even added some antibiotic ointment and Band-Aids, plus the casting material the associate producer had procured for her, along with assorted ACE wraps.

Please, Johnny, make all this unnecessary. She repacked the kit. She was as prepared for emergencies as possible.

She took it into the bedroom and added some meds from the bag to her personal ones before she stashed the bag under the bed. Then she dragged out John's backpack and dug around in it until she found the present he had mentioned. It was wrapped and had a note. She hefted the wrapped gift. *Books!*

She decided to leave the gift on the table to take a walk outside while it was still light enough. The woods were lovely, and she didn't hear anyone else around. Forcing her thoughts away from the war, she strolled around idly, picked some flowers she found and munched on a few wild berries. She was heading back to the cabin when she heard a gurgling she hadn't noted before. She followed it and was less than ten yards from the back of the small building when she found the source of the noise.

It was a spring. Water was bubbling right at the surface. She leaned over and scooped a handful to taste.

"Well, I'll be. Good enough to bottle and sell back home." Very pleased with her discovery, she scrounged around for some rocks to make sure she could find it again before heading back to the cabin.

After putting the flowers in a container – they made a nice touch on the table – she decided to open her present. The note came first.

"To Catie – the best friend a guy could ever have. Thanks for sharing the adventure! With a hug, Johnny"

"Prophetic. Oh, brother mine, prophetic beyond words. Now let's see what's in here."

She opened the package and laughed out loud.

"John Townsend Andrews, you are the best!" She took her new books, an Agatha Christie collection of the complete Hercule Poirot stories and a Nero Wolfe omnibus, to the table, smiling. At least she had something to read while she waited out the long day tomorrow. She wondered how John was getting along, and where he was serving.

*****

John stood just to the left of Myles Keogh as General Buford began his briefing.

"Sometime early in the morning, the Rebels are going to come marching up our way from the north. They most likely will be coming in strength, and frankly gentlemen, it's up to us to stop them. We hold until we are relieved. If we don't, there sure isn't anything else that will stop them. At this moment, the Army of the Potomac is strung out all the way back to Maryland. Lee is no one's fool and I don't doubt that Jeb Stuart has informed him of this. Right now, Bobby Lee is picturing his boys rolling up those elements one by one as his whole army proceeds to Washington. If we don't hold here, he'll do just that and there will be the devil to pay. So here is the plan of battle: we form a line along McPherson's Ridge and we stay there until we are dead or relieved."

Col. Devin addressed the general. "Sir I don't think it will be a hard-fought action. I feel that the Rebels are just probing to make contact and we can easily drive their skirmishers back."

"No, you won't." Buford turned a hard gaze towards Devin. "They will attack you in the morning and they will come booming – skirmishers three-deep. You will have to fight like the devil until supports arrives. We have the advantage of the high ground and I plan to use it to the fullest. "

Buford paused and looked into the face of each of the men clustered around him. "Gentlemen, I think I may safely say we hold the fate of the Union in our hands; what we do here may determine the outcome of the war. I have sent a message to General Meade. Meanwhile, we must ready ourselves. Gentlemen, see to your troops." With a nod, he dismissed them.

As the men began to move away John's arm was taken by his new friend Myles. "Come with me, John. Colonel Devin has a company that lost their Captain and you, my lad, have volunteered to take his place."

Keogh led him to his new command. Along the way, they passed the picket line for Buford's staff. Keogh stopped at the line and untied a lead.

"Here you go," he said as he handed the line to John. On the end of the rope was a bay mare with full tack. "I pulled her earlier for you. She's a good mount – I've ridden her once or twice myself." Patting the horse on the neck he continued, "She'll see you through the fight tomorrow."

John took the rope and reached to pat the horse, letting her get used to his feel and smell. "What's her name?"

"One of the troopers named her Check. She's a steady mount under fire."

Trailing the horse on the line behind them, the two men moved on to where a company was set in a cold camp. Keogh called to one of the men moving in the area. "Sergeant Hingle."

"Sir." A tough-looking, small older man came forward. Chest like a barrel, wide shoulders, and dark hair sprinkled with gray, he looked capable of keeping order by his mere presence.

"Sergeant, this is Captain Andrews. He will be in command of the company on the morrow. John, this First Sergeant Calvin Hingle. He's an excellent NCO. You can trust him to help you fit into your new command."

The sergeant saluted his new company officer, which John returned. "A pleasure to meet you, Sergeant. I shall need your help and I know I can rely on my non-coms to maintain the company."

"John, I should get back to the General," Keogh said.

"Myles, I would like to make a request, if I may."

Keogh paused, and Sergeant Hingle made to move back to give them privacy.

"Sergeant, stay. You also need to hear this." John paused, trying to phrase his favor. *Oh, hell, just say it.* "Should I sustain any injury in the fight, it is my wish I be taken to my sister rather than be treated by a military surgeon. General Buford is aware of this, but I wanted you both to know."

"Sir!" Hingle saluted.

"John, I shall abide your wishes with the General's permission."

"Thank you," John said. He shook hands with Myles, who promised to find him when the fighting was done.

John turned back to the sergeant. "Well, lead on."

"If the Captain will allow me," Hingle said, taking the horse's lead from John's hand, "I'll take you around and then I've secured a place for you to bed down for the night." John nodded.

After seeing the layout of his area and meeting his men, John soon found himself looking at a small depression near the tree line where a blanket and saddlebags were made into a bed. When the sergeant had left him to return to his other duties, John lay down on his makeshift bed. He thought about his men. *They won't let me down – here's hoping I don't let THEM down.* He stared through the tree limbs into the night sky, still amazed at the endless number of stars he could see without the city lights he was used to.

John drifted off to sleep while his mind played with the idea that although he knew overall what would happen the next day, he really didn't know what would happen minute by minute. The history books record the thoughts of the generals but little of the men they lead. Here he was in the almost same position wondering the same 'what if' question as the men around him.

CHAPTER SIX

Wednesday, 1 July 1863

6:00 A.M.

The day was shaping up to be clear and warm. Up on Check, John found Keogh had been right - his mount had a steady, even gait. He glanced over his shoulder and saw the company of troopers following.

Wow, it's just like a re-enactment. His thought suddenly stopped there. *No, they were different somehow; there was some-thing that set them apart.* He let his eyes wander over them and it hit him. *It's in their eyes ...their eyes had something about them.* He had seen that look before in some of the re-enactors who had been to the desert for their war, and sometimes he saw the same shadows in their eyes when they were on the field. The realiza-tion hit him, again. *This is the real world and not just a play-acting, fun entertainment for the weekend. Dear God, please don't let me fail these men.*

7:00 A.M.

Sergeant Hingle pulled his horse up next to John.

"There's a rider coming, sir.

A young lad rode up to them and saluted. "Orders from the Colonel. Sir."

John took the scrap of torn-out ledger paper and quickly read it.

Captain Andrews, you will pull your company

from the route of march and place it to the right

of the railroad cut assuming a defensive position

on the ridge. You may at your decision engage

any enemy you see before you. Should the Rebels

begin a withdrawal you are not to pursue them but

remain in position and await further orders.

Devin

Colonel, Commanding

John relayed the order and watched as the men quickly moved to obey. The company shortly arrived at the ridge area. "Sergeant Hingle, halt the company and have the men dismount."

He saw the now dismounted troopers standing by their mounts. John walked his horse over to his troopers.

"Company, prepare to fight dismounted."

At his command, every fourth trooper stepped forward and took the reins of his horse and those of the three troopers to his left and moved with the four animals to the rear of the line. John looked around and spotted a small stand of trees. "Sergeant Hingle, have the troopers move the horses to that copse of trees. String a line around them to use as a picket, tie the mounts there, and leave three troopers to watch them. Have the rest rejoin the company."

"Sir?"

"I'm aware that it isn't correct by the book but I have a feeling that we're going to need every man we can muster on the line today."

"Very well, sir."

When the sergeant had returned with his group of troopers and fallen into line, John continued.

"At skirmish interval…advance."

The company moved up the ridge. When they had reached the top, John gave the order to halt and surveyed the ground before them. The ridge ran off to his left and right with some low cover and some concealment for his men as well a part of a rail fence. There wasn't much to stop the Rebs' fire but what there was would have to do. John called Sergeant Hingle and his other NCO's back to him.

"Gentlemen, have your men take a position of cover as best as possible and rest in place while they can. Sergeant, pick a man to be a rider and send him to find the supply area and bring back ammunition for the Spencers, preferably double rounds for each man."

His orders were promptly carried out. John rose in his stirrups to stare down the long road before then. He thought it looked like an arrow pointing right at them.

"Begging the Captain's pardon," Sergeant Hingle said as he walked up to his new captain, a slight Irish brogue evident. "You've done fine so far, sir, but don't you think that sitting up there on that lovely bay you make a big beautiful target?" He reached for Check's bridle. "Perhaps you should dismount and join the rest of us here on the ground."

John slid off to the firm earth. "Thank you, Sergeant," he said as Hingle motioned for a man to take the horse.

John walked to the skirmish line. In the distance, he saw two things: the first was a small scouting party for the Union command and beyond it a cloud of dust rising from the road. The Union party pulled back a little at the same time the first gray-clad figures appeared. Suddenly a single shot rang out. The blue-clad soldiers immediately quickened their pace, heading to the Union line.

From where John stood, it looked as if someone had kicked an ant bed. Where there had been a few men, within a minute there were now several hundred spreading out to either side of the road.

John turned his head. "Well it looks like someone decided to start the dance," he said to his sergeant. As they watched, John saw flags rise for the first time out of the mass of men now forming into a line. Waving in the light breeze he saw the Stars and Bars and the Bonnie Blue, and a flag of which he was unsure.

"It does look like it's going to be a hot day, sir," Sergeant Hingle commented. "That flag with the green tree on it, that belongs to the Mississippi boys and we've seen them before. They have a bad habit of not liking to give up."

As John looked back at the Reb line to see the flag again, he saw a multitude of flashes followed by a blossom of smoke. He heard a whizzing drone of something passing close by him. In less than a second, his mouth had gone dry and from his neck to the top of his head he felt a strange tingling sensation. *Son of a bitch, those damn people are shooting at me. Nope – more than that - oh hell - those people are trying to kill me!* He quickly realized his biggest problem was no longer the worry of how he and Cathy were going to get home. It had been replaced by a new, larger one: *how in bloody hell do I stay alive through today?*

*****

7:15 A.M.

Cathy awakened to the sound of distant thunder, but when she opened her eyes, the sun was shining.

"What the hell?" She got out of bed and pulled the door open. "Oh, my God! It's really happening!"

She quickly pulled on some clothes, walked outside, and immediately ran back into the cabin.

"Okay, Howell, that was your idiot moment for the day," she chided herself as she changed from a t-shirt and jeans into the blouse and skirt John had given her; she ensured her weapon was in place. "Just in case someone sees me, I should be dressed for the part."

*****

7:15 A.M.

John moved to his battle line.

"Company by volley, present…fire."

He heard Hingle moving down the line, "Steady men, pick your targets…"

The gray line moving forward flowed over the ground and seeing it, John wondered if it could be stopped.

"By volley…fire!"

"By volley…fire!"

"By volley…fire!"

John saw the Confederate line drawback. There must have been a slight depression in the ground for they seemed to disappear. He realized that he was covered with sweat, but he had seen the elephant and kept his composure. He let a partial smile come to his lips.

"Don't worry, sir," Hingle said quietly. "They'll be back."

"Sergeant, if it's all the same to you, I would be perfectly fine with them laying down their arms and going home. They seem to be downright unfriendly."

Before his sergeant could reply, the gray men rose up again and the lead flew like hornets toward the blue line. The Confederates dropped into their depression again. John scrutinized his line turning to the right and then the left flank. Any smile he might still have had vanished in a hurry. The company to his left was faulting and a buckle was appearing in their part of the line. Shocked, he saw that the section had taken high casualties. Even as he looked, the Confederates were pushing to within a hundred feet of the vulnerable spot.

Oh my God, they're going to break the line but they can't. IT DIDN'T HAPPEN! My God - I can't let it happen!

John turned to his line. Moving to Sergeant Hingle, he gave his orders. "I'm pulling every third man. You have the company." Running down the left half of the line, he tapped every third man on the shoulder and had him pull out of line. At the end of his company line, he had these men form a new skirmish line.

John looked to his front. For the first time, he heard a true rebel yell and the hairs on the back of his neck stood up. The few remaining union troopers in the area were crumbling. Without hesitation John firmly called out:

"Kneel."

"By volley… fire!"

"By volley… fire!"

 "By volley… fire!"

"Rise."

"Advance."

"By volley… fire!"

"By volley… fire!"

John continued to push forward with heavy fire from his men. They moved and swung into the space that moments ago the gray warriors had held. He couldn't recall the number of times the men had fired.

"Reload."

He watched the troopers as they rapidly pulled the now-empty tubes from their Spencers and replaced them with full tubes of rounds. Hoping that no screaming Confederates would overrun his small group, he looked out to the field. The heavy smoke cleared for the moment and he could see that the area seemed to be under Union control again. He took a slow breath and had opened his mouth to give a command when the trooper in front of him screamed and dropped. John felt something hot and wet strike his face; the taste of salt and copper was in his mouth. The truth dawned on him that he was splattered with the blood of the fallen soldier.

I will not, repeat not, puke my guts out in front of these men. John heard footsteps behind him and turned to see what had to be the reserve troopers rushing in to fill the gap. John pulled his men out to take them back to his battle line.

"Captain Andrews," a voice called from behind him. John turned and was somewhat startled to see General Buford sitting on his horse, intensely watching the Confederate battlefront.

"General, we're holding," John reported. "But I'm not sure how much longer we can,"

"The infantry is ten minutes away. You must hold. Captain, I was coming to fill the hole and saw your action. I must say well done, sir."

John heard the hornet whine of a minie ball pass too close for comfort.

"General, it's about to get hot here," John stated. "It might be better if you were to remove yourself from the battle line. I think we have some more fighting to do today, sir, and we can't afford to lose you." As he said the words, John heard the report of a cannon coming from the Confederate side.

John noted that General Buford had turned slightly in his saddle and was giving him the same hard glare Colonel Devin had received the previous evening. Buford rose slightly in the saddle as if to dismount Grey Eagle.

"General Buford, with all due respect, sir, you really must remove yourself from the battle line," he said to his commanding officer.

Buford hesitated.

"Sir – for the sake of the Union, *please withdraw.*" John made it as firm as he could.

General Buford rose full up in the saddle and intently scanned at the Confederate battle line.

"Captain, I see they have moved a battery of cannon up to their tree line. Perhaps I should move back a shade." Buford touched his horse's flank and wheeled him around. He pointed the animal at an angle heading back to the center of his forces.

John started his men moving back to his company at double-time and had gone only a few yards when a Confederate shell exploded mere feet from the exact spot where the General had been. John whirled to see the area. Earth and grass were still falling from the explosion, but he saw Buford beyond it. General Buford had halted his mount and was peering back at the spot. The General slowly raised his eyes, saw John staring back, gave him a nod, and spurred his horse onward.

John took the company back from his sergeant. "Make sure all the men have drunk water and every man has a fully loaded tube in his carbine."

"Done, sir, and just in time," Hingle reported. "Here they come again and damned if I don't think there's more of them."

John saw the oncoming Rebels. "I believe you may be correct." He checked his pistol to make sure it was ready for the fight and put it into the holster at his side. He turned to look to the right side of his line – no problems there. As he turned to the left he felt someone smash his right leg with a baseball bat. He pitched forward and managed to turn his body so he landed on his back.

Damn, Catie's going to be mad. The bright sky above him turned black as he tried to speak to someone leaning over him.

*****

Late morning

Cathy looked up from her book as she heard a horse approaching. Noting that the shooting and artillery she had been hearing on and off all morning was again off, she quickly hid the book in the bedroom, and was back in the main room in time to hear a voice call her name.

"Miss Howell!"

"Yes," she answered as she opened the door, her hand going into her pocket to rest on the Beretta.

"General Buford's compliments, ma'am," said the sandy-haired uniformed young man on horseback. "He regrets to inform you that Captain Andrews has been wounded, but assures you he is alive and will be brought here as soon as is safely possible."

"Thank you, Corporal," Cathy responded, hoping she was correctly identifying the insignia on the boy's uniform. She leaned against the doorway and took a deep breath to steady herself, glad the news wasn't worse.

"Corporal William Hastings, at your service. Are you all right, ma'am? Is there a return message?"

"I'll be fine, thank you. Yes, please thank the general – I truly appreciate his kindness in letting me know. May I ask how badly wounded is my brother, and under what circumstances it happened?"

"I don't rightly know, ma'am." He started to say something but caught himself.

"Corporal Hastings, please go ahead and voice whatever it was you stopped yourself from saying," Cathy encouraged. "If it's not polite or acceptable to military protocols, I promise I won't tell."

"Well, ma'am, it's just that I've never seen General Buford do this before. I mean, sending someone outside of the battle to let a civil--, er, somebody know – or have a wounded man taken to someplace like this."

"Corporal, did you have other orders besides delivering the message, such as scouting the enemy's position?"

"I can't say directly ma'am," he replied as he dropped his eyes.

"I understand." Cathy smiled to herself as she read body language that told her she hit the target. "Do you consider General Buford to be an honorable man?"

"Oh, yes, ma'am – he's the best in the army." The boy's enthusiasm was obvious.

"That is also my estimation. Let us say he is keeping a promise and allow the subject to slip by, Corporal. Please do thank him for me, and tell him I'll be waiting for my brother to arrive."

"Ma'am." He snapped a salute, turned his horse, and was gone – away from town, which confirmed her idea about scouting.

Cathy dug into her pocket and pulled out the watch she didn't dare to wear. It showed eleven o'clock. Once again happy that she had replaced the battery before the trip to Pennsylvania, she hoped it would last the six to eight months the manufacturer claimed it would.

"Oh, Johnny, what in the world are we doing here? And how long will it be?" she moaned aloud.

She spent the next half-hour preparing the table for what she hoped wouldn't be needed, laying out one of the instrument packets, along with what her head nurse called the accessory pack in a drawer she emptied for the purpose. As she put the drawer back in place, she smiled as she recalled the conversation she had had with Gerry, when she had gathered it all up. He had questioned the need for sutures, sponges, extra syringes, vials of local anesthetics, betadine packets, alcohol preps, etc. She had replied that she didn't know but would rather be sure. – if he could see her now, he'd understand! *Thankfully, I grabbed enough to stock an urgent care unit.*

She tore a sheet for bandages, put a pot of water on the stove, dug in John's backpack for one last item that came to mind, and put a basin under the table for waste. She forced herself to quit speculating and made herself sit back down with her book, using a technique developed as a resident to break the worry of constant ER duty. "Never worry about what you can't change" is a hard lesson, but her residency mentor had been a hard master.

At two o'clock according to her watch, now restless, she got up, stretched, and put the kettle on the stove for a cup of tea after bringing in some more wood. She moved the big pot of water, which had boiled, to the side and put a smaller one to heat. She stood outside the cabin, wishing she had a bench to sit on. A bird chirping in a nearby tree made her look up at it.

"Well, at least you can keep me company for a while," she told it, but it flew off. Then she heard horses approach. She went back inside and pulled the door to, wanting to make sure they were Union soldiers before she opened it.

"Miss Howell?" New voice.

Opening the door, she saw John on a horse which was being led by the captain she had seen with Buford yesterday on another mount.

"Johnny?"

"Catie, I've been hit. I'm sorry - you're going to have to go to work," he said, trying to smile. Pain was etched in his face. "This is General Buford's aide, Captain Keogh."

She approached the horse on its left, spoke to it, and looked up at John.

"This is Grey Eagle." She turned to look at the other Captain. "Thank you, Captain, for bringing him."

"Ma'am, the general wanted to make sure your brother arrived safely into your care."

"Johnny, don't you dare faint! You fall on me, and we're both screwed," she said sharply as he wobbled. *Cripes, so much for unpolluted language.* "Where's the bullet?"

"Right leg." He groaned; she saw shock and heard pain.

Captain Keogh dismounted. "Please, ma'am, tell me what may I do to assist you."

"We're going to have to let him lean sideways, gradually pull his right leg over the saddle, and catch it before it hits anything. If you support him, I'll deal with the leg."

Keogh nodded his understanding, impressed by the firmness with which she was dealing with the situation. It struck him that the general's opinion of her, which he had shared before dispatching them to the cabin, might be well-founded.

Cathy spoke to John. "It's like the day my leg got mashed against the tree when we were little, Johnny. Remember how you got me off the horse? You need to lean over."

"I dropped you." His voice was losing strength.

"I have help, you didn't." She took in a sharp breath as he leaned the wrong way, and snapped, "Not that way - dammit, Johnny! I'll let you know when you can pass out." Holding John's arm to guide him before he fell in the other direction, she said, "Here we go. Lean towards me."

"Language, Catie, language," John mumbled as they pulled him off Grey Eagle.

"Well, you taught it to me. I shall apologize later, and I am certain the Captain has heard worse," she retorted as she caught his bad leg. "Let's get him inside."

They got the injured man onto the table. Cathy had the lantern lit. Using scissors, she cut the seam of the right pant leg open, and took her first look at the wound, midway between his knee and his hip. Someone had tied a rough bandage over it; it was caked and stuck to the open area. She poured the now-cooled boiled water over the bandage, gently removed it, and tossed it into the waste basin. She paled, took a deep breath, and let it out slowly. His thigh had been torn open. It looked like raw meat but wasn't bleeding too badly. *Good, no major blood vessels.* She moistened a clean square of material, put it over the wound, and turned to the Union officer.

"Captain, I thank you for your assistance. I know you must get back to General Buford; please give the horses some water before you leave. The stream is nearby, and there's a bucket outside the door." She put her hand on John's forehead – slightly cool if anything, indicating shock. "Johnny, I'm going to see the Captain off, and I'll be right back. don't go anywhere."

"Can I pass out now?" John tried to smile but grimaced half-way through.

"Sure. don't fall off the table."

Captain Keogh was using the bucket to water for the two mounts; they had been grazing while they waited.

"Captain, please accept my thanks again for bringing John to me, and I do apologize for my language. I would ask you not report that to General Buford - I don't want him to think less of me.

Please, though, do give the general my heartfelt thanks for his consideration."

"Ma'am, I heard nothing untoward, I assure you," Keogh said, looking down at the small woman with considerable interest. "General Buford asked me to relay his compliments to you for what you are doing for the Captain. He also wants you to know that your brother is a fine officer and distinguished himself during the battle."

"What happened overall? I'll get my brother's story later."

"We were pushed back through the town. Our lines were in danger of being broken and it was a long, hard morning. Our day may not be over, but we held long enough for the rest of our troops to get here." Keogh took a breath and let it out slowly. "Miss Howell, if you would allow it, the general would like to visit you this evening."

"Captain, give the general my thanks for the thoughts and assure him that I shall always be honored to receive him even though I suspect he has other, better, things to do with his time." She smiled up at the officer who was slightly taller than John. Dark, longish hair framed his angular face; he had a mustache and short jazz-type beard.

"Perhaps other things, but I doubt they'd be better," Keogh said, allowing himself a smile. "General Buford told me you will operate on your brother. You can manage on your own?" His skepticism was obvious.

"Yes, Captain. I do thank you for your concern, but please be assured I am well-trained. My father is a doctor, sir," she explained. "I know it looks bad, yet I have hopes that my brother will make a full recovery." She glanced back at the cabin. "Our mother always taught me to do what has to be done first, and only worry about what's next once that is accomplished."

"A wise philosophy. Is there anything I may do for you before I depart?" He was surprised at his eagerness to delay taking his leave.

"Thank you, no. My main concern at the moment is light. I have the lamp and a supply of candles, so I should be all right."

"If you need assistance, I'm afraid help won't be..." His thought trailed off.

"I've seen worse, Captain, honestly."

"I know the General is worried that Captain Andrews might lose his leg. If you have to amputate you'll need assistance," he persisted.

"I am hoping there will not be a need for it." Cathy looked up at the tall man. "I thank you, yet I assure you we should be fine."

Cathy held Grey Eagle while Keogh mounted his own horse. As she handed over the reins, she smiled up at him and added, "Captain, the General is a good and honorable man, and I believe he needs you more than he realizes. Please take good care of him."

"Miss Howell, I aim to do just that." He tipped his hat and rode off.

CHAPTER SEVEN

Wednesday, 1 July 1863

2:30 P.M.

Cathy went back inside, checked to make sure John was still with her, and before she did anything else, changed her clothes, deliberately choosing a t-shirt she felt she could sacrifice. She checked his blood pressure, grabbed a flashlight, and did a complete assessment of the wound. She gave him two shots of local, did some not-so-gentle probing, and finished by giving him a third shot directly into the wound.

"Hey," John's eyes flew open, "That HURTS."

"It won't in a while. I have given you a local anesthetic, and it should knock out most of your leg. Be grateful that I have a decent syringe. The few that are available now would scare the crap out of you. Want a pillow for your head?"

"Can I have one?"

"Yes. Give me a minute." She pulled some of the linens out of the drawer, rolled up a sheet, and braced his head a little. She also covered his torso with a towel. The room was warm, but it would help. "I wasn't sure if you'd have to be flat or not. Better?"

"Thanks. How bad is it?"

"John, your nap seems to have helped – you seem more alert - so I won't lie to you. It's a mess."

She pulled a chair over to sit by his head and turned off the flashlight to save the solar charge.

"I can do this with a local. I'm going to block some of the circulation with a tie – thank you for bringing one, Professor Andrews – so the bleeding stays reasonable. I have to get whatever is in there out or we could be looking at lead poisoning." She tied his necktie around his thigh, not tightly for now.

"It's a bullet."

"I'm not exactly certain what's in there," she said. "I see a major entry and no exit wound. There's a lot of bruising and swelling, but it looks like just one entry. I'm going to have to dig. I can't tell for sure, but there seems to be something lodged against the bone, and that could mean I have to dig out some bone fragments. You're going to have an interesting scar, but if all goes well you should heal completely. Thankfully, you didn't lose a huge amount of blood – you won't need a transfusion unless you start bleeding during the surgery. I'll know more after I get in there."

"Don't throw the bullet away – I want it for a souvenir." He grinned through his pain.

"Somehow I knew that. I'm going to give you a tranquilizer. I want you relaxed." She gave him a tablet and helped him sit up enough to swallow it.

"Will you use ether?"

"Not unless I bloody well have to. It would be difficult for - one person – it's doable but tricky. As for afterwards, I have limited meds with me - ones that I pack for any trip, some that I picked up for the re-enactment. So you'll know, I have the tranquilizers, some decently high-end pain meds, and mild sleepers. Just be glad we are isolated. I wouldn't be able to do any of this at the Scott home." She stood up and stretched her arms, shook her own hands – with one over her shoulder - behind her back, to limber up. "Johnny - I'll do my best."

"Catie, I trust you completely. I'm damned lucky to have you – any other surgeon around would see bone and probably take the leg off. You didn't, did you? I can't feel it." His dark brown eyes sought her green ones for assurance.

"Goodie – that's the local, my boy. The leg is still attached. Here," she said, taking his hand. "You can put your hand down to feel it. Want to help?"

"WHAT?"

"If I need you to hold the flashlight, will you do that?"

"Cripes, Catie – I thought you meant…" He gulped. "Yeah, I can hold a flashlight." He looked up and caught the glint in her eyes. "You were kidding, right?"

"Yep. Just making sure you are paying attention." She leaned over and kissed him on the cheek. "I'd rather you fell asleep if you can. I'm going to work." She put on a mask and opened a pair of gloves, leaving them off until he would fell asleep.

An hour later, she woke him up.

"Johnny? I'm done."

"Catie? I feel funny. Fuzzy, sort of. And I had a weird dream."

"Fuzzy is normal – some of the local hit your body in a rush when I took off the tourniquet. You can tell me about the dream in a minute. We have something to do and this time I will need your help – for real."

"Why?"

"We are going to put you to bed. I don't think sleeping on the table would be a great idea, and the bed will be more comfortable." She helped him sit up, and she gently lifted his right leg around, carefully, so the dressing didn't become dislodged.

"Catie - I can't feel my leg!" John's eyes were tightly closed and he gripped her in panic.

"Ouch – take it easy, Johnny. I promise it's still there – see for yourself. It's just numb." Cathy rotated her shoulder where he had grabbed it. "Now, swing your left leg around. You're going to use me as a crutch, and we are going to take our time."

"Did you get the bullet?"

"Can that wait?" she asked impatiently. "I want to get you moved before the local wears off. It's going to hurt like hell when it does."

It was slow and stumbling. John dragged the numb leg and hopped on the good one. They almost fell once. Finally, he was in bed. She positioned him with pillows and let him catch his breath while she cleaned up her instruments and other tell-tale signs of modern medicine. Dirty linens and such went into the basin to be washed. She poured hot water over them for the time being. She figured she'd add her t-shirt and jeans to the mess when she took them off.

"Catie?" John's voice was tinged with anxiety.

"Coming." She came in, drying her hands with a modern towel.

"Will I be okay?"

"I think so. I didn't use the penicillin, it's not quite ready. I only have a light dressing on the wound with some antibiotic ointment – I cleaned it up, but I don't want to close it yet. There's a lot of swelling from the impact and I want it to drain. I cauter- ized a couple of minor bleeds - don't ask about that part.

"I think I can curb my curiosity."

"My main worry at this point is infection. That wasn't exactly a clean wound." She folded the towel, put it on the chest, and dug in her jeans pocket. "Here."

She tossed a small zip lock bag to him.

"My bullet! And...?"

"A silver dollar and one bone fragment." She grinned. "You're not going to believe this, but apparently the bullet hit the silver dollar in your pocket and drove the dollar into your thigh. The coin partially embedded in the bone and cracked it. When I pulled it out that fragment broke off. I cleaned everything, and I'll take the bone bit as my souvenir if you don't want it. I haven't worked that hard in a while." She smiled at the grimace he made.

"The dollar is bent." He held the coin, which now had one bowed side.

"That coin saved your leg," she said, sitting on the chair. "It not only blocked the bullet from shattering the femur, it actually stopped it - preventing more damage." She smiled. "How do you feel?"

"My leg is still numb. How long was I out? Better yet, why was I out?"

"Ah, my professional secrets." She chuckled. "You were exhausted but wired when you got here, in a slight state of shock. I risked giving you a tranquilizer as a pre-op, which took away the anxiety and nervousness. Your body did what it was supposed to – you fell into a deep, exhausted sleep. I woke you up when I finished, about an hour later."

"I had a weird dream."

"Tell me about it."

"I heard my mother singing to me. You know that song she sings? *'Look for the silver lining when e'er a cloud appears in the blue, remember somewhere the sun is shining and so the right thing to do is make it shine for you,'*" he sang. "That old song she loves."

"Umm, that was me. I remembered that Joyce used to sing to us when we were sick or hurt or scared." Cathy hummed a few bars. "I needed it too, you know, for comfort. If it helped to keep you relaxed, so much the better."

"Yeah, you're right - comforting. Reminds me of home."

"*'A heart full of joy and gladness - will always banish sadness and strife. So always look for the silver lining, and try to find the sunny side of life,'*" she sang softly. "Me, too."

"Mom would be proud of you. She always has been, you know." John swallowed hard. "May I have some water?"

"Sure. Hungry?" She had her blood pressure cuff on his arm.

"Not really, maybe later?"

Cathy got them both a drink of water and then spent some time positioning his leg. The dressing showed oozing around its edges, no signs of hemorrhaging, which was excellent after the jostling to get him in bed. She checked his vital signs, thankful she could. His temp was low-grade, and his blood pressure was normal.

"So far, so good. I'll probably annoy you every now and then the rest of the afternoon and during the night, checking on things. I want you to sleep."

"Where are you going to sleep?" he asked, looking at the way she had positioned him on their only bed.

"I'm going to double the sleeping bags to use as a mattress on the floor. I figure it's safe since you can't get up to step on me. I have the small, wind-up alarm clock from your pack, and I'll make sure you have meds on time. Yell when you need the chamber pot. I wake up easy."

"I don't know what I'd do without you. I'll make it up to you somehow."

"You have already. You're alive." Cathy shuddered. "When the corporal rode up, I was afraid he had the worst news."

"Corporal?"

"He said his name was Hastings."

"One of Buford's messengers and scouts," he nodded. "Nice kid."

"He came at around eleven o'clock with a message from General Buford that you had been wounded and you would be brought here as soon as possible. At least then I knew you were alive." A thought struck her. "Johnny, before he left, Captain Keogh said that General Buford might visit this evening. Was he kidding?"

"Maybe not. The general may think I saved his life."

"What the hell have you been up to?"

"Buford put me in as a replacement officer for the 9th New York Cavalry unit, under Colonel Devin. I tried to balance things between following orders and letting things happen, you know, not interfering. Our job was to hold until General Reynolds brought up his men to relieve us. One of our lines was starting to cave, and I had reorganized the men to push back when the General came to our lines. I was already working on what he saw." John stopped, frowning as he tried to recall the scene. "Catie, the General actually commended me!" John's tone held a note of awe.

"I'm proud of you! But why does he think you saved his life?"

"Well, he wanted to stay with us, and we were the forward line," he admitted wryly. "I know I promised you I'd stay back, but I couldn't. Anyway," he continued quickly before she could argue, "I had a bit of a heated discussion with him, finally pointing out – probably not gently – that the army could not afford to lose him, and he agreed to move to the rear."

"I see," she murmured.

"Buford rode off to see Colonel Gamble, and I stayed with my men. Then the Rebels did another push; there was a lot of confusion, and that's when I was hit. Buford thinks I took his place and helped save the line and him. He could be right, but I can't remember it all." John winced as he moved his leg. "My leg is beginning to wake up."

"No problem." Cathy grabbed the med bag from her duffle. "This will probably put you back to sleep. Take it and let me get you a piece of bread and some of the ham. I know you're not hungry, but you need something to eat to balance the med or it may make you nauseated."

She watched as he finished the snack, drank another cup of water, and fell back on the pillows.

"I have to go outside for a bit. I want to rinse some of the cloths and sponges I used. I can boil them later, but I want to get the blood out. don't worry if it takes me a minute to get back if you yell. I want to get this done while I can, especially if we are going to have company."

"Okay – no problem."

Finishing the clean-up of the linens and modern instruments, and securing them back in her kit took her until after six o'clock. "Keep busy, keep busy," she told herself, knowing she was going to have a stress reaction to the events when she finally stopped.

Cathy gently woke John and handed him an empty canning jar she had cleaned for him to use as a urinal, then told him to go back to sleep, fully aware that he wasn't going to remember most of what had happened since he got back to the cabin - probably for the best.

Once that was done, she changed into a clean blouse, and put on the skirt she had worn that morning. She took the jeans and t-shirt and washed them in the stream. John hadn't bled all over everything, but there were a few splatters. She took his uniform pants and considered washing them, but wasn't sure how, so she settled for carefully folding them. She found his watch in his vest pocket and put it away.

Finally, she sat at the table, put her head down, and let go. The tears and shakes were normal, the price she paid for staying emotionally distant long enough to do what had to be done. She thought again of her emergency residency mentor. *I hope he'd be proud.*

She lost track of time and dozed. A sound at the door brought her to alertness. A glance at the window told her it was now dark.

"Miss Howell?" Not a new voice, this one was deep and familiar. Buford's voice.

"Just a moment, sir." She wiped her eyes and blew her nose. Opening the door, she looked up at Grey Eagle and his rider.

"General Buford! Captain Keogh said you might come by, but I didn't think you'd have the time."

"Ma'am, for some things I make time. I won't come inside, as I don't wish to disturb you. I wanted to make sure you and Captain Andrews were safe. Will he recover?"

"Yes, sir, he will. He's resting."

"Will he lose his leg?"

"No, I don't believe so. The bullet he took drove a silver dollar he had in his pocket into his leg. The bone didn't shatter – it chipped a bit and I was able to remove that, the bullet, and the coin. His leg muscles were torn, but the damage will heal." She frowned. "Assuming he will be patient with himself and give it the time it will require."

"You are a doctor." It was not a question.

"A doctor, sir?" Cathy tried to look and sound innocent.

"Miss Howell, I had a talk with your brother after he fell in the fight." Buford looked down at the petite woman. "You are a doctor," he repeated.

"Yes, sir, I am." She sighed. "I see he told you."

"Yes, he did. Colonel Devin had him taken to the field hospital, but he wouldn't allow the doctor there to touch him. In fact, he got downright mean about it. Captain Keogh had reported that your brother was down and asking to speak with me. As soon as I could I went to find him. When we were alone, he told me you are a doctor."

"He must have told you a few other things as well. I can't imagine you coming out here otherwise, on your own, at this time." She looked up at the man, who seemed to be part of his horse.

"I want you to know that your brother performed a great service during the battle. Without his leadership, our line might well have collapsed. Ordinarily, I would send word to his commanding officer recommending him for promotion, but that does not appear possible." Buford reached into his tunic and removed a folded piece of paper. "I would like him to have this."

"Are you certain you won't come in, General?" Cathy asked, accepting the paper. "It would mean so much to Johnny – I assure you it would not be a bother."

"If I dismount, can you help me back into the saddle? I need assistance." He grimaced as if the admission was painful in itself.

"There's a chair inside we could use as a mounting block – between that and my help, yes, I believe it can be done," she replied. She kept it matter of fact with no unwanted sympathy. "Let me fetch it to show you, and you can decide."

Cathy ran into the cabin, grabbed the chair, and was heading back out when she heard John's voice.

"Is that General Buford? He's here? I thought I heard his voice."

"Uh-huh. And you told him." She went to the doorway.

"I had to." He sat up and moved as if he were going to get up.

"I can handle this, now that I know what he knows. He wants to come in to see you." Cathy scowled at him. "Stay put, or I swear I'll hit you with something."

She returned outside with the chair.

"Pardon the delay, General. I had to stop to threaten my patient." She put the chair down at Grey Eagle's side. "Will this do?

Use my shoulder – I'm stronger than I look. I won't help, just support and steady you."

Carefully, Buford got down off the horse, then the chair. "You threatened your patient?" His voice held a note of amusement.

"He wanted to get up to see you and I stopped him." She shrugged. "It's simple, really. He'd undo everything."

"May I see him?"

"He's waiting for you. If you don't go in, he'll try to get up and I'll have to make good on my threat."

"Which was?"

"To be blunt, I told him that if he didn't stay in bed, I would hit him with something."

Buford laughed out loud. "I knew you weren't one to cross."

She led the way into the small partitioned room. "Johnny, behave yourself – you have a visitor." She put the other chair next to the bed for the general.

"You two make quite a pair." Buford regarded them with the hint of a smile as he eased onto the chair.

"You're not the first to say so, sir," John replied. "I told you Catie would take care of me."

"Excuse me, General? Now that he's awake, I'd like to check his leg. Will it bother you?" As he shook his head, Cathy pulled back the covers. "Johnny, wiggle the toes of your right foot." She took a pedal pulse and watched as the toes moved. "Good! I want to bend your knee – let me support and move it." She cradled his thigh and slowly moved his lower leg. His face reflected the pain of the motion. "Excellent!" She carefully positioned his leg and replaced the covers.

"That's amazing." Buford shifted in the chair. "I reckoned he'd lose the leg."

"I cleaned the wound, got the bullet, the dollar, and the bone fragment out, repaired the muscle, and set the dressing."

"So the silver dollar saved his leg?" Buford looked puzzled.

"It's bent," John said, handing over the coin, "But here it is. It's my new good-luck piece."

"Amazing," he murmured, turning the coin over in his fingers and handing it back to John. "Miss Howell, you make it sound easy."

"It wasn't. It was a matter of knowledge, tools, and practice, General. Luckily, I had tools, and probably most importantly, I had the time to use them. Your field surgeons probably don't have the luxury of taking that time." Cathy smiled at the care-worn man. "You have your own knowledge, and your tools are your men. Today your actions…" She stopped, unsure of how much she should say.

"Today, General, you have helped to save a nation," John finished for her.

"The Union will be preserved? That is a fact as you know it?"

"Yes sir, it will. It's going to take a while longer, and there's a lot of blood yet to be spilled before it is over, but if all happens as it should, the country will stand as one nation, reunited." John smiled at the older man.

"Then I was meant to survive today's fighting." Buford's voice had a shading of awe.

"Yes, General, you were. You have more to do."

"Is that why you did what you did? Even at the cost of your wound?"

"I merely made a suggestion, sir." John struggled to sit up a bit, with Cathy's assistance.

"That was a suggestion? It sounded more like an order," Buford said dryly, "And bordered on insubordination."

"You didn't need to be in the middle of that firefight. Thankfully, you took my, umm, suggestion. My apologies if I was out of line, sir," John replied, not looking sorry in the least. "Your actions today, and those of your troopers, will be remembered years from now as part of the turning point in the tide of the war to the Union's favor."

"Johnny." Cathy, who had been watching, trying to memorize the scene for recall later, cut in. "Enough?"

"The United States of America survives this," Buford said softly. He was smiling as he held up a hand. "That's enough for me. I don't think I want to hear any more."

"You should probably forget you heard that much, sir," John said, falling back against the pillows.

"Heard what, Captain?" John Buford grinned, suddenly looking years younger. "I wasn't even here."

"General," Cathy spoke up, "Won't your absence from your command be noticed?"

"Captain Keogh will swear I never left him." He shifted in the chair, obviously in pain.

"Johnny, one good night's sleep? Please?" She looked at the man in bed, pleading.

"Catie!" There was force behind the warning.

"What do you mean, Miss Catie?" Buford asked, and realizing his informality, added, "Oh, pardon me."

"You're fine, General. That's my name, and I'd be honored if you would use it. I was asking Johnny if I could give you one night's relief from your pain so you could sleep."

"You can do that?"

"General, I'm a doctor. It's my observation that you have what you call rheumatics, although I would call it something a bit fancier and I know you are in considerable, constant pain. I have a medication that could ease the pain temporarily. No morphine, no laudanum, nothing that would impair your judgment. It would relieve the pain and enable you to get a solid night's sleep. With all due respect, sir, you look as if you could use it."

"Miss Catie, I appreciate the thought, but it is not necessary. You told me a dream will come true, and now I can believe in it. That's enough to help me sleep." He rose slowly and reached to shake John's hand.

"Johnny, where's my phone and battery?"

"W*HAT?* Catie, are you *nuts?*"

"No more than you," she countered. "Don't *you* want a photo?" She watched his face as caution fought with desire. Desire won, and he grinned.

"My shaver kit, back of the drawer."

"General, may we delay you for a few moments, please?"

"I am listening to birds sing in a dream, which is not especially difficult since I truly have no idea what you are saying." Buford was smiling to himself and totally at ease.

Cathy found her cell phone, installed the battery, and stood back far enough to get the shot.

"Gentlemen, please shake hands, and as you do so turn to look at me." She took two photos, checked them, and handed the phone to John. "General? Please, if I may?"

"It would be my pleasure, whatever it is. Be assured I won't believe any of this happened, even if I do remember it," he said, chuckling as he stood by her side. She took his arm, and the light flashed twice. "Miss Catie, will you escort me outside to Grey Eagle?"

"It will be my honor and pleasure," Cathy told John to go back to sleep and followed the general.

"Are you certain you will be all right out here on your own?" he asked as Cathy placed the chair she had left outside by his horse. "This fight isn't over, and it could wander around some.

"As long as the war doesn't land on my doorstep any more than it has we'll be fine, but I do thank you for your concern." Cathy paused. "General, how much did John tell you?"

"He talked about time. Some of it – most of it - didn't make much sense, but what I understood was you are not from here or now, but from some other time in the future."

"You put that very well."

"I'm concerned that you have no income here."

"While Johnny recovers, I will be working in a store in town, and that will give us food," Cathy replied. "We've made some good friends."

"May I ask a question?"

"Ask whatever you wish. I feel we owe you much more than explanations."

"Are you two really brother and sister, or step-brother and sister?"

"No. We have known each other since we were four. We grew up together as close friends. I like to think we are family in spirit - his parents and mine are close friends, and we became as close as siblings, probably closer considering most siblings fight." She smiled. "We have a saying back home: 'you can pick your friends but you can't pick your family.' If I had been able to choose anyone with whom to share this, I couldn't have chosen better." Cathy shrugged. "We have never been romantically interested in each other, but the trust between us goes deep."

"What was that device with the light? It could not have been a camera, yet I heard you use the word photo."

"The small device did take your photograph, sir. It's a type of camera we have. When we get back home, we may need those to convince ourselves that we weren't dreaming, to borrow your phrase." She helped him into the saddle with the use of the chair. "General, you are an honorable man, and I am proud to have met you. Please, sir, take care of yourself as the world needs men like you to save it from its own folly. Go with God, John Buford, and may He keep you safe."

"Miss Catie, I say again that it has been my honor to make your acquaintance. May God keep you both safe." He tipped his old hat and rode into the night.

She took the chair back into the cabin and was sitting down when she heard a piece of paper crackle. Standing up, she took Buford's letter out of her pocket where she had stashed it before helping him dismount. She placed it on the table.

"Another piece of evidence that I'm not dreaming," she murmured to herself. "This and Johnny's souvenirs."

She looked at her watch. It was just nine. She checked John's wound and vital signs. He never opened an eyelid, she noted. She changed into a sleep shirt, spread the sleeping roll, set the clock, and was asleep in less than ten seconds, knowing it would be a long night.

*****

"Catie?"

The note of panic cut through her sleep.

"Right here," she answered, sitting up and noting the time as ten-thirty by her flashlight.

"You weren't.... Oh, there you are. I couldn't see you." He rubbed his eyes as she lit the lamp.

"It's okay. Dreaming?"

"Yeah. My leg hurts, too, and I have to go to the bathroom."

"We can deal with all of this. Here's your nineteenth-century urinal." She handed him the canning jar.

"Sorry to be such a bother," he mumbled a few minutes later, after taking the pill she offered.

"Just sleep, Johnny. It's the best thing for you."

"Can you leave the lamp on?"

"Sure." She hummed his mother's song until his breathing became regular, and then fell asleep herself.

CHAPTER EIGHT

Thursday, 2 July 1863

Cathy heard birds singing. The sun was up. It was the first time during the night that she woke on her own. Quietly, she turned out the lamp and rolled up her bed, ending what had been a difficult night. She thought she had heard thunder, but obviously, she had been mistaken.

"Is it morning?" John's voice was still sleepy.

"Barely. It's about five-thirty. How are you doing?"

"Better now that the sun is coming up." He wiggled around in bed. "Pain is okay for the moment. How come it always seems to hurt more at night?"

"During the day, you have other things to think about. At night it's just you and the pain."

"Simple, when you look at it that way. Was I horrible?"

"No, truly not. But you're in for it today," she teased. "I have a few things to do, and I'll be back with implements of torture. Doze off again, if you can. I'll be a while. If you need me, yell." She put the clock where he could see it.

To John it seemed that Cathy came back immediately with water, washcloth, some soap, and a towel, but the clock said she had been gone for almost an hour.

"Bed bath time!" she announced with a grin. "After that, I am going to change the dressing."

"The torture you promised. Do I have to look?"

"Nope, not unless you want to."

"I'll pass."

It was a tiring, painful process. Once finished, Cathy was as tired as John looked, and she wasn't going to ask if he felt man-handled – she was afraid of the reply. He was clean, wearing a clean shirt and the covers were straightened. His wound was properly dressed with a poultice and two drains contrived out of tubing, one for each end of the incision she had made. A loose elastic wrap was in place around the bulky dressing to keep everything in place. John was asleep. Sighing, she vowed to never again berate a nurse for resting for five minutes.

She deposited the wash water into the outside sink, drew some more from the creek, and got herself cleaned up. She carefully used some wood to make a platform and laid out the wet things, making a note to herself to ask Miss Martha for some laundry line. Trees she had, all she needed was a piece of rope. She wanted to be back inside before…

Artillery fire. In the distance, but definitely artillery. *Day Two of the battle, and here we go.*

She got back inside as John woke up. He was sitting up with a panicked look on his face.

"It's okay – it sounds like it's in the distance." Cathy sat on the bed. "Will it come our way?"

"What?" He tried to shake off the dream the firing had triggered. "Oh. No, I don't think so. The big stuff today will be to the south and west of us. I wish I had brought a book about this with me. Should have."

"Speaking of books," she said with a grin, "Johnny, I opened my present yesterday. Thank you!"

"Did you have those?"

"No. I've seen the television and film versions of some of the Christie's, but it's always fun to read the original stories. The Stout omnibus is out of print. How'd you find it?"

"Easy – the internet. I got the hardbacks – I figured they'd last longer." He winced as he heard artillery fire again.

"Have you read them?"

"Mystery has not been my reading genre. Watching, yes. How about we read some of them out loud? It may help pass the time. I have a feeling we'll have plenty to fill."

"We do have other entertainment. I brought the cribbage board."

"Maybe later we can play cribbage," he smiled. "Hey, you may even win."

"Yep – with you at half-power, maybe I will," she teased, as he was a fiend when it came to the game. "And of course, with the board we have cards. I brought two decks."

"Good. I can finally teach you how to play poker."

"Careful, I'll get even by teaching you bridge." She laughed – the face he made matched the one she had pulled at the mention of poker. "Meanwhile, I have a question for you. When will it be safe for me to go into town?"

"Tomorrow is the last full day of fighting, but it will take a few days for things to settle down." John frowned. "Saturday is July 4th but no one will be bothering much about it. Sunday might be possible."

"I was wondering about that. Mary and the Scotts are going to be worried about us, and I don't want them to have to walk all the way out here. If you are okay, I might walk in. Sunday also means church. Normally I don't bother, but it would probably be good for me to go. I certainly have things to be thankful for." Cathy touched John's hand. "You're going to be okay."

"There will be a lot of wounded men in town. Almost all of the houses and churches were used to shelter them during the battle, so I doubt they'll be holding services. If you do go to see the Scotts, don't be surprised if the parlor and dining room are lined with bodies. On second thought, you may want to wait until Monday, just to be sure."

"Cripes, what a mess." She shuddered. "You need to go back to sleep, and I have some chores."

While John slept, Cathy spent the rest of the morning seeing to their food stores. Between what the sisters had given them and what was in the cabin, she wasn't too badly off. The one thing she lacked was milk. Dismissing thoughts of having John invent the refrigerator for her, she decided she could try milk-less biscuits with water and added molasses to give some substance to them. If it worked, she could also use them to keep the mold culture going. She spent the early afternoon baking, cautiously pleased with the results. While they would never win a county fair prize, they were edible and she didn't burn them.

"Catie," John yelled from the bedroom, "Am I dreaming or do I smell baking?"

"You are awake and your nose works," she called back.

"YOU are baking?"

"After surviving a battle, don't have a heart attack because I tried something," she laughed, coming in and offering him a biscuit. "I'm trying to remember everything my gran taught me when I spent summers on her farm in Illinois. Miss Martha helped by giving me some recipes."

"Not bad," he said after taking a bite.

"Well, I'm missing some ingredients, but I wanted to give it a whack. I'm working up a list of things I'd like to have, but you're the historian. How do I keep things cool?"

"We could bury a covered crock by the stream. That might help keep things like butter, milk, and eggs fresh for a bit." He finished the biscuit.

"Okay! I used a spare pail and a flat stone I found and cleaned."

"I always knew you were a smart lady. So what's for supper?"

"Protein bars." She smiled at his grimace. "You need protein and we have them, so there. I'll bring you a snack in a bit. How's the pain level?"

"Not great."

"Can you handle some serious talk?" Cathy took a deep breath as he nodded. "We have to figure we're stuck for a while, and I have a limited supply of meds. Other than the initial pills, which were four hours apart, I have held you to six hours. I'd like to see if you can handle eight hours in between."

"I can try," he said, with noticeable reluctance.

"I know it hurts, and I'm not trying to minimize that – hell, I put you together. But pain is one of the great clues of life. If you experience a sudden increase in discomfort or a sudden burning sensation, it would let me know that something is wrong." She sighed. "I shouldn't have to touch that dressing for two, possibly three days, if that will make you feel better."

"Isn't the third day the worst?"

"Generally, yes. If you had been shot at home, I would have used a general, IVs, and all sorts of wonderful things to control the surgical pain. I also would have had help. Here I used a local, and you're already on your own. Think about what the dentist did when you had your tooth prepped for capping." She sighed. "You may have a bit of a shock reaction, but I'm not anticipating much."

"Oh. Okay."

"I won't leave you lying there in agony, I promise, but I'd like to try to balance the meds a bit – I don't want to risk running out."

"Gotcha." He looked at her, sitting with him in her pretty blouse and skirt. "Catie, I'm sorry if I'm being a dork. You've been wonderful and I know you have got to be bored out of your mind."

"You aren't, and I'm not, really. The challenge of day to day living – without benefit of electricity or gas, or any modern con-veniences – is going to keep me busy. Believe me, I have plans. I'll let you know when I get bored."

"Make sure you do."

"You're the one who will get bored, you know. That leg is going to need TIME to heal properly. Once you feel better, you're going to want to get up. Like John Scott."

"I wonder how he's doing."

"If he tried to help yesterday, he's back in bed today," she stated. "Guaranteed. Miss Martha has enough aspirin to help him, though, for a while."

"I could always write a book," John ventured.

"Describing our great adventure? Disguise it as a time travel novel. The thing would sell itself," she suggested slyly.

"You are a warped person, Catie Howell."

"I'm a doctor – it's in my job description right under illegible handwriting." Cathy sighed again. "We know no one will believe us when we get back, so we might as well try the sci-fi route."

"Any more biscuits? And how about some water or tea?"

"Coming up."

She came back in with a tray, loaded with cups and a plate of biscuits and chicken.

"Afternoon tea is served. Supper will be available later."

"Where'd the chicken come from?"

"Miss Martha sent it home with me after you went off with Buford. The ham needed to be finished first."

"We owe them more than we can possibly repay." He took a sip of tea. "Wow, this tastes great. I mean, really good – not just because I'm thirsty. What's in it?"

"My twenty-first-century tea bags with clean 1863 spring water."

"Spring water? Real spring water?"

"Uh-huh. There's a little spring behind the cabin. It's wonderful. You've been drinking it since you were wounded, but I'm not surprised you didn't notice. I didn't find it until the night before the battle." She described her walk and finding the water source.

"Hmmmm." He swallowed a piece of the chicken. "Hmmmm."

"I know that sound. What is going through your warped engineer's mind?"

"Remember you woke up the other day and were disappointed that we weren't back home?"

"Yep. I also woke up this morning hoping that yesterday was a nightmare, and we were back in the tent." She made a rude noise. "Oh well. Reality prevails."

"Yeah." John shivered. "Anyway, I've been thinking about the cabin, and how lucky we have been to find the things we've needed, and such. Doesn't it seem as if it was planned?"

"Planned?"

"Well, like you found the spring last night. The water in the creek being clean, the cabin set up for reasonable survival – it seems to go way beyond coincidence." He paused for a moment, lost in thought. "Even the Scotts and Miss Mary are cooperating as if they were guided to do it."

"They did take us in quickly, and I'm way past grateful. We haven't had time to catch up since you got here last evening, so I'll tell you now. Remember the day dress outfit I wore to meet General Buford? When I got back to the house, I changed back into this skirt – I was really afraid I'd mess it up her lovely dress – and she insisted that I keep it. Miss Martha said that Mary just got another summer day dress. So now I have two skirts, two blouses, a summer day dress, and a winter day dress. None of it is fancy, but it's all there."

"That's quite a wardrobe for this era. Many women only had some everyday clothes, one summer church dress, and one winter church dress. So you are properly outfitted." He paused. "It's as if they know we need the help and they are the ones who need to provide it."

"I was accepting it on the grounds that in this era, suspicion of strangers isn't as entrenched as it is back home." She sighed. "By the way, that is the phrase I am using – I said it to the general last night."

"It does sound better than something like, 'one hundred and fifty-two years from now', doesn't it." John smiled. "I like John Buford. He's not quite what I expected, as a person. The man on the battlefield was amazing. He was cool and collected during the mess yesterday, definitely in command. I may see if I can find a biography when we get back."

"I like him and admire him. His sense of humor sneaks up on you, doesn't it? Before you ask, you can't see the photos. I checked them before I took the battery out again when I went to bed. All four shots are good." She slapped her forehead. "Damn – I forgot. General Buford gave me a letter for you. Back in a jif…"

She ran out and came back, holding out the folded piece of paper.

John took it, carefully unfolded the paper, which was thicker than what they were used to, and read aloud.

"'To All Who See This: Know that Captain John Townsend Andrews, Third Missouri Volunteer Cavalry, demonstrated considerable leadership, tactical skills, and bravery while temporarily serving under my command during the battle which took place on the first of July, 1863 in and around Gettysburg, Pennsylvania. In the brief period he was with my forces, he gained my full and complete confidence. John Buford, Brigadier General, First Division, Cavalry Corps, United States Army'"

"Wow," Cathy said. "Is that normal for an officer to write something?"

"Buford feels I saved his life. He offered to write to my commanding officer, and I told him that wouldn't be possible."

"That's what he told me when he handed it to me. Can I see it?" Cathy held out her hand to take the letter. "Between this, your bullet, the coin, and the photos, we may be able to convince ourselves that we didn't go nuts and imagine all this. Too bad you can't frame this."

"Are you kidding? I'm *going* to frame it. I don't care what people think, that's going on my office wall. It will probably be taken as something I got my re-enactment commander to write. Only you and I will know the truth," he said, grinning. "Thanks for the nudge about the photos."

"We can always pass them off as trick photography." She grinned back at him. "I know it's against the rules, but we'd already broken so many it didn't seem to matter. The General commented that even if he related all of it to someone, no one would believe him."

"He's probably right. He's not a gossip, and he doesn't open up to people. Most people in this era don't."

"What does happen to him?"

"Short form? He has some personal tragedies this summer – some of his family members die, including one of his children. He takes a leave, not sure when, to go back to Illinois and put things in order. When he returns to duty, he goes through a few battles, has some sharp words with his superiors, and in November, he becomes seriously ill. He dies in December, Catie."

"Sad, and such a waste. When he left last night, I told him he was an honorable man. The last thing I said was to go with God."

"He probably appreciated that."

"So you did save his life?"

"Thinking about it, yes. A moment after he left my area, a shell exploded where his horse had been standing. That does bring us back to why all this happened. We are meant to be here. There is something we have to do."

"Well, according to what you said the other day, once we do it, we should get back to where we belong, right? Then saving Buford wasn't it."

"Or wasn't all of it."

"Damn it, I feel as if we are stuck in a role-playing game without any instructions. I know this is real. I have operated on you, washed your blood out of bandages, and muscles I haven't used much are aching. But the whole thing feels more than a bit spooky." Cathy sighed. "At least we met John Buford. I'd really freak out if we met President Lincoln."

"He won't be in town until November, Catie. He comes for the dedication."

"Right – the Gettysburg Address."

"Can you even imagine being able to see THAT? Talk about living history! To hear Lincoln, himself, give that speech – wow. I've got goosebumps just thinking about it," John stated, giving a little shiver.

"Down, boy. It would also mean staying for several months. It's now the beginning of July, and if I recall, the dedication is in mid-November."

"Thursday, the 19th of November, to be precise."

"Johnny, that's almost five months away."

"Are you sure we won't be here? How long is this thing going to take to heal?" He gestured to his leg.

"Best guess, assuming you cooperate," Cathy glared to underline the phrase, "Somewhere between six and eight weeks. The bullet drove the coin into one of the quadriceps on the outside of your thigh. The quads control movement of your knee and hip. That's why I moved your knee last night. I wanted to make sure the muscle was properly attached, but I didn't want you to do it. Muscle tissue doesn't take to stitching well, so I repaired the fascia – that's the strong membrane around muscles. Once it heals, it's going to take a bit of physical therapy to be able to get it functioning properly and build up strength so you can walk normally. We could be looking at up to three months total recovery time."

"What about the bone whose bit I have with my souvenirs?"

"Bones heal when they have a chance. The coin was driven to the bone, cutting through your leg muscle on its way. That's one hell of a projectile, but if the coin hadn't been there, the bullet would have shattered the bone, which is another problem entirely – I didn't pack any titanium plates. As it is, the bone cracked from the impact, but only separated when I pulled the coin out. So what happened resulted in the bone being bruised and only marginally more than chipped. There may be some other cracks, but I'm not as concerned with the femur as I am the quads." At the blank look she got, she added, "The coin did as much damage as the bullet, but not nearly what the bullet would have done on its own. I had to make an incision so I could see what I was doing and get everything out, but it's neater now."

"Wow." John was quiet. "I can't believe that the coin saved my leg."

"Yep. Imagine how I felt when I found it!" She grinned. "I freely admit I was startled. The bullet was easy to remove. I saw a piece of metal, and I figured it was a bit from a shell casing or some such, but it was your silver dollar. That bullet was well-aimed. If it hadn't been to the side, it would have missed the coin and hit the bone squarely. It's also the only reason you made it back here on horseback. If it had been towards the inside, you wouldn't have been able to sit on the horse, even if it was Grey Eagle."

"Buford had me put up on a horse, but I didn't realize it was *his* horse." John smiled dreamily. "So I did ride here on Grey Eagle. I don't remember all of what happened when I was shot."

"Shock does odd things to the memory."

"Was I in shock?"

"A bit." She looked at him and sighed. "I was pleased to see you were as alert as you were when you got here. The first set of vital signs I took was more than a relief. You were in a light state of shock. Your forehead was cool to the touch, but you weren't going deeper. I was concerned about the length of time between the shot and your arrival, but you did well."

"I don't remember much, except having an argument with Devin about the surgeon, and talking to General Buford." He thought about it. "Oh, I did ask for some water, and they gave me some. But most it is a real fog."

"It may come back to you." She chuckled. "General Buford did tell me that you got downright mean when you refused to let Colonel Devin have you taken to the field surgeon."

"Well, I wasn't about to let anyone but you touch my leg."

"Good thing, too. It wasn't as bad as it might have looked to someone other than me, and with so many wounded a military surgeon would not have taken the time I did to put you back together, assuming he had the knowledge."

"You're saying the wound itself was lucky, in a way."

"You mean the way the damage was done?" She considered that. "I suppose, in that sense, yes, it was lucky. The damage was not as bad as it might have been, and it was repairable. No tendons were involved, and the femur wasn't shattered. No major blood vessels were clipped, either, which was actually the biggest piece of luck. Lastly, I had all that I needed to do the repairs."

"I may look the next time you do the dressing change," he said.

"It won't be a pretty sight," Cathy replied honestly. "I haven't closed it yet – too much of a chance for infection, which is why I applied the poultice."

"How would I have fared without you? Was Buford's assessment right?"

"Seriously? I think they may have gotten the bullet out along with the coin, and the wound would have been closed. The muscle may have healed, but only if you hadn't developed an infection. On its own, even without infection, you may have healed but limped." Cathy smiled as he shuddered. "I have placed drains, and packed it with the dressing, which has a variety of antibiotics so the fragment pathway can benefit."

"The bread mold."

"That's part of it. Staph infection should be stemmed by the penicillin mold, but I also used some more of the antibiotic ointment I discovered in the field kit. Speaking of antibiotics, I am going to start you on an oral one – I found a bottle of a strong, broad-spectrum one. I have enough for two five-day runs, and I'd like you to take it as a preventative measure." Cathy chuckled. "I didn't do all that work just to have you succumb to a massive infection, and the penicillin may not get all of it."

"Catie, I promise I will try to make it up to you – thank you."

"Don't thank me until after the physical exercises. You won't enjoy them, I promise."

"Okay, but thanks anyway." He yawned. "Can I do anything about exercising now?"

"Let me think about that. Your whole leg needs time to recover from the bruising and swelling the impact caused. I will have to decide on a balance between healing and exercise." She stretched. "It's been a long time since I had to do all this on my own, you know. I usually have a whole team of people."

"Oops."

"Well, it's good for me," she said with a grin. "Keeps me on my toes. Meanwhile, would you like more for your theory about our situation?"

"Sure."

"I have a 'way past coincidence' for you, then," she said. "Think about this and add it to your collection for thought. We are two people, fairly ordinary, right?" At his nod, she continued. "You are an engineer, and I am a doctor, neither being particularly rare for our own place and time. Yet I am beginning to notice how well equipped are we for what we have landed in. You are a living historian with a good working knowledge of what is here and now, this place and time. I have the skills I need to deal with the slightly archaic language and dress of this time, and my summers on Gran's farm are going to come in handy."

"Your vegetable garden." John nodded thoughtfully. "You're right. We have the skills to blend in, the basic knowledge to know when to intervene or not, and other skills to survive."

"There's something else that's even more important, I have realized."

"What?"

"It is taking both of us to do it. Neither one could have managed this alone." She smiled at him. "We have each said it from the first: if I had to be stuck here, I'm glad I'm stuck with you. We have always complemented each other – we are known for it. Now our survival and mission, if you want to call it that, depends on our ability to complete each other's skills set."

"Good Lord. It's scary." John took a deep breath and exhaled slowly. "Geez," he added and then spoiled the effect with a yawn.

"Why don't you take a nap? As far as I can see right now, you have one job: heal."

"Chamber pot time first." He scowled. "I may come to totally resent bodily functions."

"'Function' is the keyword there, my boy. As long as you function, don't knock it. Can you manage?" she asked, handing it to him.

"I think so. Any tips?"

"Use your good leg and let the wounded one stay on the pillow if you can. Roll if you can't lift up enough. Call me when you're finished. I'll bring a square of material for the last touch." She gave him a quick hug. "We'll get the hang of all of this, regardless of the whys and whats. At least while we are on our own, we can speak normally."

" *'Look for the silver lining'*, I guess," he quoted.

"Now more than ever. We both have to."

The rest of the day passed quietly inside the cabin, but as she read Cathy heard the sounds of war in the distance. At least it was in the distance, she thought to herself and hopefully would stay there. She stood up and stretched, checked on John – sleeping – and went outside. It was hot and still. She propped the door open on her return for airflow and decided that she'd get more water when the shooting stopped. She brought her sleeping roll into the main room and took a nap under the table.

*****

Cathy went into the bedroom with a stack of clean cloths, the empty canning jar, and the chamber pot.

"Wakey, wakey."

"What time is it?" John said with a slight groan.

"Almost six. I thought you might need these," she said, handing him the receptacles, "And once you're through, we can each enjoy a protein bar along with the last two biscuits. After supper, I will challenge you to a hot game of cribbage."

They were in the middle of a game, which Cathy was wining, when there was a knock on the door.

"Uh-oh." Cathy checked the room for anything 'illegal', tossed the covers over John's leg to hide the elastic bandage, and headed to the main room.

"Miss Howell?" Keogh's voice came through the door as the knock was repeated.

"Yes, Captain?" she said, smiling as she opened the door. "Please, do come in."

"I am here with General Buford's compliments, Miss Howell. He sent me to check on you both," he said, taking off his hat as he entered. "I'm glad to see you well."

"The General is most thoughtful, Captain. Johnny is in the other room. We are playing cribbage, and for once, I am winning. Please come this way, as I know he will be delighted to see you." She smiled as she led the officer into the sickroom, thankful she could change her language at will.

"This is most unexpected," John said, offering his hand to his fellow officer. "Please, Myles, be seated."

"I won't stay but a moment," he said as he sat. "I have been instructed to make sure you are both safe and well. How's your leg, John?"

"Tell the general it is still firmly attached," John quipped. "And likely to remain so." He grinned.

"He is attempting to be humorous, Captain, however, he is correct. Please assure General Buford that there have been no complications," Cathy replied. "Although it is early days yet, I am confident John will make a complete recovery."

"You are quite skilled, indeed, Miss Howell. I saw the wound yesterday and feared the worst. The bleeding was not overmuch, but the flesh did appear to be badly torn. I hope I did the correct thing by covering it."

"Captain, you bandaged it with a clean cloth, and that was fine," Cathy reassured him. "Keeping a wound clean is one of the best things to do."

"I am relieved, and the General will be most impressed."

"May I ask how the battle went today?" John asked. "Were the brigades involved?"

"We were not part of the major battle this afternoon, having been moved to the rear to guard the supply trains. At the moment, most of the troopers from both brigades – what is left of us – are now south of the state line. The General is meeting with other commanders to determine whether the fight will stay here or move south."

John nodded at this. *That tallies with what little I can remember about the aftermath of Day One for them.* He asked, "Did we lose many men yesterday? Once I was taken from the field, I lost touch with the rest of what was going on."

"Entirely understandable," Keogh told him. "From the brigade reports we received last evening, we lost about thirty men and another hundred or so were wounded, with a few missing. Of those wounded, there are several who may not survive, yet some will be able to recover enough to keep fighting. The general told me you will probably not rejoin us, considering the severity of your wound."

"I'm afraid it will be a long time before he can walk again," Cathy put in asserted quickly, "quite possibly three months."

"I would have thought it might be longer," Keogh stated, nodding. "I am glad, however, that you will recover in due course, even if it will not occur in time to rejoin our unit. Perhaps you can go back to the Third Missouri."

"Possibly, however, be assured I will look for news of the brigades as this war continues," John told him seriously. "I was proud to serve with you. I was hoping to continue with the men for longer than a day," he added ruefully. "Please remember me to them."

"I shall."

All three were silent for a few moments.

"I was told to inform you that I am not here, though this does seem strange to me," Keogh began hesitantly. "I do want to add that it has been my honor to serve with you, John. The action yesterday morning was very confused, and I was unaware of the importance of your role until a short while ago as I was engaged on another part of the field. The general explained some of what you did for your men as well as for him. You were quite correct - the Union cannot afford to lose her officers, especially one the caliber of the General, and I want to extend my thanks."

"None are necessary. I did what I thought to be correct, and would not hesitate to do so again, even at the risk of raising the General's ire," John replied easily. "I do have one personal concern, however, and would like to request a favor of you. Should you find a moment to do so, please tender my apologies to Colonel Devin for my behavior yesterday after I was wounded. I was rude and argumentative, and I would like him to clearly understand that I was not directing any criticism towards the Colonel personally. I was proud to serve under his command and would not wish him to remember me with rancor."

"I believe the General has done so and you may relieve your mind on that score," Keogh replied. "However, I will add my assurances on your behalf the next time I have the opportunity."

"I would be much obliged."

"There is something else I would like to say to you both, but I am not certain how I should phrase it."

"Speak freely, please, sir," Cathy encouraged. "We both feel obligated to you for your actions on our behalf yesterday."

"The general never left my sight last evening, as you know," he began, looking at the ceiling and turning his hat in his hands as if embarrassed, "Yet he seems to be much relieved in his mind regarding the ultimate outcome of the war. Seeing his mind eased has, in turn, helped relieve my mind about General Buford. He is a true patriot and desires to see our country remain whole. I believe I have you both to thank, or I would if there had been some communication between you." He dropped his gaze to Cathy. "Miss Howell, before I take my leave, I was instructed to hand this to you." He extended a letter to her as he rose.

"Captain, I again thank you for all you have done for us, as well as all you will do in your continuing service to General Buford," she said as she took the letter. "I shall always remember your courtesy and kindness for bringing my brother safely here yesterday, as well as your assistance." She rose to show out the officer. "Allow me to show you to your mount."

Keogh saluted John, who returned it and followed Cathy out of the room. Once outside, he stopped, again seeming to hesitate.

"Miss Howell, I find myself at a loss for words, something highly unusual for an Irishman." He smiled down at her with charm and a flash of humor she found appealing. "There is something I should like to present to you, but I do not wish to presume on so short an acquaintance, as it might be considered impertinent. To be truthful, I had hoped and wished for the prospect of spending more time with you; it would have been proper before giving this to you. However, circumstances do appear to be against this. As times are uncertain, I pray you will not be offended by such informality."

"Captain, your duties must come first, and I understand that. Truly, I beg you to speak frankly – I have never stood upon formality." Cathy guessed that Myles Keogh was not generally as ill at ease with ladies as he appeared now, and she found it touching. "I shall take no offense."

"I did mention this to the general in private, seeking his opinion. I was thankful that he found my suggestion worthy - if somewhat unorthodox. He did not think you would take it ill." He drew a small cloth bag from his tunic and extended it. "Please accept this, and consider it as coming from two that have seen your courage and strength in the short time we have known you and accept it as a token of our genuine admiration. The general wants you to know you have his highest regard, even if you did discourage a suggestion of his."

"He told you I had discouraged a suggestion of his?" Cathy was puzzled.

"That is indeed what he said. I admit I did not understand that particular reference, but he was smiling when he said it."

"Captain, you have now aroused my curiosity," Cathy replied, frowning slightly until she remembered her first conversation with Buford. Laughing as she took the offered bag, she added, "I believe I can explain. General Buford may have referred to our first meeting. I do recall he asked Johnny if I could ride a horse. I quickly stated that I gave it up as soon as I was forced to wear petticoats and use a sidesaddle. For a moment, he seemed inclined to enlist me!"

"Ah," Keogh said, joining her laughter, "I believe I now understand."

"May I open your gift?"

"Please," he assented.

Cathy opened the drawstring bag and found a pair of captain's insignia shoulder boards.

"Captain? I am not sure I understand. These are military insignia."

"They are mine. Please accept them as a token of respect and admiration from two soldiers." As she hesitated, he added, "I have been informed that I will shortly have no need of them. General Buford is recommending me for promotion to major."

"Since that is the case, I shall treasure them, along with the acquaintances which prompted the gift. You are very attached to General Buford, and as I said yesterday, he does need you." Cathy bobbed a small curtsey. "God keep you safe, Captain."

"And you, Miss Howell." He took her hand and raised it to his lips.

She rejoined John after securing the door.

"Johnny, Captain Keogh and, by extension, General Buford, have given me a gift." She showed her insignia to him and related what had taken place.

"Wow – I knew Myles was very taken with you. He saw you on the street and at the hotel and asked me several questions about you. I gathered from some of the other officers that he's quite the ladies' man." John grinned. "He asked how he might write to you and asked my permission as your brother if he might write to you. I gave him the Scotts' address, by the way."

"Good grief - that would be akin to courting. Still, I can easily believe it. When not being formal he oozes Irish charm. But his insignia? I thought that was against the rules."

"Yes and no. As he told you, he will be promoted to major shortly."

"Do you know anything about what happened to him?"

"Only vaguely. I know he was with General Buford when the general died – he was, umm, is very devoted to Buford. After the war, I think he stayed in the regular army cavalry and went out west." John frowned, trying to pull information from memory. "I think I read somewhere that he worked with General Custer."

"Well, that wouldn't work out too well – if he was at Little Big Horn, it would spell curtains."

"Yeah, probably."

"When we get back, I have *got* to find a book on this battle. I want to know what the hell is going on, or went on, while no one was visiting us," she said to John. "Where are they all now?"

"Buford's troopers are on their way to Winchester. I think they are camping tonight in Taneytown, which is over the Maryland border."

"Is the General with the other commanders?"

"Possibly. But, for the record, he wasn't here last night."

"And Keogh wasn't here today."

"Right. Aren't you going to open that?" he asked, pointing to the letter still clutched in her hand. "Read it out."

"'Dear Miss Catie, I would like to thank you for saving the life of the man who saved mine. I now share your conviction and belief that our victory is coming, and I trust it will happen even if I do not live to see it. When I do leave this life, I look forward to seeing you in the next life. My faith tells me that we shall once again meet, along with your brother and my wife. Until then, may God always keep you safe. Yours sincerely, John Buford'."

Cathy looked up at John, tears welling in her eyes. "He's a bit of a fatalist."

"Uh-huh. He may realize that he can't live with the rheumatoid arthritis forever if nothing else." John smiled at her. "Frame it."

"Oh, yeah." She carefully put the letter with his, adding the ziplock with the bullet and bone fragment to her small bag. She knew better than to ask for the dollar. "Quite a few souvenirs. Before we get back to the game, can you tell me what happens tomorrow?"

"In plain speaking, a slaughter. Tomorrow's main action is what becomes known as 'Pickett's Charge.' It takes place in the afternoon. We'll hear it – there's a major exchange of cannon fire before the men start fighting."

"Buford's people are elsewhere?"

"They have left the battlefield. He still has battles to fight, but not here."

"You said tomorrow is the last day of the battle."

"Yes. Then the cleanup starts. I warn you, it's going to be a real mess. Bodies, dead horses, wounded – it's all going to have to be dealt with and none of it is pretty. The whole area was said to reek with the smell of rotting flesh for weeks."

"Should I volunteer to help?"

"No, I don't think so," he said thoughtfully. "You might interfere with something without realizing it."

"Like you did with the General."

"Look, the historical knowledge we spoke of was put to use. I was able to stop something from happening. Buford had to survive and the line *had* to hold…" His voice trailed off. "Cripes. I really was in the right place at the right time, wasn't I?"

"Yep, and now we have to figure out what comes next." She thought for a moment. "Is there anyone who is wounded who SHOULD survive?"

"Huh? Oh, I see what you mean. Someone who should make it but needs special help. General Winfield Scott Hancock is – or will be – wounded tomorrow but survives. Lewis Armistead is mortally wounded and dies. The only other one who comes to mind will be Colonel Joshua Lawrence Chamberlain, but his really bad wound won't happen until 1864. Hopefully, we won't be around."

"Chamberlain went into politics, didn't he?"

"Very successfully, yes. He was the Governor of Maine for four one-year terms, and then became president of Bowdoin College. You recognized the name?"

"One of the residents in the ER went to the University of Maine for undergrad work, and when I mentioned I was going to a Gettysburg reenactment, he told me that one of his heroes was Chamberlain."

"Chamberlain got – or will get – a Medal of Honor for what he did today. It takes thirty years, but he does receive it."

"Anyway, I have your care to attend to. I should probably plan to use it as an excuse not to stay in town and help."

"Yeah. I know it's going to be frustrating staying out of it, but it's for the best. The Army will step in shortly and organize a field hospital outside of town. It was – or will be – called Camp Letterman, after the head of military medicine. So relief will start to flow in."

"Wounded from both sides will get care, then?" At his nod, she continued. "Good, that will make it easier for me. I am trained and knowing what I know makes it hard for me to just walk away."

"Now, let's see if I can manage to pull this out," he said, gesturing at the game.

"Not a chance," she answered as she shuffled. "Not a chance."

After her victory, she offered to let him get even, which he did although not by much.

"I'm going to keep score," she told him as she put the game pieces away. "I've never won against you by that much before." They both laughed.

"How about a book?" he asked. "The Christie volume is stories, right?"

She chose the first story in the Poirot collection, and read aloud until John let her know it was time for him to sleep for the night.

"Good thing we have always been our own best company," he commented as he took his medications. "Skillsets aside, I can't imagine going through this with anyone else." He reached up to hug her.

"Do you want the lamp on?"

"Do we have enough oil for it?" he asked, then added quickly, "Never mind. You're going to sleep on the floor?"

"Until I'm reasonably sure that I won't bother you by moving back to the bed, yes."

"Okay. I'll be fine without it."

"Wake me if you need me." She settled onto her bedroll.

"Trust me, I will," he said. "Catie?"

"Yes?"

"Thank you for sharing my adventure."

"That's what you wrote in the note with the books. I'll bet you never dreamed how much of an adventure it was going to turn out to be."

"Cripes, no. What did you think when you read it?"

"Well, it struck me as being overly prophetic and unintentionally accurate. In view of what happened, it does rank as the understatement of all understatements." She chuckled. "I did make a vow to myself this morning, though. After doing your bath and changing the dressing, I decided I would never berate another nurse for taking a breather again."

"A wise decision. Never argue with a nurse."

"I'll remind you of that the first time you balk. Go to sleep."

As she lay there thinking over the day, Cathy heard John humming. "Look for the silver lining." It's our theme song, she decided as she finally dropped off.

*****

"CATIE!"

It was a scream.

She jumped up so fast that she had to grab the bed so she didn't fall over. John was gripping the covers, and obviously in agony. She raised the covers over his wounded leg. One glance told her what the problem was.

"Leg cramp?" she asked, eyeing his foot, which looked contorted.

"Like I've never felt before."

"Let me see if I can ease it," she said, tossing the covers over. She started to massage his foot, working up his calf, and trying to feel the injured quads in his thigh. "It seems to be mostly in the lower leg," she said as she worked.

"Got anything in your bag for this?" He was sweating, trying not to scream.

"Can you take over the massage? It's helping. I think I can find something to ease this." She helped him sit up so he could reach around the bandages.

She dragged the duffle out from under the bed and practically dove into it.

"Hey," he said, still clenching his teeth, "You look like Mary Poppins digging into her carpetbag."

"Gee, thanks," came the muffled reply.

Moments later, she resumed her place on the bed with her small med bag, popped open a bottle of tablets, and handed him one.

"I'll be right back with water," she said, dashing out to the main room.

He heard the door bang, silence, then another bang as it shut. She came back in with a pail of water and a cup. He took the tablet, not even bothering to ask what it was. Meanwhile, she dug into what he privately thought of as her Bag of Tricks. She handed him a half-tablet, which he took. Then she handed him a small food bar.

"Eat it and drink another cup of water." She sat down in the chair.

"What happened?"

"I said, 'eat.'" She pointed at the bar. "It will help. Honestly? I slipped up."

"What?"

"Johnny, I should have realized this might happen and taken steps to head it off. I'm sorry." She slouched in the chair.

"You can't think of everything, and it's going away. What happened, really?"

"Your circulation is skewed, you have major muscle and tissue damage, your calf and foot muscles haven't been exercised as they normally would by walking, and you built up lactic acid. Hence, cramps. Your electrolytes are probably out of whack as well. I gave you a potassium tablet, a half a tranquilizer to help calm everything down – you clench muscles when you're in pain, everyone does – and the food bar should help take care of the rest."

He handed her the cup, which she refilled and handed back. "You also need water."

"I know if I don't eat a banana and drink water after a run, I get cramps."

"Same principle. Bananas, and believe it or not, potatoes, are high in potassium. The other key is hydration. The lactic acid is the result of cell metabolism. If the buildup can't get out of the tissue, blammo. I packed the potassium tablets because your living historians might have needed them for the same reason you just named. Exercise, without replenishing potassium and without drinking extra water, can often lead to the spasms and cramping you just went through."

He finished the bar and handed her the wrapper. "Talk about a useful skills set."

"Better?"

"Oh, much." He wearily leaned back into the pillows. "Wow. That was…."

"Yep, I know. Again, sorry." She put things back into the field pack, put it back into the duffle, and put it all back under the bed.

"Don't worry about it – I'm okay now. Did the spasms do any damage?"

"I doubt it. First, you'd know. It would have been a different sort of pain if anything had torn open, and it would HURT with worse pain than the cramps."

"How about a few more pages of Hercule's little grey cells, so we both calm down?"

After reading for a while, Cathy noticed that John was drifting off. She put the book away, mumbling, "Let's try this again," to herself. She got halfway through their song before she fell asleep.

CHAPTER NINE

Friday, 3 July 1863

John woke to hear birds singing, looked around to see sunlight coming in through the window, and peered over the edge of the bed. Cathy, still asleep, was curled on her side much as she had been the night they were drop-kicked in time. He couldn't see the clock they were using, and his pocket watch was in his uniform vest pocket. It occurred to him that he had no idea where his uniform was. *The pants would be another souvenir, even if they were bloody.* He made a note to ask.

He felt bad about dragging her through this whole thing, but at the same time, he realized that he hadn't known anything unusual was going to happen. *Certainly nothing like falling back through time over one hundred and fifty years – never, ever could I have pictured this.* He thought back to their conversation yesterday. *It's taking both of us to do whatever was keeping us here.* That brought up the thoughts about President Lincoln. *Naah, meeting John Buford was treat enough. Almost worth getting shot.* He thought about his encounters with the troopers and the general. He and Cathy had their letters and they had the photos. *I'll get the photos printed and have them matted and framed with the letters. One set for me and one for Cathy. I might even have the frame shop put the bullet in, too. Sounds like a plan. Maybe have the bone bit put into Cathy's mat, as long as I don't tell the store exactly what it was....*

He stretched a bit and realized immediately that it had been a mistake. Somehow, it woke up his bodily functions. He hated to do it, but he needed to wake her up so she could hand him the jar.

He was just about to call her name when an arm popped up next to the bed, holding that very item.

"Morning. Need this?" Her head came into his field of vision.

"Uh, as a matter of fact, yes. How did you know I was awake?" He took the offering with a chuckle.

"The bed makes some noise when you wiggle around. I was waking up and heard it. The rest is just logic."

"Does the sound wake you up? I hope your sleep isn't that light."

"It's hard to explain," she replied as she got up and rolled up her bed. "I hate to put it this way, but it's a doctor/nurse thing. Probably also what my mother calls a 'mommy thing.' You are aware of a noise on some level, but it won't wake you up completely unless it needs to." She looked at his face and laughed. "I know – not much of an explanation."

"Not really, no. Strange thing is, it almost makes sense." He handed back the jar and winced as she looked at it closely. "You are kidding me? You're looking at it to annoy me, right?"

"Not entirely, although that's a bonus," she grinned. "Okay, I'll be serious. It's clear, not cloudy. No obvious blood, pus, or gross evidence of infection."

"Gross is right."

"I can't run tests, on this or blood. But if there was an infection building, this is one place it would show up. For real."

"Oh." He thought for a moment, and asked warily, "How much torture will you put me through today?"

"None, really. You got a bit sweaty last night with the cramps, so I thought you might like to sponge off. I'll even do your back. Also, we need to work out how to turn you onto your side so you can give your back a break for a while."

About an hour later, cleaned up and comfortably lying on his side with the pillows positioned to support his wounded leg, he had to admit – again – that Cathy was a first-class health practitioner.

"How about some biscuits and tea for breakfast?" he asked when they were done. "Those were good."

"I'll consider it," she said as she sat down. "I heard some rumbles a while back."

"Skirmishes and a bit of a running battle over Culp's Hill, all to the south of us. You'll know when the serious stuff starts later today, believe me."

"I think I'll stoke the stove and bring some fresh water in. I don't want to be outside when the shooting starts, even though you have said it won't be around here."

"Some of it went around here on the first day. A group of Devin's men were reasonably close to the cabin, but I wasn't with them at the time."

"I think I'm glad I didn't know," she said with a shudder.

"What were you doing?"

"Reading, mostly. Trying to prepare for whatever emergency you showed up with and hoping like hell none of it was going to be needed." She got up to do her chores. "By the way, as the wound heals, I may see if I can cast the leg. Once the swelling goes down, it may help immobilize and support it – which would also give the bone a chance to heal - and it would make you a bit more mobile."

"Speaking of mobility, what happened to my uniform?"

"It's a bit of a mess, but I haven't thrown it into the fire. I thought you might want to see your pants, maybe even keep them as another souvenir. I only cut the one leg, and I can stitch that. The bullet hole can be your badge of honor."

"My watch is in my vest pocket."

"No, it's not. It's in the dresser with your other clothes." She got it and handed it to him, putting the windup clock where he could see it.

John set and wound his watch. "We could use a couple of bedside tables, huh."

"Yep, and you can build them once you get better." Suddenly a thought struck her and she actually giggled.

"The idea is funny?"

"Not that – I know you could easily build something we could use, no problem. It's just that yesterday, I decided I was going to skip asking you to invent the refrigerator." He opened his mouth, and she added, "I know. I'm not a well person." They both laughed.

She left the room, and he heard the cabin door open.

"John Townsend Andrews," he said to himself out loud, "You are the luckiest son-of-a-bitch in the Union Army, no matter what century you happen to be in." As he lay there, he tried to think of ways to thank her once they made it back. He was trying to figure out her favorite restaurant when he fell asleep.

*****

Cathy was wondering where she was going to get some eggs and milk, even as she made some more biscuits. The protein bars were saving them, although she wished she had packed more food stuff, like energy drink tubes. Oh well. She made a note to never leave the house without a week's worth of supplements. Biscuits done, she woke John up with a cup of tea and a couple of her latest baking efforts. He straightened up in bed to eat.

"Once you finish that, you get to take a few pills – vitamins and the antibiotic. The protein bars help, but I think we should do what we can to build you up. Nutrition is not even on the horizon at this point in history."

"Neither is germ theory."

"I'm aware. I have a small bottle of multivitamins, and I think you should take them."

"What about you?"

"I'm not the one with the gaping hole in my leg." She held up her hand as his mouth opened. "Never argue with your nurse, especially when she's also your doctor, not to mention in charge of things like the Mason jar."

He closed his mouth.

"That's my boy," she said with a smile. "Oh, I have a task for you."

"Like what? You said I didn't have to invent the refrigerator."

"No, but I wish you could. Seriously, can you design a crutch that we can make? Something I can make with your guidance?"

"I'll think about it. It would be easier with some tools. Besides the shovel and the ax I saw by the woodpile, do we have anything?"

"I don't think so."

"Make a list. What will you do today?"

"I thought I'd start mapping out a garden and maybe turning soil until the shooting starts. Do you happen to recall when it rains?"

"I think it starts up again Saturday or Sunday. I'm not sure." John looked at his watch. "It's about eight-thirty. You have a while before all hell breaks loose, and outdoor activity would probably be better before noon due to the heat."

"Here." She handed him a vitamin, a capsule, and a cup of water. "I'll rinse out the jar and leave it with the pot in your reach. You can have my clipboard and a pencil if you want to try to write anything. Or you can fall asleep."

"Why am I so tired? I feel like a wimp."

"You're not a wimp. The next time I change the dressing, you can take a look at the wound. Healing takes energy." She regarded him as she changed into her jeans and a t-shirt. "You've never really been sick, have you?"

"Measles as a kid. I still have my tonsils and appendix." He stretched his arms. "I'll take the clipboard and pencil."

"Johnny, you can move anything that doesn't hurt – arms, left leg. Sit up, turn. I don't want you to try any movement with your leg without me. Just don't jostle the wound. You won't like it."

"I don't doubt that for a moment." He looked at the window, which was open. "If I yell, come running."

"Gotcha."

Once she left, he started to try to organize his thoughts about the battle. Some of it was still too blurry, so he shifted to what he and Cathy had discussed. Was this all part of a master plan?

What was the goal? He made some notes, and after a while put it all to the side so he could nap.

Cathy, for her morning, stepped out a garden in an area of the clearing that got the most sun and proceeded to turn soil with the shovel. Slow going, but when she quit, she had a respectable amount ready to plant. She went inside to work on a map of what she wanted to put down, hopefully, tomorrow.

She peeked in on John. He was dozing but opened his eyes at her soft call.

"Mary, Mary, quite contrary how does your garden grow…"

"I wouldn't call it a garden yet, but I should be able to start planting. I want to make a sketch of the plot, so I can map out what will go where." She started working on the clipboard.

"Can I help?"

"Sure. Tell me what veggies you don't like, for a start. I don't want to slave over a garden only to have you turn your nose up at what comes out of it."

"I love vegetables. Almost all of them, except Brussel Sprouts."

"Well, maybe I'll try those for just me. Spinach? Green beans? Radishes? Lettuce? Cucumbers? Corn? Kohlrabi?"

"Not familiar with the last one but I'll try it. Were all of these around back now?"

"Does it matter?" she asked, chuckling. "I figure as long as it's just us, we're okay. We need vegetables, and I need a hobby. Ergo, we will have a garden. Once you can move a bit, you can come out and supervise." She looked at the grin on his face and added, "Yep, you'll enjoy telling me I missed a weed. I wish we had some sort of bench we could use to sit outside."

"Put that on the list. So I need to design simple tables, a bench, and crutches."

"Which I can build under your guidance. Crutches should come first."

"Yeah. I'll make a list of stuff we'll need to do this. Nails, hammer, and saw come to mind."

"You said you think it may start to rain tomorrow?"

"From what I can remember," he said, frowning, "The weather cleared almost exactly for the battle itself. Before it started, it rained, and it picked up again afterward. If that is true, it should start tomorrow and maybe rain all weekend."

"I should probably leave the visit to town until Monday," she said. "I'm going back outside to mark off where I want what. I won't be long."

Less than an hour later, Cathy stood back to look at her garden plot. Rows were marked with sticks, and she had divided the two rows for the beans into sections for staggered planting. She had two cucumber hills laid out, rows for spinach and lettuce - also sectioned – with a row for radishes, two short rows for corn, and one for kohlrabi.

Not the amazing garden Gran has, but it will do for the two of us. She regretted the lack of tomato plants and seed potatoes, which were the other two things she would have liked to grow. *Maybe Miss Martha would know where I can get some.*

She washed her hands in the stream and then went to the woodpile, which thankfully did not seem to be diminishing much, and grabbed an armload to take back into the cabin. She had come to terms with the thought of having to keep the stove lit and burning in the heat of summer, as it was their only source for cooking, not to mention hot water, but chopping wood was something she'd rather avoid. She banged a log on the doorframe as she tried to juggle the load through the door.

"Catie," John called out, "Are you back inside yet?"

The next thing he heard was the sound of logs falling, followed by some modern colloquialisms.

"Are you all right?"

"No damage. Do you need help or can I pick all this up?" came the reply.

"Take your time," he answered as he stifled his laughter.

A few minutes and considerable noise later, Cathy came into the bedroom. She had both hands behind her back.

"Do you need anything?"

"Well, water would be nice. Did you get the garden laid out?"

"Uh-huh. I won't plant today – heavy rain will wash out the seeds." She handed him a cup of water, which she had behind her back. "Anything need to be emptied?"

"Not at the moment. What's next for you? And why is your other hand behind your back?"

"It got scraped a bit when I was arguing with the wood. I wanted to make sure you were okay before I tend to it."

"Can I help?"

"Nah, I'm going to wash it off and then apply some of the antibiotic ointment. The doorway isn't as wide as I thought it was." She grimaced. "Johnny, I haven't heard any major booms. When will it start?"

He glanced at the clock and then at his watch. "It's a little after eleven now. In about an hour, maybe a bit more, there will be a bombardment from both sides across a wheat field not far from where we started. After an hour or so of that, the Confederates will start across to attack the Union troops. The heavy fighting will come between two and three this afternoon. Once the fighting starts, it won't take long."

"Will we be able to hear it?"

"We'll hear the bombardment. Remember yesterday's noise?" As she nodded, he continued. "This is going to be worse. The Scotts were probably warned to evacuate, but I doubt they did. Most of the people stayed put." He sighed. "I'm glad I won't be on the field. It's going to be a bloody day."

"So what do we do?"

"Let's see how loud it gets. If we can, I think reading or cards would be good."

"Before it starts, let me see what I can find for lunch."

It was still shy of noon when she came back in with a tray.

"Add a lap table to your list of things to make," Cathy commented as she placed the tray on the bed.

John looked at their lunch, eyes wide. They had a selection of cheese and hard sausage, plus Cathy's biscuits.

"Where did all this come from?"

"Guess."

"Miss Martha?"

"When I left their home Tuesday evening, I had a full bag of what Miss Martha called 'all sorts of useful things.' I've barely dug into it all. We had flour, but she gave me a box of baking soda, some baking powder, and some tins of meat. This sausage, though, probably came from someone local. People around here, and up near Carlisle, are known for making it, she told me."

"My God, Catie, we owe them."

"No joke. Eat up. Then after I clean the dishes, I'll bring in more water, and we can play cards."

During their second game of gin rummy, the sound effects began. John recognized it for what it was, but Cathy thought it sounded like rolling thunder with punctuations of louder bangs.

"It's the acoustics of the sound waves over the distance between us and the origins," John explained to her. "Remember your basic physics?"

"Probably not more than you remember of your basic biology," she said, putting down the ten of clubs.

"Being in a wooded area helps absorb the sound," he said, picking up her card. "Gin. Another game?"

"Why not." She gathered the cards and shuffled while they both listened to the distant barrage. "Will there be less noise or more noise when the actual fighting starts?"

"Honestly, I'm not sure. The barrage will last about an hour or slightly more. The Confederate troops are assembled behind some trees at the edge of the field and will step off at about two o'clock, marching across about three-quarters of a mile while under fire. It's a testament of the bravery of those men that they went at all." He sighed. "I've always wanted to hear the troops cutting loose with the rebel yell as they charged, but I don't think the sound will carry this far."

Cathy dealt the cards. "Rebel yell?"

"The Confederates had a yell that they did when going into battle. I've read that it was something to both help their own courage and at the same time intimidate their enemy. I always thought the impact was exaggerated, but Wednesday I heard one. I can't really describe it, but it gave me shivers." He picked up his cards.

"Berserkers scream and screech, martial arts practitioners use kiais. Indians used the war-whoop as they went into a fight," Cathy reasoned as she picked up her cards. "So why not the Confederates?"

The barrage died off slowly as they continued to play. John checked his watch.

"Now they start marching," he said, noting it was two o'clock.

"I'm glad you aren't with them." She picked up her newly dealt cards.

"So am I." After sorting his cards, he put down the four of hearts as his opening move.

"Gin." She picked up the four, put down her discard, and displayed her hand with a huge grin.

"What? I think it's time to change games here," he said with mock anger. "How about poker with no instructions?"

"Spoilsport," she retorted with a chuckle. "Why don't you take a nap?"

"What will you do?"

"I'll think of something," she said, straightening the bed-clothes. "Want to know a secret?"

"Okay," he said cautiously. "What?"

"When I was laying out the garden, I realized that in spite of all the problems we have here, I'm enjoying not being tied to my cell phone. Or being on-call to a bunch of interns and residents."

"Seriously?"

"Yep. don't get me wrong – you know I love my job. However, I turned off the cell phone when we got to the re-enactment site and haven't missed it a bit."

"Catie, thank you," John said, absolutely serious. "I needed to know that. I've been feeling guilty about dragging you into all this, and worried about how you were handling it."

"I thought it might help. You are going to be okay and in theory, the worst will be over today, right?" She smiled. "We can probably deal with anything else. Since the noise has calmed down, sleep for a bit. I'll stay inside. Someone gave me a couple of great books and I'll be fine."

*****

"Johnny?" Cathy carried a tray into the bedroom and put it down on the chair. "It's almost six."

"What's happening?"

"Not much. It's been quiet for a while. Is it over?'

"Probably. After the main action, both sides took time to gather up their wounded as best they could. The Confederates will start pulling back tomorrow, and there may be some problems in town, but the battle as such is over."

"I want to check your temp before you have something to drink," she said as she popped a thermometer into his mouth. She was more than relieved to see it was normal and said so.

"That means what?"

"The bread mold seems to be a success. If you were developing an infection, it would probably be showing by now. Increased pain, increased temp, and so forth. It's still a concern, which is why you are taking the antibiotic – that was a dirty wound as both the bullet and the coin went through cloth and could have carried threads into you. I'll change the dressing tomorrow, and hopefully partially close the wound if all looks good." She laughed as he grimaced. "Don't worry – I'll use a local and I won't put the needle straight into the wound this time."

"Promise?"

"Promise. I've also been thinking about exercises for your leg that you can start."

"Can I eat something first?"

"Absolutely. Have a mixed-centuries supper!" She took the towel off the tray with a flourish to show a variety of snacks with two protein bars.

"It's amazing how good some of that tasted," he commented after they were finished and she had cleared the dishes. "The local, contemporary stuff seems much more real somehow."

"Artificial shows doesn't it," she agreed. "Modern covers the protein, though, and you need it. I'm glad we can mix both, at least for the time being. Thankfully, because we don't have sources of fiber – the vegetables – and it will do until I can get some growing. The idea of balanced meals doesn't exist. I guess people ate what was at hand and what could be preserved."

"Yeah – we're a sturdy species to survive all of this."

"Johnny, you will heal faster than someone from this century simply because you are from a time when nutrition, vitamins, and exercise are practiced."

"Catie, you have a gift for segue ways. What exercises do I start?"

"You don't want to strain the sutures I put in, but you do want to maintain muscle tone of the whole leg," she answered, ignoring the comment. "I think flexing and relaxing the muscle groups would be a good place to begin. You can flex and extend your foot without putting too much on the thigh muscles, and that should help the bruising heal. I can help with passive movement of the quads, the way I did that first night."

"Okay."

After some experimentation, Cathy laid out a series of stretching moves and number of reps he could do on his own. The more passive movements caused some pain, but John swore it wasn't too much.

"The more muscle tone I can keep, the faster this will go, right?"

"Within limits. You tear anything open and I promise I'll suture you back up without the local," she threatened, checking the dressing. "It would be easy to overdo it. I'm trying to balance this."

"Can I sit in the chair?"

"Let's wait until after I close the wound completely." She looked up and added, "I don't want to risk too much jostling until it is closed. Until then, move it as much as you want to without using the thigh muscles."

"Catie, I promise I'll be good." He caught the look she gave him, and hastily added, "Okay, I promise I'll do my best to be patient about it."

"That's a better way to put it," she replied. "How about a game of cribbage?"

"You just want to win as much as you can before I can think straight," he teased. "Sure, why not?"

Cathy won, but narrowly.

"You're feeling better, I can tell," she laughed as she put the pieces into their place on the board. As she was putting the board away, she suddenly stopped. "OH!" It was a cross between an exclamation and crying out.

John turned and looked at her. "Something wrong?"

"Johnny, I just thought of something," she said as she sat on the chair. "Maybe saving Buford was the reason we are here – our purpose, as you call it."

"Then why are we still here?"

"That's what I was thinking about. The answer I came up with is so simple it's easy to overlook."

"Okay, I'm listening."

"We have to assume that when our job – or mission or whatever – is complete, we'll be whisked back to where we started – the morning of the 28th of June 2015. Right?"

"Right. We won't move location, which means we could end up in someone's back yard or the middle of a mall parking lot, but yes, it would be Sunday, the 28th of June, 2015."

"We can't do that yet." Cathy made it a flat statement.

"Why not?"

"Look at your right leg." She paused to let that sink in. "When last seen, we had just retired to your tent to sleep the night in preparation for the next day's shooting of a civil war documentary. How would we explain it if we were next seen popping up heaven-knows-where with you recovering from a real Civil War wound?"

"Damn! You're right! Even if there's no other reason for us being here, I have to heal before we can go back."

"Completely heal, to where there is no sign of any injury. No limp, no nothing."

"Oh, crap! Catie – I'm sorry! I guess I do have only one job – heal. I promise I'll be good."

"Amen to that," she said smiling. "I know you think that there's some higher plan controlling all this, and if that's so, we're stuck until you can walk out of here. Whoever or whatever is managing all of it can't move us back until you can."

"I've been thinking about how we got here," John admitted. "You know, going over it in my mind. I saw a major pattern of light. If time was compressed so we could move through it, then energy was generated. Maybe that is what I saw."

"You're saying that it was a sort of light strobe effect?"

John thought about it. "Sort of. It seems like there was more to it than that. John began glancing around the cabin.

"What are you looking to find?"

"You remember when you started humming and looking for Mr. Serling. I think we might need to look for a retired admiral with a cigar and a little machine that squalls But regardless of how it happened, we had to go through each and every day – one hundred and fifty-two years of days and nights."

"Well, we certainly have, pardon the expression, *time* to consider it. I told you that at best we have another six or eight weeks, and it could be closer to three months. Does anything major happen in this area?"

"You're not going to believe this, but once the Confederates clear out, two groups of people are going to start flooding in. Relief workers, including medical personnel, and tourists."

"TOURISTS?"

"People want to see the famous battlefield. Many bodies are 'buried' under a few spadesful of dirt, and the rains will start to wash that away, so wandering around could be a grisly experience. There was also some souvenir hunting. The official burials won't begin until October. The plan for a national cemetery hasn't been brought up yet."

They each sat for a moment, lost in thought, until John broke the silence.

"We'll deal with all of it, Catie. We're each good on our own, and together, we're amazing. Meanwhile, how about some more Poirot? We left him in the middle of a puzzle."

"God bless Miss Agatha Mary Clarissa Miller."

"Who?"

"Agatha Christie."

"Was that her full name?"

"No, that's the one she started with. Her full name - and title - would be Agatha Mary Clarissa Miller Christie Mallowan, Dame of the British Empire." Cathy smiled. "Just think of it – she won't even exist until 1890. There's a mystery about her I'd love to solve."

"There is?"

"Oh, yes. She disappeared for ten days in December 1926, and it's never been properly explained. She herself never talked about it. One film tried and even used a disclaimer about being an imagined solution to it, but her estate tried to sue the producers. Twice."

"Wow – that would be something, wouldn't it! A real-life mystery about a real-life mystery writer." John grinned. "Oh well, here's to one more advantage to being from the 21st century – we have her book!"

"And a good choice it was," Cathy stated as she retrieved it from her bag.

She read aloud. John listened, sometimes closing his eyes for a 'theatre of the mind' experience. When she finished the story, Cathy closed the book.

"Enough for now?"

"Yeah, I think so."

"Let me help you get ready for the night."

After making sure he was settled, Cathy went back out to the main room. She tended the bread mold, which she knew she would be using again the following morning. She cleaned out a small jar she had found, set it in boiling water for ten minutes, and transferred more of the purest-looking culture to a new biscuit half.

Back in the bedroom, she put out the lamp and stretched out on her makeshift bedroll.

"Catie?" John's voice was sleepy.

"Yes, Johnny? We'll be okay."

"I know that, Catie. Good night." He closed his eyes and listened as she sang his mom's song.

"Yes," he thought to himself, "A comforting bit of home."

CHAPTER TEN

The First Weekend

Saturday, 4 July 1863

John woke to the sound of rain falling on the cabin roof. He had vague memories of waking in the middle of the night, but just once – and Cathy had been right with him, as usual. He remembered he didn't even have to call her name; she just seemed to know when he needed something. He guessed it was that 'doctor thing' she described.

"Good morning." Her voice came from the floor. "The rain sounds lovely, doesn't it?"

"It sure does, especially since it's just rain, not distant artillery fire."

Cathy sat up, hugging her knees. "How are you doing?"

"The usual," he admitted. "Mason jar time. Plus can I have a pain pill?"

The jar came into his field of vision, and he reached for it. Cathy stayed where she was, thinking about what she wanted to do. When she figured John was finished, she got to her feet.

"Let me give you a pain med now, and I think we should have something to eat. That will give the med time to act before I change the dressing," she told him, handing him half a tablet and water. "Let me get some biscuits going and I'll be back. Feel free to doze off as it could be a bit."

Cathy pulled on a t-shirt and her jeans in preparation for her day. Sighing, and wishing she had an assistant, she stoked the stove, brought in more water from the spring and put it to heat in a pot. She made biscuits – adding an extra spice to keep things new – and brought in more wood. Hoping the outside temperature would stay reasonable – she thought it had been around 90 the day before – she went back to the bedroom to get her medical kit out from under the bed. After she got what she wanted, she put the bag back and put her supplies on a towel on the dresser.

"Johnny, I don't think we have to move you to the table in the other room. We have enough linen to completely change the bed afterward if we need to, and I'm not anticipating complications."

"I was wondering about that. I wasn't looking forward to that long hopping trip again," he grinned at her. "You did say breakfast first, though, didn't you?"

"Yep – coming up." She left the room, returning shortly with a tray with mugs of tea, plates, her latest biscuits, and some slices of hard sausage. "Will this do?"

"Absolutely." He took a sip of tea. "I can't get over how good the water is."

"Ummm, I know what you mean," she agreed. "By the way, you did a good job placing the sink where you did. It's not likely to contaminate the spring or the stream."

"Thank you. I was tempted to put it closer, but I decided it was better to have to walk a few extra yards then risk polluting our water supply." He glanced at Cathy. "I assumed you checked the spring."

"Of course. I admit it tasted it before I did it, but the tests showed that it's good enough to bottle."

"Hey," This is better!" John exclaimed after taking a bite of a biscuit, "This is better. What did you do?"

"Ginger and cinnamon. I guessed that both would add to the molasses," she said, smiling that she had pleased him. "I wanted a bit of a change."

"Since most of the soldiers are living on hardtack and whatever they can scrounge," he commented, "This would be considered a feast."

"I saw local people asking some of the Union soldiers to supper. Isn't that a bit much?"

"Not to the soldiers. When Buford rode through town Tuesday, there was a group of young girls on a corner singing to them. I saw women running out into the street handing out loaves of bread, cookies, and cakes. Believe me, every bit of it was appreciated. Buford's men had a long, hard march to get here."

"When I got back to the Scott's house, Miss Martha and Mary were baking bread. I suggested tearing up a few sheets for bandages, too." Cathy sighed. "I hope they are all right."

"From what I remember of my history, the only civilian killed was Jenny Wade, who was shot through a door while she was making bread. Famous incident. Others may have been wounded, and there won't be any horses worth having left in town, but most people found themselves hosting wounded – from both sides."

"When is Camp Letterman set up?"

"I'm a bit sketchy on this, so don't take any of this as gospel," he said. As she nodded, he continued, "I think once the reports of the casualties reached Washington, orders went out to set up some sort of major field hospital near the town, adjacent to a railway."

"That would make sense – they would need supplies and people, and a way to get them both here."

"It seems like the whole thing got a start on the fifth of July."

"Uh, Johnny? That's tomorrow. Will all the wounded be taken there?"

"Eventually – I think they start moving the wounded out of private homes into makeshift hospitals today and tomorrow. The Scotts may have their house back by late Sunday, although a few could be left with them."

"Where was the camp located?"

He thought about it for a minute and gasped.

"What?"

"Cripes! We saw the marker the day we drove in. You asked for a short tour of the town, remember? We stopped at the gas station to fill up, went to that restaurant, and the waitress told us that the hospital was basically across the street. We walked across the street and looked at the site."

"Okay, I remember that, although admittedly it means more now. I have no idea where we were at the time - I have a lousy sense of direction," she reminded him.

"Catie, we were on York Road on Friday. And again on Sunday. We walked along it the first time we came out to the cabin."

"You mean York Road is what used to be the York PIKE? That's not far from here, is it?"

"I think Camp Letterman is further east of here, maybe a bit to the south. I'm still not sure of exactly where the cabin is, or would be, or will be in 2015."

"I have a feeling we are going to find out. Hopefully it won't be in the Wal-Mart parking lot. Waking up there would be embarrassing."

"Yeah, it would kind of be an anticlimax to the whole thing." He finished his tea and handed her the mug.

Cathy collected the dishes, took them to the dry sink, and she came back into the room with a cup of water. She dug into her small med bag and offered half of another tablet.

"The first half was a pain pill. This is half a tranquilizer," she explained while he took it. "This is going to hurt. I'll give you another pain med after I'm done."

"Okay," he said. "What, exactly, are you going to do?"

"Unwrap your leg, remove the dressing, and check the wound for infection. I will hopefully close the wound at least partially, redress it, and bandage you up again."

"Okay," he said slowly. "You're looking for signs of infection?"

"Johnny, at the risk of repeating myself, that was not a clean wound. I didn't expect it to be. The first thing I did was irrigate it with spring water I had boiled, to try to jump ahead of it. Infections used to kill people more than anything else." He nodded, recalling his history. "My first goal was to see if I could prevent a wound infection. Today is when I'll see how well I did."

"Better than anyone else would have, here and now."

"Yep. I took a course in the history of medicine – there are some real horror stories of minor wounds in the Civil War becoming fatal due to current practices. One that I remember clearly was a soldier who got a couple of sword cuts. Would have been really minor in a modern ER, but it was so badly handled that the kid died. They hit him with purges, and things that were considered routine – including turpentine and ammonia. don't ask how they were used – you really don't want to know." Cathy was watching John for signs that the medications were beginning to work. "Medicine was slow to change – and the first big changes came during this war when it began to dawn on practitioners that keeping things clean helped. But anything new was slow to be adopted."

"Which brings us back to my leg?"

"Yep. First, I want to finish cleaning up breakfast. Rest and let all that take effect. I'll be back shortly."

He heard the sounds of her washing dishes. It wasn't long before she was back in the bedroom. John watched as she began to prep her area, eventually asking him to help by rolling to his other side so she could slide in a sheet she had folded in half. She padded the area with towels, then turned to the dresser and arranged her instruments. Back in the main room, she carefully prepared a poultice dressing and another piece of tubing to use as a drain, both of which she covered with sterile 4x4 gauze, before going back into the bedroom. She then announced she was ready if he was.

Once the outer bandage was unwrapped, she sniffed a few times before proceeding.

"Doctor, may I ask questions?"

"Sure."

"Did you just *sniff* the wound?"

"Uh-huh," she replied a bit absently as she pulled on sterile gloves. "I told you, I'm looking for infection. They have a distinct smell."

She then uncovered the wound. John, curious, looked at it. All he saw was a gash that ran from the middle of his thigh to around the side, and it was open. He quickly decided that he really didn't want to look further and laid back.

"Here comes the local," she informed him, syringe in hand. She looked up to see his reaction. She smiled to herself – she didn't blame him and told him so. He just nodded, still swallowing hard.

"Take a few deep, slow breaths," she advised. "You'll feel better."

"How does it look, Doc?"

"Decent – honestly, I'm pleased. The dressing wasn't soaked, and I don't see a staph infection. I think we're going to get lucky," she sort of mumbled, half to herself.

Cathy worked as quickly as she could without risking missing something. She inserted the new drain, secured it with two stitches, and decided she could close most of the wound and keep an eye on it. The swelling was starting to go down, thankfully, and missing was the typical blotchiness of cellulitis – the sign of a staph infection. The area beyond the bruising was pinkish-to-flushed, with no angry red areas. *No surprises. Thank God!* She closed intermittent areas to give the wound a better chance to start healing, dressed the whole length of it, and bandaged it carefully, making sure to support the remaining drainage tube in the bandaging. She collected her towels and sheet, positioned John on his back with his leg elevated, and smiled at him.

"Done." She sat on the chair next to the bed. "How are you doing?"

"I was just going to ask you that."

"I think we got lucky. Keogh wrapped a cloth around your leg – he told us that – and it was apparently reasonably clean, which is almost amazing. I am cautiously pleased, as the saying goes in the emergency department."

"What's next?"

"You mean besides washing and boiling what I just used?"

"Yeah, I know that has to be done. I meant what's next for me, as far as the leg goes."

"Let's see. Today is Saturday. Tomorrow I'll see if the drain can come out, and I'll do another dressing change on Monday, unless something develops in the meantime. I'm erring on the side of caution with the drain, but I've never had less to back up my judgment. I don't have a microscope, lab for blood work, IV antibiotics, etc. Still, one drain is out and I closed some of the length of the opening. Right now I think you should stay put." She chuckled at his smile.

"So you think it's going to be okay."

"Yes. But before you ask, there are still open areas. Once I close those, and I should be able to do that Monday, you can start moving around more." She looked at his face. "I know, it's not exactly what you want to hear, but there isn't any leeway here."

"Well, it is frustrating."

"Yep – and it's the hard part. I can't speed things up, and you're not the most patient person I've ever known." She held up her hand as he started to speak. "I know, you've promised to be good. Seriously, how do you feel overall?"

"Like I wish we had crutches. As grateful as I am that we have the cabin, these are not the most interesting four walls I have ever seen."

"I understand," Cathy admitted with a sigh. "We can't do much about that, either, I'm afraid. Is the area still numb? I didn't use as much local this time."

"Still numb."

"Okay, let me do the clean-up. Just take it easy. Want the Wolfe book?"

"Yeah, that would be nice." He frowned. "My memories of the battle are still fuzzy. I mean, I clearly remember what happened before I was hit, but the circumstance of getting hit and what happened after that are really blurry. Will it come back to me?"

"Probably. Give it some time," she said, handing him the omnibus. "And stop thinking you're a wimp – you're not. The battle was real, and although you thought you were prepared for it from your reenactments, you probably weren't. It was bound to be a bit overwhelming, and part of your mind has to come to terms with that before everything can be clearly recalled."

"So you're saying this is a defense?"

"In a way, yes. It's no reflection on you or your sanity, either. It just needs time." She saw he needed a bit more. "You were dealing with real bullets, real men, and your actions had real consequences."

"Okay. I noticed that you haven't asked me about it since the first time."

"I don't want to push. Besides, I know that when you do remember, you'll tell me." Cathy sat on the chair. "We know that you did well. You can recall most of the details of the actual battle, and the rest will probably come back. You do remember what you said to Buford, and later to Devin – that's a good sign. As for how and what was going on when you were hit, that will probably show up during a dream, which you will then be able to re-member."

"Didn't I have one like that?"

"You were dozing the other morning when the shelling start-ed, and when I came in I noticed it took you a moment or two to come out of it. The artillery sounds probably triggered things you aren't quite ready to recall fully yet."

"How come you're so smart and reassuring?"

"I'm a doctor", she began with a smile, "It's -"

"It's in your job description. Yeah, okay." John smiled back at her. "Go on and clean up. I'm okay."

"Johnny, you are more than okay – and you always have been," Cathy remembered something she hadn't relayed to him. "I forgot to tell you something that General Buford told me the night he wasn't here."

"Such as?"

"He said he wanted to recommend you for promotion, but since that wasn't possible – you told him about us being from the future – he wrote that letter instead." She picked up what she needed to wash, leaving John to think about it all.

John lay back on his pillows and reflected on what Cathy had just told him. He remembered Buford commending him on his actions while they were in the field, which had given him a real boost. But to recommend him for promotion – wow. *Too bad I can't tell anyone I would have become a major!*

Cathy finished rinsing her instruments and put them in a small pan of spring water to boil. The towels needed washing, but when she looked out the door, she noted the steady rain was heavy, and while she watched, she saw some lightning. Definitely more than she wanted to deal with by staying outside. She settled for grabbing a pail and quickly got water from the stream, putting it in the basin and placing the basin on the stove. She made it back just in time – the rain became a downpour right after she got back inside.

All the towels went into the water. Stains were okay and boiling killed anything else. She'd have given a lot for an autoclave, but boiling water would have to do. After she was through with those chores, she made herself a cup of tea, using the loose tea – and strainer - the sisters had tucked in the bag of 'useful' items. John was sleeping, and he looked comfortable.

She sighed, realizing how much of the medical procedures she was making up as she went along. John's faith and trust in her abilities was touching, and she knew she was doing all she could, giving it the best she knew how and relying on her knowledge to fill in gaps. But, as she had told John, she was used to a full support team and lab at hand to check what her instinct told her and find any surprises she might have missed. Her residency mentor always warned his classes that emergencies could happen at any time under any circumstances, and they might not have everything they were used to. "Be prepared to improvise, using tools at hand, your intelligence, and your experiences." Boy, was he right!

Tea finished, she stretched and opened the door to the cabin. Only the sound of the rain greeted her, but she noticed that there was still some thunder in the distance. At least she hoped it was thunder. If there were birds around, they were quiet.

"Catie?"

She closed the door and walked to the bedroom, as his voice was not panicked or pained. John was sitting up in bed, an odd look on his face.

"Need something?"

"I was dreaming – but now I can't remember it." He sighed. "I don't think it was about the battle, but I can't remember what it was. It's frustrating because I have the feeling it's important."

"It will come to you. The subconscious mind is amazing." She perched on the edge of the bed. "How are you doing? I was going to put some lunch together if you're interested."

"Umm, something else needed first," he said, with a slight grimace. "I hate having to ask you for every little thing," he added as she handed over the jar.

"No problem. I should have offered it."

Tactfully, she turned away until he told her he was finished. Once she took care of that, and cleaned up, she gathered up a lunch, taking it in on the tray.

"Lunch is served."

Cathy felt she needed to address John's concerns – she knew him well enough to realize that being waited on, even though he needed the help, was going to grate on him. She was trying to figure out how to begin when he brought it up.

"Catie, you know I don't mean anything against you when I say I hate having to ask for everything."

"I was going to say something similar," she replied with a smile, "But I do want you to know that I know you hate having to ask – but right now you don't have much of a choice. We can let this become a problem or we can deal with it openly."

"I vote for open."

"Oh good – that makes it unanimous," she said, letting the smile become a grin.

"Seriously, with all you are doing for me – especially the little details like the jar – I feel as if I should be doing something in return."

Resisting the urge to suggest he continue to lose at cribbage, mainly because it was too flippant for the circumstances, Cathy also decided that trite reassurances would be equally inappropriate.

"Johnny, we're out of our norm here, with only each other to rely on for everything. Right now, you are unable to do much because you are injured. If our positions were reversed, say if I was the one in need, you would be waiting on me with just as much attention. Try looking at it that way?"

"I suppose," he said, "Although that isn't much help."

"Okay. You need to feel useful, and I can understand that. Do something that is normal for you. Design something, like crutches, or sketch the table you want to build – things that we need."

"I can do that," he replied. "I'll also make a list of materials that we'll need to do them. Crutches first, right?"

"That would be the best. I know it won't be the easiest project, but I want you mobile and that's the only way it's going to happen."

"Compared to what you are doing for me, it doesn't seem like enough."

"Well, I can't do it." Cathy regarded her best friend. "It is going to take both of us to get through this, Johnny. No secrets, no moping, no egos. You're in for a long haul, and so am I. I'll get to where I have to let off steam myself. We'll both get discouraged, frustrated, and impatient, but we can come back to one thing: at least we have each other."

"I'll make a deal with you," he said, smiling a little. "When I get cranky, you bring it up. When you get cranky, I'll do the same. Deal?"

"Deal." They shook on it.

Cathy handed her clipboard to John with a pencil.

"You can start by designing the crutches. Don't make it so complicated that I can't understand it, because you may have to coach me through making them, unless you can figure out how to make them yourself, which would be a much better idea. Monday I'll go into town and see what I can find in the way of materials. While you do that, I'll clean this up."

As she rinsed the plates and cups, Cathy realized that what they needed was a routine. So far things had been dealt with as they had been reacting to the drastically altered circumstances as it happened. They needed to settle into a pattern of activities. Nothing boring, just a basic pattern. Keeping John occupied was going to take tact, not her strongest point. But then, tact wasn't his either, she reflected.

What would make the most difference would be getting him out – first out of the bedroom, then out of the cabin. But how? John was very intelligent, even brilliant in his own field. *My ballpark. Damn. I'll have to think about it.*

John decided to do a small sketch based on what he recalled of what a crutch looked like before he started working on the technical details. The first was a definite 'nope.' He erased it and tried again. Again, nope. He closed his eyes. *Crutch. Start from scratch and picture a functional crutch, not just what I've seen. I'm not re-inventing the wheel here, just a crutch.* He chuckled to himself, just a crutch. He set to work on that and was soon lost in designs.

Cathy peeked in a few times, pleased to see him totally immersed in what he was doing. When she had finished her chores, she stepped back to the partition opening. John looked up from the pad of paper.

"Well?" she prompted.

"Take a look," he said, handing it over.

The design looked like a variation of a classic crutch, rather than a copy of the standard device.

"This looks good," she mused after studying the design. "I mean this looks really good. Basic crutch construction hasn't changed much in decades, and this may be an improvement over 'standard.' It's not quite ordinary, but it isn't what we call Canadian crutches either."

"I'm glad you are pleased," he commented, inwardly delighted. "I tried to keep it simple, and it shouldn't be too hard to make. I haven't put in the dimensions, because I don't know what they are yet, and it would probably work better in aluminum tubing, but wood should work."

"I don't have a tape measure, but I'll bet Miss Martha does. Mary mentioned a sewing room, and you don't have one without the other." She looked at his design again. "Will the wood be hard to bend here?" She indicated the lower part of the length.

"Hopefully it can be done by soaking the wood first, and letting it dry in place – it's not a true curve."

"You're the engineer. Make a list of what you'll need at the bottom of the sketch and I'll take the paper into town Monday after I do your dressing change."

"Maybe I should invent the refrigerator," he said with a grin.

"Before you tackle that, I thought you might try the bedside tables and a front bench," she replied, smiling, "Or take a nap," she added as she saw him yawn. "Before you complain about being a wimp, remember what that wound looks like."

"I'm trying not to," he mumbled, putting the clipboard to one side.

Cathy helped him settle onto his side, and left the room, mentally blessing the idea to have him do something normal and useful. It seemed to have had the desired effect of lifting his spirits. She decided she would show his sketch to an orthopedist she knew 'back home' for his opinion. The crutch looked as if it might be a genuine improvement on the standard model. *Silver linings indeed.*

While John napped, she disappeared into the world of Nero Wolfe – she always loved reading Stout's detective yarns, even ones no longer new to her. She saved the Christie stories for reading aloud.

It was around four when she heard John stirring.

"How are you doing?"

"It hurts."

"Pain med coming up," she said as she got the small med bag. After he took the pill, he asked for a game of cribbage.

"I think we need to set up a general routine," she murmured. She grimaced as she regarded her six cards and tossed two of them into her crib. "I think it will make the days go faster."

"Sure," he said as he put down a card. "Seven."

"Fifteen for two," she stated, putting down an eight in front of her and moved her peg.

"Twenty-three for two," he added, putting down another eight and taking the points for a pair.

"Thirty-one for eight," she said with a flourish as she moved her peg, taking six points for the three eights and two points for ending on thirty-one.

The play continued, and Cathy was pleased when she won by a few points.

"I'm winning more," she said pleased with her victory.

"You're less distracted than you usually are back home," he commented wryly. "Normally when we play, part of your mind is always on your work. Here you haven't got those distractions."

"Hmmm, good theory."

At five-thirty, they stopped and John asked if she had done any baking.

"Is that a hint?"

"Well, the biscuits are good," he replied with what he hoped was an encouraging smile. "If you don't want to, that's okay."

"Turn on your side and do some exercises, and I'll tend to it. The pain med should cover the discomfort."

"It's a deal," he said as she collected the cards.

Cathy served their dinner on the usual tray, and as requested, it included biscuits along with the protein bars. Cathy knew she was going to have to find a way to introduce some variety of food before much longer, but as John reassured her, at least they were eating better than most of the people in either army.

Once the meal was cleared off, Cathy offered John the volume of Poirot.

"I think it's your turn to read," she said as he took the book. "I'll sit and listen."

John had a good speaking voice, and his students always commented that his lectures were fun because his delivery style was good. Cathy sat on the chair with her feet up on a corner of the bed, listening to his well-modulated baritone. After one attempt at Poirot's accent, she suggested he give it up, but other than that she gave her full attention. The evening passed.

"Johnny," she said later as they began their preparations for the night's sleep, "I really am pleased with the progress you are making."

"Honestly?"

"Yes, honestly. Remember, it hasn't even been a week."

"Why didn't you completely close the wound?"

"Fair question," she conceded. "Initially I expanded the wound, making an incision so I could get to what needed to come out. The poultice dressing I used has the penicillin – the bread mold – and I want to give it the chance to act directly in the wound. It's not a topical like you would put on a rash. If there is no sign of a staph infection Monday, I can finish closing, and do a proper post-surgical dressing that will protect the sutures."

"So the bread mold on plain skin won't work?"

"Bread mold on intact skin is just moldy skin – there's no carrier agent like a topical med. In order to work, this has to be in contact with the bacteria. The bonus is that it may also act systemically." She paused, studying his expression. "Does that make sense?"

"So the biggest risk here is infection."

"Yep. The skin is the body's biggest defense. Any time there's a cut or opening, bacteria can get in and set up housekeeping. The dirtier the wound, the less sterile the wound, the greater the risk. Antiseptic theory hasn't got a foothold in this era yet. Some doctors are beginning to pay attention, but the practice of keep an open wound clean for maximum healing hasn't caught on."

"Which is why so many wounded died from injuries that weren't fatal in themselves."

"Exactly. With no way to sterilize an open wound, all kinds of complications set in."

"What about tetanus?"

"You've had tetanus boosters, right?" As he nodded, she continued, "Good. I forgot to ask, but I did assume your immunizations are current. Since you brought it up, one common source is animal dung. The bacillus lives in the ground and thrives in dung. If a soldier fell in battle with a shell fragment wound and happened to land near horse manure, tetanus was a major possibility. In this era, there was nothing to be done except watch."

"Cripes, that's a horrible way to die."

"Absolutely. Thankfully, it's one we don't see often in our era because of immunization programs, and of course, there is an antitoxin which is given in case of exposure." She made a face. "Johnny, this is not a wonderful bedtime conversation."

"I understand, but I was curious." John grinned. "You don't talk shop often, so I thought I'd take advantage."

"No problem. As a matter of fact, I saw a case of tetanus once, brought in too late for us to be able to counter it. It's a very nasty thing, especially since it's easy to protect against." Cathy shuddered. "In case you were wondering, if you were going to have a problem with it, you would have felt it long ago."

"I wasn't wondering."

"Any other fun topics you would like to discuss? Gangrene, maybe? It's not a worry in your case, by the way."

John laughed. "Nope, at least not for now."

"Good." Cathy stretched. "Johnny, it's been a long day, and if okay with you, I think I'll end mine. Anything else you need at the moment?"

"Not a thing." He turned on his side. "Catie, thanks. For everything."

"Goodnight, Johnny."

*****

Cathy woke up with a start. She thought she had heard a man's voice but she knew it hadn't been John's.

It was still dark in the room. She lifted her head to see the clock on the dresser. It showed midnight, but she couldn't hear it ticking. She sat up and checked to see if John needed anything, but he was still asleep. Oddly, she couldn't hear him breathing although when she touched her ear she could hear that small sound. Laying back down and closing her eyes to concentrate, she tried to remember what – exactly – she had heard or thought she had heard.

Her mind and inner senses seemed sharper, and she felt as if someone had charged her with energy the way you charged a phone battery. Ignoring the feelings of confusion, Cathy fought to keep her mind clear of speculation and focused inward, as if she were in a mediation class.

A man's deep voice seemed to resonate in her head rather than as an audible external sound. "*You will come full circle.*"

What the hell?

Whoever, or whatever, was in her mind appeared to find her thought amusing, for her reaction seemed to prompt a deep chuckle. Then she 'heard' the same phrase again:

"You will come full circle."

The voice was soft, yet somehow reassuring. She wasn't frightened. Trying to avoid speaking out loud, so John wouldn't wake up, Cathy didn't know if she was imagining this or simply dreaming. Focusing on keeping her own thoughts as words, she *thought* – rather than spoke –

I'm confused. Are you real or in my mind?

"Both." Again the soft, deep chuckle. *"Be assured when the time is right, you will come full circle."*

Are you the one who put us here?

"When the time is right, you will come full circle."

You keep saying that. If I am not imagining this, can I ask questions?

"Full circle."

Cathy felt the extra sharpness of her mind slowly fade. She could once again hear John breathing and the ticking of the clock. Whatever had happened, it was over. Suddenly she felt overwhelmingly tired as if something or someone had drained her energy or a sleeping pill had taken effect.

She slept, deeply, with no further interruptions.

Sunday, 5 July 1863

Cathy awoke to the sounds of birds. The sun was shining, but she also thought she saw some shadows in the light, so she figured there were some clouds in the sky. She lay on her makeshift mattress and thought about her midnight caller, whoever and whatever it had been.

Full circle. We will come full circle. The voice had been oddly comforting. Trying to remember exactly what had happened, she realized that she had felt as if she had been enveloped in a cozy cocoon, almost a safe haven from anything that could harm her. Whatever it was, it had been wonderful.

She heard the bedsprings squeak as John moved.

"Catie? Are you awake?"

"Yep." She reached for the jar and raised it to where he could grab it. "Present for you."

"Gee, thanks." John wiggled in the bedclothes for a few moments. "Okay."

Cathy got to her knees, rolled the mattress up, and stood. "Back in a few," she said, taking the jar.

John turned on his good side and waited for her return. He knew there was something he should remember, something important, but it wouldn't come forward. He closed his eyes to concentrate.

"You're scowling," Cathy's voice sounded close to his head.

"I can't remember something, and it's going to drive me nuts," he mumbled crossly. "I'll almost have it and then it just fades."

"Well, for now, how about getting cleaned up a bit before breakfast?" She got dressed. "I'll be back with soap, water, and a towel. While you tend to that, I'll get biscuits in the oven."

After he was finished, she collected his bath stuff before bringing in a tray.

"Ta-da!" She took the dishtowel off the tray to reveal a selection of cheese, hard sausage, and biscuits in addition to their usual mugs of tea.

"Looks good," he said, taking a sip of the hot beverage, "And I think I will be totally spoiled for life about biscuits. I doubt any of the canned ones are this good."

"I think you're exaggerating, but I appreciate the compliment."

Cathy was silent for a moment. John noticed she appeared to be concentrating on something serious.

"Catie? Something on your mind?"

"Yes." She took a deep breath and related her midnight experience.

"Cripes."

"Yep. Spooky. What do you suppose it means?"

"'When the time is right you will come full circle'," John echoed the words. "Maybe it means when we have done whatever it is we need to do, we'll go back to where we came from."

"Okay, if that's it, and I think I agree, it also means that you are right when you say there's a logic to all this. Someone or something really IS controlling this." Cathy shuddered a bit. "I wish they'd let us in on the game plan. It's comforting, yet frightening at the same time, to know that we were put here by an intelligent entity. I hope we're up to the task."

"I know what you mean." John suddenly sat up straight. "Catie, THAT's what I've been trying to remember!"

"Huh? At the risk of sounding dumb - *What* is what you have been trying to remember?" Cathy realized how her sentence sounded. "Or words to that effect."

"The other day when I had the dream I couldn't remember – it was that same voice saying the same thing. I guess I was too drugged or still in shock to be able to recall it." John fell back against his pillows. "The same single sentence. '*You will come full circle.*' Wow."

"Wow is right. I'll bet, though, that if there is something more than saving Buford on the first day of battle, you're going to have to be completely healed to do it." Cathy regarded John. "So we're back to the notion that at the moment, you have one job: heal."

"When are you going to finish closing the wound?"

"I'm hoping for tomorrow. Tomorrow's Monday, right?" Cathy looked to John for confirmation.

"You're asking me? I'm the patient around here," he said, grinning to take the sting out of the words.

"I think today is Sunday. Wait a minute. I have a pocket planner," she said as she dragged the duffel out from under the bed. After digging for a moment, she held up a small booklet about the size of a checkbook. "Here!"

John took the planner and turned to June. Sure enough, he saw the notations "road trip" and "re-enactment" on the appropriate days in her precise printing. He turned to July. Sure enough, the fourth was a Saturday.

"Cripes," he began. "I know we decided that the days and dates of 1863 and 2015 match, but to actually see it – it's startling." He handed her the planner.

"I know. I think I'm going to pencil in a few things. Like when we met John Buford, when you were shot – you know, all the fun stuff." Cathy looked up in time to see John make a face. "Seriously, I should track when I do the dressing changes. Possibly put in when I plant what in the garden. Once we get back, I'll put this one in the deep freeze. I know I have another one."

"That would probably be for the best," he agreed.

"Tomorrow, after I tend to your incision, I'll walk into town. I don't want Mary walking out here, and we know she will if she doesn't hear from us. I'm also hoping that I can take your sketch and list for the crutches and come back with at least an idea of how to get what we need."

"Okay."

"We need to find out what's going on in town. I am concerned about the sisters and John. From what you've told me, it's been a real circus."

"I understand, and I agree. We owe them so much, and I'd hate to have them think that we have forgotten about them." John stretched and yawned. "But that's tomorrow. What about today?"

"Let's keep to what we've been doing and take it easy. Tomorrow we can kick into a higher gear." Cathy laughed at the look on John's face. "I would like to remind you that you were shot less than a week ago."

"Yeah, yeah, I know. I'm sorry, Catie – I'm getting really tired of these walls." John yawned again.

"Why don't you give up and take a nap? I'll keep busy."

The rest of the morning passed quickly. Cathy spent some time reorganizing their food stores, and after peeking in on John, sat down to read her Wolfe book. Shortly after noon, she put together a tray of snacks and tea, and took it into the bedroom.

"Lunch!" She put the tray down. "Need the jar?"

John sat up and stretched. "Oh yeah."

As they ate, John brought up the subject of the midnight caller. "If that voice is what we believe it to be," he said, "We at least know he is paying attention."

"I wonder if he reached out to me when he saw you weren't getting the message."

"Probably. Without the injury, I would have been sharper." John grimaced. "I'd like to think that I would have remembered eventually."

"No argument. I have a question, though."

"Shoot."

"We went to bed in 2015 and woke up in 1863. You told me that you saw a bright light."

"So?"

"Think about it and describe it to me."

"It was bright enough to wake me up and illuminate the whole inside of the tent." John closed his eyes. "Hold it. There was something else!"

"You hinted at that before, which is why I asked."

"It's a vague impression, but I think there was a pattern within the flickering of the days and nights passing."

"A pattern?"

"Yeah, it seemed familiar, but I can't quite pin it down."

"Well, don't worry about it – it will come to you." Cathy began to gather the dishes. "Let me take care of these. How about a hot game of cribbage after that?"

"You're on."

They played three games. John won two, with one being really close, and Cathy won the other.

"You're getting better at this," he admitted. "You're really challenging me!"

"It's good for you," Cathy said, laughing as she put the game away. "Are you ready for a nap?"

"Not quite yet."

"No problem. Any ideas?"

"Gin?"

"You are a glutton for punishment today," she replied, taking out a deck of cards and handing it to him. "I'll even let you deal first."

They played four games, each winning two.

"We do seem to be evenly matched," John stated as Cathy put the cards away.

"We always have been," she agreed. "You should be about ready for your nap. Let me get you a cup of water first."

John stretched and yawned. "Okay."

After seeing him settled, Cathy opened the cabin's door. The sun was still out. The ground was moist but not muddy. If this keeps up, she thought to herself, she would be able to plant the start of her garden tomorrow or Tuesday if she didn't have time tomorrow. She grabbed a bucket and drew more water from the spring, mentally planning their supper. She wanted to try a few things.

John woke to the smell of cooking. Meat. He smelled meat. Meat?

"Catie?" He called his question, after checking his watch – it was almost six.

"Give me a minute," came her reply.

"No rush," he called as he heard the clank of a pot on the stove.

"Can I get you something?" she asked, standing in the door-way. "Supper is almost ready."

"Just the usual," he said with a small frown. "What's for din-ner? I thought I smelled meat cooking."

"Your nose still works," she replied, chuckling as she handed over the required container. "I'm playing at cooking."

"If it's as good as the biscuits you've been making, no argument." John turned on his side and watched her leave the room. *At least she seems to be enjoying herself.*

John honestly figured she'd be bored by now. *Maybe it was because she had the time to do things she couldn't do 'back home' – like cooking, and gardening. Sort of like the way she was improving at cribbage. She could focus on what she was doing, without worrying about the phone ringing or having to drop everything and run to the hospital for a major emergency.* He knew she loved her job with the medical center emergency department. He smiled as he remembered how proud she had been to get the promotion to medical services director for the ED. They had gone out to celebrate, and he had bought flowers for the occasion. Her parents had been thrilled, too, seeing her fulfill her ambitions to run an ED that was also a major teaching facility. The bonus was that they were both at Mizzou.

His parents had taken a while to understand why he wanted to teach rather than go into private practice as an engineer, but they came around in the end. He did enough designing to keep him happy, and like Cathy, he enjoyed the challenge of opening the minds of his students. His life was his own, and Cathy had her world. They met often enough to be happy but never crowded each other. He was sociable enough to go to faculty parties, which he did more than Cathy did, and he went out on casual dates.

John sighed as he recalled the last time they were together with both sets of parents – he and Cathy got the impression that all four parental units were waiting for an engagement announcement, which of course didn't happen. He had tried to explain to his mother that he did go out on dates and that he and Cathy were more like brother and sister, but he knew it hadn't taken root. His parents, like Cathy's, were set on their getting together. So were his secretary and Cathy's director of nursing. Oh well. He enjoyed the company of other women, and he tried not to compare them to Cathy, but somehow it was never the same.

"Here comes dinner," Cathy called out as she approached the doorway with the tray. "Ready or not."

John straightened up in bed as she put the tray next to him and removed the bowl she had used as a cover.

"Hey – it's a real meal!" John was looking at two plates with what appeared to be open-faced biscuits with meat in a sauce on them. "Smells good, too!"

"I used one of the tins of meat and tried to make gravy with the juices. Hope it tastes okay," she said as she sat down. "I wish we had some vegetables, but this should do."

"Mmmm," was John's reply as he took a bite. "Definitely edible. The biscuits are different. What did you do this time?"

"I used a bit of the gravy and added some cheese." She laughed, adding, "I guess it's really a matter of just trying things."

"Congratulations – you're really cooking!"

"How about that? I don't have time back home – it's easier to toss something into the microwave or open a can."

"Uh-huh. We get so busy we don't have time to do a lot, much less remember how to do it."

"Well, here and now, I have to do it all by hand. I think I'm going to enjoy it, at least for a while, but I'll bet I go right back to modern conveniences when we get back."

"Probably. But I'm glad you can do this much now." He frowned slightly. "It's the skills set thing again."

Cathy nodded.

After she cleared the meal, they played cards for a while and John read from the anthology. As she drifted off to sleep, Cathy realized that today had been their first really uneventful day. Her last thought was that it had been nice.

CHAPTER ELEVEN

Monday, 6 July 1863

Morning dawned with birds singing and sun already streaming through the window. John opened his eyes and saw Cathy sitting up on her bedroll. Her t-shirt was rumpled, as was her hair.

"Good morning," she said with a smile as she stretched. "It's peaceful, sunny, and what Mom calls a good day to get things done."

"Well, I have a first order of business," he began as he reached out his hand.

She handed over the jar, got up, and rolled her mattress up, turning back to him only after he said he was done. She pulled on her jeans and disappeared.

John leaned back on his pillows. According to Cathy's medical plan, today would tell for certain how his leg was doing. The initial pain had been incredible, but now it wasn't unbearable. Cathy was correct in assuming nothing in the re-enactments had prepared him for actually being injured – and he knew that the combination of the coin and minie' ball hadn't done as much damage as a minie' smashing into his femur would have done. He was taking pain meds, but he had noticed that Cathy was stretching them, and he thought she was using plain acetaminophen part of the time. *So far so good. Maybe after she did her thing today, I can get out of bed.*

Cathy, after taking care of herself, put together a light breakfast, complete with pain meds for John. She wanted them to take effect before she did anything to his wound.

"Here we are," she said, bringing the tray into the bedroom.

"Back to food bars?"

"Protein, my boy, plus all sorts of other nutrients." She unwrapped her bar and regarded it. "Okay, it's not haute de cuisine, but it will do for the moment. If you're lucky, I'll be able to make something nifty for supper."

"I'll hold you to that," John replied as he took a bite of his bar. "The tea is still great, though. What's the game plan for today?"

"First, I want to dress your leg – I should be able to close it completely. Once that's done, we can get you out of bed for a while. I want to see you do the transfer yourself, so I know you can."

"I wish I could leave the room."

"How's your upper body strength?"

"Okay, I think. Why?"

"I was thinking about a serial sequence of chair movements." She laughed at his scowl. "We have two chairs. You're an engineer. Work it out."

John's scowl slowly became a grin. "You know, that might work."

"Tedious, but doable?"

"Catie, you are amazing. I don't think that would have occurred to me for at least another day or so."

"One of the physical therapy people told me about a patient of hers who did it with two lawn chairs after falling in a yard. It's not fast, and it can get tiring, but it's doable if you get desperate."

"You mean once my leg is officially bandaged, I can move around."

"I wouldn't recommend dancing or trying to bear weight on it, but yes. You'll know if you overstep your boundaries. I'll do my best to make sure you can't do major damage without realizing it."

"So my leg is first. Then what?"

"I thought I'd go into town and see what's going on. Maybe I can find a set of crutches to borrow, and hopefully, get some eggs." Cathy paused, with a slight frown. "I feel I owe it to Mary and Miss Martha to check on them."

"Yeah, I agree." John swallowed the last of his tea. "When does my torture commence?"

"As soon as I clear this away and set up for it." Cathy picked up the tray. "Rest. I'll be back in a few."

John turned on his side and closed his eyes. And fell back asleep.

Cathy came back in with her prepped tray, saw him asleep and smiled as she dug the med bag out from under the bed. She got what she needed, put it back, and stood watching him.

"Hey, sleepyhead. I'm afraid you need to be awake for part of this." Cathy nudged his shoulder.

"Huh? Sorry, I didn't mean to do that." John sat up. "How do you want me positioned?"

"I'll do it," she said, pulling out linens. She carefully positioned the folded sheet and placed John's leg the way she wanted it.

"Are you going to numb the area again?"

"Probably." Busy setting up, she heard him gasp and quickly added, "Sorry – I was thinking of something else. Of course, I will. Don't panic. You won't feel a thing, except some tugging."

"You scared me for a moment," he said. "Okay, it's the same drill."

"I can give you a half a tranq if you want one." Cathy glanced up from her preparations and regarded her best friend in the world. "I'm sorry, Johnny – I didn't mean to scare you, honestly. I was thinking about closing the wound."

"I'm fine – I promise. I just didn't relish the thought of you going in there without some painkiller."

"Understandable." She finished her prep. "I'm going to give you the local now and go make the dressing."

A few minutes later, Cathy carefully removed the wrap and the dressing. John, watching her face rather than what she was doing – he had learned his lesson the first time – saw her start to smile.

"Are we winning?" he asked.

"Definitely. The drainage from the tube is clear, and the site is clean. I'm going to close it, redress it, and bandage." Cathy's gaze met John's eyes. "We did good. The bruising is subsiding and the swelling has gone down."

John relaxed as she worked. *Damn, I was lucky to have her with me – if she hadn't been...* He knew he would have been at the mercy of the surgeons of this time period. *I would probably have lost the leg, most likely to infection.*

Once she finished wrapping the actual bandage, Cathy sat down in the chair.

"I think we should wait for this to wake up before you try moving to a chair, but it shouldn't be long."

"No argument. Will I be able to move my leg more?"

"Probably." Cathy rose and gathered up what Gerry, her head nurse, always referred to as the medical leavings. She privately thought of it as medical clutter. "I'll be back in a bit once I get this stuff cleaned and stowed. Any discomfort? I didn't use much local."

"A vague ache, nothing more." John grinned. "Compared to what I felt when it happened, I'm fine."

"I love a satisfied patient," she said with a grin.

Cathy put all her items in the pan of water she had boiling. She was reusing more than she would back home, but boiling would sterilize and clean everything from her instruments to the cloth sponges. Since she was burying their trash, she was trying to keep it to a minimum. Done for the moment – she was giving the water bath time to act – she went back to the bedroom to check on John.

John had picked up her clipboard and was busy sketching. He held up his latest design for her inspection.

"A bench!" Cathy took the clipboard. "It looks nice."

"It's simple, and shouldn't be hard to build, but it should be sturdy enough to use," he said, pleased with his doodling. "Big enough to hold the two of us." He laughed at her expression. "What?"

"I thought you'd do the bedside tables before the bench," she said, "But this is good."

"I told you – I want to go outside."

"Figures," she laughed as she started to change out of her jeans into a blouse and skirt. "I think I'll take the walk into town."

"Pack the Beretta. There still could be some trouble."

"No problem," she replied. "I was going to ask about that. What should I expect to find?"

"The town will still be in shock. The whole area was under siege from both sides for about four days, remember. Some of the wounded will be Confederates who haven't been moved, and there may be some deserters from each side around. You may see damage to property and buildings, too."

"Cripes."

"Oh, yeah." John smiled. "It's a matter of putting things back together for the townspeople. This has made headlines all over the country. Relief stores and personnel should also be coming in. You may even run into a journalist."

"I was indoors with my head down."

"Exactly."

Cathy turned around for his perusal. "Acceptable?"

"Absolutely. The petticoats hide the gun's bump. Can you still reach it?"

"Yep – I cut the seam open to match the hole in the pocket." She reached into the folds of her skirt and pulled out the handgun. "See? I'll admit it's harder to get back in, but I figure that is less important."

"Oh yeah." John wiggled his leg a bit and Cathy saw a slight frown come across his face. "It's waking up."

"Since I'm going to be gone for a bit, let me leave you a couple of the acetaminophen tablets – you can take more in six hours," she said, opening the dresser drawer where she kept them. "And before I leave, let's see if you can make it to the chair."

Cathy told him to support the wounded leg with his hands and slowly lower it over the side of the bed as he turned his hips, then stay put until things stopped swimming. Once ready to move, she instructed him to stand and pivot on his good, left leg and maneuver into the chair.

John followed her directions and found himself sitting in the chair.

"I can't believe how good this feels," he commented. "Can I stay here for a while?"

"I want to see you get back in bed – just to make sure you can do it." Cathy grinned. "Once you prove you can, I'll take off." She checked the watch in her pocket. "It's about eight-thirty now. If I leave and don't take overlong in town, I should be back by two o'clock. Now, get back in bed."

"Can you leave some water and maybe a food bar?" he asked once he was back under the covers.

"Coming up."

Cathy disappeared into the main room. John heard the cabin door open, then close, and shortly after that, Cathy came back in carrying a small pail of water and his cup, which she put on the chair at the bedside. She also put the empty jar and chamber pot on the chair, covering both with a hand towel. As John opened his mouth, she held up a hand.

"I'm not through yet."

She left the room and immediately returned carrying positioned the second chair in a way that would make it easy for him to transfer from the bed to the chair and stood back.

"Better?"

"Yeah – this should be okay."

"Have you got your watch?"

"Uh-huh." John pulled it out from the covers. "I have thirty-four minutes after eight."

"That's what I have," she said, checking hers. "Then I will go." Cathy leaned over and gave him a hug. "I'll try not to be too long. don't start to worry seriously until it starts to get dark. I don't know what I'm going to find at the Scotts'."

"Understood – we owe them big time," he said, nodding his agreement. "I'll be okay. You're taking the carry bag?"

"Of course. I hope the sisters don't think it's a hint for more handouts. Oh – one more thing," she said as a thought occurred to her. She ran into the main room, returning with the Stout omnibus. "Here."

"Thanks," he replied as he took the book. "This will give me something to do."

After she left, he started his day by falling asleep.

*****

After spending almost a week in the cabin, Cathy enjoyed her walk into town. She felt a little concerned about leaving John alone, but she knew he'd keep busy. It felt odd to be on her own, much as it did the day before the battle after John left her at the Scott's. She used the shortcut, partially for time, partially to make sure it was still clear, and partially to avoid running into anyone. Once she was in the town proper, she saw the signs John warned about – the streets showed wear, and an odd smell pervaded the air. She walked down Chambersburg Street to the Scott home and knocked on the door.

"Cathy!" Martha Scott threw open the door and gave her a hug. "Thank heaven you are all right! We've been so worried about you and the Captain! Mary," she called over her shoulder, "It's Cathy!"

"Thank the Lord! We've been wondering about you and your brother!"

"Is everyone here all right?" Cathy inquired after giving the sisters hugs. "We have been so worried about you both and Mr. John. I was so afraid you would be hurt or the house would be damaged. John told me it was very bad."

"Is he not with you?" Martha Scott asked, looking past Cathy to the street. "We had hoped to see you both."

"John was wounded the first day of fighting," Cathy explained, adding, "I believe he is going to be fine. At the moment, he's back at the cabin. This is the first day I felt I could make good on my promise to come back to see you. We have been praying all was well here."

"Let's have some coffee in the kitchen so we can visit," Mary put in sensibly. "Would you like some bread? Martha just baked some."

"I'd love some," Cathy said, smiling. "It smells wonderful. How's Mr. John?"

"He tried to assist with the wounded, and ended up back in bed," Martha told her, "Just as you predicted."

"We still have wounded here," Mary put in as Cathy came into the house, "And we're doing our best for them. Most of them were taken to hospitals yesterday. These men are waiting to be moved."

They passed through the front parlor into the dining room, and Cathy saw a dozen men, lying on the floor. Bandages, some around amputated limbs, were evident. The men were clean, and some smiled at her.

The three women went on to the kitchen, and Martha poured coffee while Mary sliced the bread and buttered a piece for Cathy.

"Oh, this is wonderful, thank you," said Cathy, tasting the warm offering. "Oh my - butter! I've been using what you gave me sparingly, only for baking. It's lovely to have some *on* something rather than simply *in* something!"

The sisters chuckled at her exclamation.

"How have you been managing?" Mary asked as she sat down with her cup of coffee.

"Yes, and tell us what happened to the Captain?"

"General Buford kept his word to send John to me," Cathy began as she related an abridged version of the events at the cabin since Tuesday. "Johnny still isn't completely clear about exactly what happened, but the general wrote a lovely letter of commendation about his service," she finished.

"We have seen so many limbs amputated – it's miraculous you were able to save his leg," commented Mary. "He is truly blessed that you are with him."

"Amen," Martha stated firmly.

"Can I be of assistance here?" Cathy asked. "We both feel we owe you so much. The bag of useful things you gave me last week has been so welcome, we can't thank you enough. I also want to thank you for the cooking lessons. Johnny was very impressed when I was able to make acceptable biscuits, too, so your baking instructions were well worth the effort."

Again, the sisters chuckled, and Martha asked, "How did you make them without milk?"

"I tried using water and added some molasses to add some substance. I found some ginger in a cupboard, and once I added that to the mixture, they were truly quite tasty."

"Hmmm," mused Martha, "I may try that."

"Honestly?" Cathy was surprised. "I am flattered, although I would heartily recommend you use milk when you do. I'm sure yours would be much improved over my efforts. Johnny will be most pleased with the notion that you might learn something from my meager efforts."

Martha asked if Cathy would mind looking at their patients.

"I would be delighted to do so; however, I would very much like to begin with Mr. John. Is he upstairs in his own bed?"

"Yes," Martha replied as Mary picked up the dishes for washing, "And did we have a time convincing him he should stay there!"

Cathy climbed the familiar stairs to John Scott's room.

"Cathy," he said, a bit sheepishly, "I should have listened to your warning more carefully."

"Well, you can't say I didn't warn you," she replied kindly. "Still, how do you feel now?"

"About the same way I did the first time you came into this room," he admitted ruefully, "I didn't try to do that much, at least it didn't seem to be that much."

"Yet it proved to be too strenuous," Cathy said. She proceeded to examine him, finding that most of his problem seemed to be the usual aftermath of a virus: general weakness akin to exhaustion.

"How is he doing?" asked Martha from the doorway.

"All things considered, he's not doing too badly," Cathy replied, "However, he doesn't need to be running up and down the stairs." She turned to John Scott. "If you take it easy – and I do mean EASY – you will find you get better faster. You can go downstairs to SIT, not to tote or help move people around. Or you can stay up here and fret. Your choice."

"I think I'll start by taking a nap," said John, "And maybe come downstairs for lunch."

"Wise of you, very wise of you," Cathy said with a chuckle. "Behave yourself and you'll be able to stay up for a whole day in about two days."

"Yes, ma'am." He lay back on the bed and closed his eyes.

Cathy joined Martha, whose hand clamped over her mouth did nothing to hide the laughter in her eyes as the two went downstairs.

Mary was in the kitchen, preparing a basin of warm water and a stack of clean squares of material when they rejoined her.

"Before we proceed, I would like to know what we have in the way of wounds," Cathy stated.

"Mostly open wounds, where a bullet passed through or bayonet or sword has stabbed," replied Mary. "We've been trying to keep them clean and mainly take care of bathing, plus giving water and what food we can supply. We got some stores in last evening when some farmers brought in things like eggs and milk."

"Basic care is always the best way to start," Cathy agreed. "Does anyone need amputation or surgery?"

"The two that probably do have told us they don't want a surgeon taking their limbs off," Martha cautioned her. "They appear to be more afraid of being crippled than of dying."

"Let me see those two first."

Cathy, knowing full well she could be messing with the timeline, began her rounds with the two men mentioned by Martha. She convinced the first man she could close the wound without taking off his arm, even though it was a deep cut. The damage was primarily to muscle, and it wasn't as badly torn as John's had been. A surface closure and keeping the limb immobilized would work after she cleansed the wound. Her problem was figuring out what everyday items could be used to do it – her field kit was back at the cabin.

"Miss Martha, would you have any silk thread with a small needle that you could boil for five minutes?"

"Do you want the needle threaded before it is boiled?"

"Yes, please. Also, do you have any whiskey or brandy in the house?"

"I don't think we have any in the house," Mary answered. "However, I should be able to get something at the tavern down the street."

"Anything alcoholic, other than beer or ale, will do," Cathy replied.

"Ma'am, begging your pardon, I don't take spirits," the young soldier interrupted, sitting up, "even as medicine."

"I would not ask you to do so in contrary to your beliefs," Cathy soothed the wounded man. "I have another use in mind – I have to cleanse your wound before I stitch it together. It will hurt, but it may prevent infection."

"I can stand the pain, ma'am, if it will do some good. I am a watchmaker by trade, and I need my arm to do my work." The man – who looked about twenty – leaned back.

"I will do my best," Cathy promised as Martha went upstairs to her sewing room and Mary left the house to find some whiskey.

Cathy prepared her area by washing the man's arm carefully. after laying down a towel she had picked up in the kitchen.

"Ma'am?" the man began, "Are you a nurse? Begging your pardon, you seem to know what you are doing."

"Yes, I am. I teach nursing, and my father is a doctor whom I assisted many times," Cathy told him. "My brother, who was badly wounded on the first day of fighting, was brought to me, and I saved his leg. I believe you can trust me to do this."

"Michael," he said. "I didn't mean to be disrespectful."

"Michael, I will do what I can. It looks as if you were stabbed."

"One of the rebels caught me with a bayonet as I was fighting during the big charge on Friday. I was brought to town and I've been here ever since. The ladies here have taken real good care of me, but I didn't want a surgeon. I was afraid he'd take my arm off. I need it for work and to hold my baby boy."

Martha came back into the dining room. "I have the needle threaded with silk and it's boiling."

"Good. If you have a small bowl and a tablespoon of salt, I can use that as well. May I have a few more squares of material? When the thread has boiled for five minutes, take the pan off the stove to cool a bit before bringing the whole thing to me with the bowl. I'll also need a small pair of scissors and material for a sling."

"Certainly."

A few minutes later, Martha brought salt in a small dish, the pan and scissors. Mary turned up with a half a bottle of whiskey, which she handed to Cathy saying it was the best she could do.

"This will be fine. This is going to sting." Cathy poured some of the water into the salt, took a clean cloth, dipped it in solution, and gently wiped out the wound. She then poured some of the whiskey onto a cloth and, warning the soldier that this is what was going to hurt, pressed the soaked cloth directly into the wound. Michael gasped, crying out. Mary knelt on the floor to hold him steady, and he clutched her arm with his good hand.

"My apologies, ma'am. That truly does sting a mite." He took some deep breaths, and slowly let go of Mary's arm. "Begging your pardon, Miss Mary."

"There's no need to apologize," Mary said, dipping a cloth into the basin of warm water and wiping his face gently.

"You're doing fine," Cathy assured him. "If it helps, imagine that stinging to be killing the infection that's starting."

"That helps some," he said. "Is that the worst?"

"I'm going to do that one more time, rinse it with the salt water, and stitch you up. I'll leave it so someone can just cut the stitches out with a small pair of scissors or a clipper after you heal." Cathy soaked another cloth, letting the excess drip on the wound. "Here we go with another dose of whiskey."

She changed out the cloths, tossing the now-bloodied one to the side. Michael cried out again but gamely hung on as best he could. Cathy started humming her theme song, which she knew was also a risk, but it seemed to help Michael. She rinsed the area with salt water in preparation for the stitching, which was quickly done. Cathy made sure there was a tail to each stitch and put in a row of ten and bandaged the closed wound. She and Martha fashioned a sling.

Cathy sat back on her heels, knowing that she had done more than a contemporary surgeon would have. The wound was reddish around the edges but she didn't see any major signs of infection. Michael, who had closed his eye during the last part of the procedure, opened them to look at her.

"I think you'll be fine. I'm sorry it was so painful."

"It feels much better now. How can I thank you?" Tears came to his eyes, and he brushed them away with his good hand.

"Get better, survive the war, and go back to your family," Cathy said, smiling as she got to her feet after washing her hands in the pan of now-cooled water. "Now, who's the other man who needs my attention?"

"We have a Confederate lieutenant who took a bullet in his leg," Martha said, collecting the clean cloths and the bottle of whiskey while Mary picked up the basin. "He's over in the corner, by himself. He told me this morning that he has decided to die. His leg hasn't gotten any better since he was brought here on Saturday morning."

One look told Cathy that if she was going to save his life and his leg, he was going to have to help. The wound was in his calf and it was very swollen and infected. She wouldn't know for certain what she was dealing with until she took the crusty bandage off. The bandage was crusty and would need to be carefully removed.

"Lieutenant? My name is Cathy Howell, and I'm a nurse. May I have a look at your leg?" she said as she knelt beside him.

"Miss Howell, ma'am, I fear I am beyond help now but you are welcome to do so," replied the handsome officer whose voice was surprisingly deep with only a trace of a Southern accent.

"I'm told you refused to have a surgeon."

"Ma'am, if I am to die, I want to die whole." The response was firm, flat, and devoid of emotion. "I have made my peace with God. It's in His hands now."

"I'd still like to look at the wound."

"It's not a sight for a lady."

"I'm made of sterner stuff, Lieutenant, and I'm a nurse, not necessarily a lady," Cathy replied gently with a smile. "Let me be the judge of this."

"As you will, ma'am," he said. He lay back and closed his eyes.

Cathy carefully soaked the unwrapped the bandage with warm water, and slowly drew it off. She then lifted and turned his lower leg. What she saw made her draw a sharp breath. The man opened his eyes to look at her; he saw she was meeting his gaze steadily.

"Sir, if you are willing to put up with some very sharp pain, I may be able to help you survive this with your leg intact. Whatever hit you is still in the wound, and it seems to be festering. I do warn you, however, that this it will not be pleasant." Cathy sat back on her legs. "Do you have a family?"

"No, ma'am. I had a wife and two children, but they died this past spring during an outbreak of the fever while I was gone."

"Lieutenant, if you have truly given up on life, nothing and no one can help you. I'm willing to try, but," she said, looking him square in the eye, "I won't touch this if you won't meet me halfway."

"Miss Howell, I loved my family – they were my life - but now I don't have much to go home to. If I survive the wound, I will be taken as a prisoner of war. I don't want to go through that."

"As someone trained to help heal the sick and injured I feel I should argue with you," Cathy stated simply.

"Ma'am, I'm not afraid to die," he said sincerely. "My preacher taught me to believe that when I do pass from life, I will be reunited with my family. Death will come as my friend."

"Sir, I will honor your convictions, and abide your decision. Miss Martha?"

"I'm right here." Her voice came from behind Cathy.

"Will you get me some strips of sheeting so I can re-bandage this man's wound?"

"You're going to leave it as it is?"

"I am going to respect his wishes," Cathy said.

"Ma'am, I thank you with all my heart." The lieutenant smiled.

"Sir, I bow to your beliefs," Cathy told him as she wrapped clean linen around his leg. "May God take you with as little pain as possible."

"God bless you, ma'am." He reached out his hand, and when she took it, he raised it to his lips. Letting go, he lay back and closed his eyes. "May He keep you and yours safe."

Cathy found herself shaking as she got to her feet. "Before I go on, may I have a cup of tea?"

"Certainly," Martha said quietly.

As Martha made tea, Mary asked why she didn't argue more with the man.

"Do not imagine that it was easy for me. That may well have been the most difficult decision I have ever made as a healer. It is hard for me to stand back and do nothing - very hard. I had a procedure in mind, but the man had already decided to die. I was being honest when I said that nothing and no one could help him if that was truly his desire." Cathy blinked back tears. "With no family left, and facing a prison camp, he is putting his faith in God that he will be reunited with his wife and children. I cannot and shall not argue with him."

"So sad."

"Yes, and a waste of a fine gentleman, but he's being realistic and I must honor his wishes." Cathy took a deep breath and changed the subject. "Mary, you and Miss Martha have done a remarkable job here. From what I have seen – and I will make rounds - All those men are clean, with clean bandages." Cathy stretched using her favorite posture of shaking hands behind her back. "The biggest secret to controlling wound recovery is to keep everything as clean as possible. Once foreign objects are removed from a wound, they will heal by themselves if given a chance. Infections are the enemy, and cleanliness is the best weapon." Cathy sighed. "My apologies to you both. I did not mean to start a medical lecture."

"Watching you work is a privilege," Martha said, with Mary nodding. "You knew what to do and what you needed. The first man you tended will recover?"

"Unless I was too late and infection sets in, he should. His will to live is strong, unlike the lieutenant. He has a wife and baby boy, and a job to which he will return." Cathy sighed again. "There are no guarantees. I have to believe that he will recover and, more importantly, I have to make him believe that he will recover. I know I did what I could to give him the chance. Now, are there any other bandages that should be changed?"

"Unfortunately, there always seem to be," Mary said. "These are our last patients, however. For a while, we had men all over the house, but most were taken to the new hospitals yesterday evening."

"Were you attacked during the fighting?"

"Mary dodged bullets to go to the church the first day to help with wounded there."

"When I finally was allowed to come back, I found men all over the house," Mary added. She smiled, almost wickedly. "We did have some fun Friday with a pie that Martha baked."

Cathy looked at Martha. "Truly?"

"I baked a berry pie, and some Confederates were walking by and smelled it and asked for some," Martha related with a broad smile. "I cut two pieces for them, but they insisted that I eat a piece before they would touch it."

"Why? Did they think you had poisoned it?"

"Apparently. When I refused to eat it, they decided that if I wouldn't eat it, they wouldn't eat it." Martha grinned. "I protested, but they didn't seem to trust me."

"It was delicious pie," Mary added, also grinning. "We served it to the men here."

"Johnny is going to love that," Cathy said, chuckling. "Let's get back to work."

The three women spent the next hour changing bandages, helping with letters, and seeing that the men in the house had water and something to eat for lunch. Cathy was able to give the sisters some tips on how to wrap a wound and keep things clean but repeated that overall they were doing a magnificent job. The sisters beamed.

"As much as I would like to stay and help, I need to get back to the cabin," Cathy said reluctantly after they finished feeding the men and John Scott, who did come down for the meal. They were in the kitchen, cleaning up. "I will come back, probably not tomorrow but most assuredly before the week is out. It is going to depend on how Johnny is doing. If he feels he can, I'm certain he will accompany me."

"Of course, we understand. Did you have any trouble getting here?" Martha asked. "There are still stray Confederate men around, mostly deserters."

"I stayed off the roads by using the shortcut, which is still clear. Johnny warned me that there might be some trouble from stray soldiers in the area, so I was careful."

"You brought your carry bag, didn't you? Let me give you some eggs and meat."

"You are wonderful, and eggs will be most welcome. I did remember to bring the crock for molasses, and we would be obliged if you would fill it again. Johnny has become partial to my molasses biscuits."

Mary took it to her large crock and filled it, "I'm happy to do it. I filled my crock at my store the other day." She shuddered at the memory. "Some Confederate soldiers were there helping themselves and were very rude. I thought they were going to physically accost me, but one of our patients made sure I could get safely back inside the house."

"How terrible for you!" Cathy paused. "Mary, Miss Martha, please know you have our thanks for all you have done for us. We don't know how we would have managed without your kindness," she said sincerely. "Oh my goodness! I totally forgot one of the things I was going to ask you."

"We have been busy, you know," Mary said with a smile. "What have you recalled?"

"Would you possibly have some rope or twine I could use as a wash line? I've been using some logs as a drying platform, and a line would be so much easier. I would also like to ask you for some sturdy material I could use as a windbreak for one side of the privy sink John dug for us. He put some canvas around it, but it needs one more panel."

"That will be no trouble at all. I have extra line that I was going to take back to the store, and I think there's a piece of canvas you can have." Mary opened a cabinet and pulled out a coil of clothesline, which she put into the bag with the folded material. "Is there anything else you need?"

"There is one other item we need, however, I suspect we are going to have to make it. Johnny is in dire need of a pair of crutches as he can't bear weight on his wounded leg yet. He can make them with some pieces of wood, a few nails, and a small saw," Cathy related. "The poor man has been in that small bedroom in the cabin since the night he was brought to me, and he would love to be able to get around a bit more. It's been almost a week, and he's getting quite anxious, looking at the same four walls," she said with a sigh.

"Crutches?" Martha pondered for a moment. "Mary, didn't Father use a set of crutches before he passed on? What did we do with them?"

"They should be in the small box room at the top of the stairs." Mary came to the kitchen table with some eggs, carefully nested in cloth in a container, along with a small smoked ham wrapped in paper and some fresh green beans. She took one of the loaves of bread and added it to Cathy's bag as Martha left the room to go up the stairs to find the crutches.

"As usual, I am at a loss for the words with which to thank you both," Cathy began. "Your generosity is always overwhelming, and we owe you so much."

"Nonsense," Mary replied. "Your skill as a healer pays for everything. We are all doing our part to get through this. The Captain served with honor, and you are caring for him, yet you came here and helped these men. We see them as men, regardless of on which side of the battle they fought."

"They are all Americans, which is why we are fighting," Cathy said softly.

"Precisely."

There was a clatter on the stairs. Alarmed, both women ran to the foot of the stairway.

"I found the crutches," Martha said wryly as she bent to pick them up from where they had fallen. "I didn't mean to alarm you – I simply lost my grip on them."

"As long as you didn't fall with them, that's fine." Cathy was amazed to see that they really resembled the older wooden ones she was used to seeing. She took the two awkward crutches with a big smile. "Johnny will be so pleased - now all he has to do is build a bench so he can sit outside while I plant my vegetable garden."

"A vegetable garden? Will you be able to grow anything planting this late in the season?" asked Martha. "We are already picking green beans."

"I sincerely hope so, and I do have seeds with me." Cathy smiled. "My grandmother has a green thumb. I may not have in-herited it, but I learned gardening from her. I turned soil on Friday. Johnny will probably send me back to town for the wood and supplies he'll need to build a bench – he showed me his de-sign this morning. He believes he needs to do something useful now that he can't get around well, but I think he wants to super-vise while I work so he can pick on me when I miss a weed!"

The three ladies laughed.

"He designed a bench?" Mary asked. "I didn't realize that he designed furniture."

"He's a civil engineer, more accustomed to designing things like bridges, so it was probably child's play for him. He also did a sketch for a set of crutches and told me that I could build them." Cathy made a face at the thought. "I cannot tell you how happy I am that you have a pair we can borrow! The bench is on his list of things to make, along with some side tables for the bed-room."

"Can you manage all of this on your walk home?" Martha asked, eyeing the now-filled bag and the crutches.

"I shouldn't have too much difficulty," Cathy said as she put one arm through the top opening of the crutches and picked up the carry bag. "I will take my time, I promise."

Mary insisted on accompanying her to a home a few doors down the street, where Cathy picked up a real treat. It was going to take her a while longer to get back to the cabin but would be worth every step.

*****

John checked his watch – for the fourth time – and sighed. It was three-thirty, and there was still no sign of Cathy's return. He had spent his day alternately napping, practicing moving from the bed to the chair, and reading. He even managed to get dressed. However, by two o'clock, he was getting concerned, and by three he was getting downright worried by her absence. He kept imagining all sorts of horrible things that could have happened to her, which didn't help.

He tried reading some more pages of Wolfe and Archie but couldn't get into the plot. He was about to check his watch again when he heard someone outside. His watch said it was close to four o'clock.

"Johnny! I'm back," Cathy called as she opened the cabin door. "And I have a few surprises for you."

"You're okay?"

"Yes, I'm fine. Sorry, I took so long," she said, coming into the bedroom. She raised a crutch in each hand. "Look! The sisters had a pair and send it with their regards and hopes for a fast recovery. These belonged to their father."

"CRUTCHES!" He started to get up, all worry banished.

"Hold on, my boy," she said, laughing at his eagerness. "Have you ever used these things?"

"Uh, no."

"As with most things, it's not as easy as it looks. First, sit on the edge of the bed. It's higher," she explained, "So you won't have to lift up into them as you would in a chair, which will be easier until you get used to them."

"Okay." He took them, and placed them under his arms, looking up for approval. "Yes?"

"Yes. Now, carefully, stand up on your good leg and get the feel for balance." She waited while he did so. "I know you want to tear off across the room swinging both at the same time, but first try one at a time and hopping. You can't bend your knee much – remember it's going to drag a bit. Take SMALL steps." She watched as he struggled to control all four 'feet.' "You'll get the hang of it – you're coordinated enough. Just give it time and don't fall down."

"Yeah," he said, frowning in concentration. "Anything else?"

"Try not to mash your palms on the hand-rests. I don't want to think about dealing with carpal tunnel – keep your wrists as straight as you can. You're lucky – these are about the right height for you."

"Gotcha." He maneuvered across the bedroom, back to the chair, and sat down. "That's work."

"Yep." She smiled. "I'm going to leave you to it while I take care of the supplies I brought back. We have a couple of bonus items from the sisters and a lovely extra from one of their friends."

"Go. I need to learn this."

Cathy put things away in the cabin and took most of the eggs and the surprise bonus out to the cooler pail. As she came back towards the cabin, she saw John in the doorway. He was wearing the grin of a conquering hero, obviously very pleased with himself.

"Well look at you! Dressed and outside!" She applauded his efforts. "Let me get the chairs moved to the kitchen and you can watch me figure out what we're going to have for supper."

"I had my food bar at one," he said.

"You got dressed. How did you get to the clothes?"

"I moved the chairs until I could get to the dresser. I figured I should be dressed in case Miss Mary came back with you." John looked at her. "So what have you been up to?"

"At the risk of screwing up the timeline, I spent most of the day being a doctor." Cathy related her activities briefly as she made them a cup of tea. "I know I may have altered a few minor things, but I couldn't sit and do nothing. The young soldier I helped may still die – I improved his chances only with what was at hand. The men in the house are so grateful for any help – it's really touching."

"Catie, I knew that something like that was bound to happen." John shook his head. "It must have been hard to back away from that officer. What were you going to do?"

"Bandaging that leg without doing anything was one of the hardest decisions I've ever made," she admitted. "I was going to remove the bullet - or whatever - that was still in his leg. It was at the back of his calf and would have been easy to extract after I made a small incision. Then I was going to ask Miss Martha for a small knitting needle."

"A knitting needle? What for?"

"After it was boiled, I would have wrapped a whiskey-soaked cloth around it and inserted it into the wound to cleanse it the way I did the other one."

"I'm proud of you – you did what you thought was right in both cases and, more than that, you stayed within period tools. A knitting needle and whiskey! Good heavens." John smiled at his best friend. "I noticed you didn't get their full names."

"I did that deliberately. I decided I didn't want to know for fear of complications."

"Good thinking." John shifted his leg. "Can I put the crutch under my rear and use it to prop my leg up?"

"Cripes, are you an engineer or what? Yes, it's one of the tricks of the PT trade."

"Now, what's for dinner?"

"Be prepared for a feast!"

John watched as Cathy took some eggs, chopped some ham and shaved some cheese, putting them all together in omelets while she boiled some of the green beans. She served it all with slices of Martha's wonderful bread. She made tea but didn't place the mugs on the table.

"I have one more really great surprise," she said, taking an extra cup outside.

Utterly perplexed, John could only wait for her to return. She came back in and put the third cup on the table. John picked it up and looked.

"MILK!!!"

"Yep. And I want some in my hot tea – I've really missed it." She put the tea mugs on the table.

"Where did you get milk?"

"A friend of Mary's has a cow, and she insisted that I take some with me. It was a major juggling act to get it all home, but worth every bit of trouble. I snuck a bit into the omelets, too.

They ate slowly, savoring each bite and sip. During their dinner, Cathy related the story of the berry pie to John, who – as predicted – loved the way the sisters had out-foxed the two Confederates.

As Cathy cleaned the dishes, John realized how much work she had been doing.

"Catie, that was amazing," he started, "But I don't think I appreciated how much you have had to do because I haven't seen it until now. I never fully considered that every bit of water has to be brought in and dumped after using it. The same with wood and ashes from the stove."

"Mom's philosophy of doing what needs to be done first, then figure out what has to be done next has been a big help," she admitted. "There have been a few times I would have felt totally overwhelmed if I hadn't stuck to that. I also freely concede that there have been times in the past week when I would have killed for an assistant."

John yawed and frowned. "I'm whacked."

"Go back to bed, soldier boy. You've had a long and busy day – and you should sleep very well after all the exercise you got. I'll be there in a few."

As John made his way on the crutches, Cathy went to the spring to draw more water for the night. Darkness wasn't far off, and she preferred to see where she was going. They ended the evening with Cathy reading aloud until John couldn't stay awake.

"Good night, Johnny. You're doing really well, and from now on, your recovery should be downhill."

Her answer was a soft snore, which made her smile. She hummed Joyce's song and reflected on her decision to let the Confederate lieutenant's wound alone. The ones you walk away from are the hardest, she knew, but she also knew that as a doctor, once a decision was made, she couldn't second guess herself. Sleep was slow in coming, but it did finally arrive.

CHAPTER TWELVE

Tuesday, 7 July 1863

John woke up with a grin – he knew he could move around now with the crutches. He was starting to get out of bed when he realized that if he did, he'd step on Cathy. *Nope, not a good idea – it would be a horrible way to repay her for everything she's doing for me.*

"Good morning," she said from the floor. "Please remember I'm down here before you step on me."

"Uh, that thought just crossed my mind."

Cathy sat up and faced him. "If you're going to be mobile, I need to rethink where I sleep. First, let me roll this up and get out of your way. You can do almost as much as you want to – just bear in mind that if you tear the wound open doing something stupid, I have promised to stitch you up without a local." She grinned, grabbed some clothes, and left the room.

He pulled the crutches to him and maneuvered to the dresser where she had put the jar. He felt ridiculously proud of himself after he used it and got dressed. He couldn't quite figure out how to take the jar to the other room, so he left it on the dresser, and made his way to the table.

Cathy was busy making something – biscuits, he guessed – but turned to watch him thump across the room.

"I knew you'd get the hang of it. Maybe later we can take a walk outside," Cathy said, smiling. "Johnny, be warned. You're still going to get tired easily and you're still going to need naps."

"Okay, okay," he said. He was smiling broadly at the thought of leaving the cabin. "What are the plans for the day?"

"I think my priority will be to start planting the garden."

"If you put a chair outside, I'll watch. But first, I'm hungry."

Breakfast – eggs and biscuits with some ham – was soon ready, and once cleaned up, Cathy took care of some housekeeping details before preparing for gardening. She was wearing her 'young boy' clothes – she was not about to mess up a skirt kneeling in dirt – and put the seed packets she was going to use on a plate with the sketch of the plot. Chair and plate went outside near the plot she had turned.

"Okay, I'm ready for you," she said, coming back in. "The ground is nowhere near level, and there are lots of things to trip over, so for heaven's sake take it slow. I'm going to spot you until I'm sure you are okay."

John opened his mouth to protest, realizing just in time that she was being sensible, and closed it.

Cathy, knowing what he had been about to say, laughed. "Very commendable restraint. Now, let's go."

John carefully picked his way across the yard. She was right about taking it slow. The ground was not even, there were branches and roots everywhere, and it would be easy to fall. He made it to the chair and gratefully sat. Only then did he look around.

The cabin sat at the edge of a true wood, and there was just enough clear land to afford them the yard. Cathy had chosen the garden area for maximum sun exposure while staying reasonably close to the primary stream they used for water. The sink he had dug was off to one side of the clearing, away from the stream. Cathy had added a canvas panel to the ones he had put up, so there was more of a windbreak. From where he sat, he could see the area behind the cabin.

"The extra panel around the sink looks good," he said, "But what are the rocks behind the cabin?"

"That's how I marked the spring." Cathy knelt on the ground and smiled up at him. "How does it feel to be outside?"

"Amazing. It's a beautiful day, and this is so peaceful," he began. "It's just plain great." He took a deep breath. "Clean air, too."

"The air in town is starting to stink," Cathy told him. She put the sketch on a rock and anchored it with some small stones. "It wasn't too bad, but I suspect the rain had something to do with that." She carefully opened a packet of seeds and poured about ten into her hand.

"Those look like beans," John observed.

"Yep – green bean seeds. They should grow quickly, too. This is rich soil, and moist." She planted them between two of her marker sticks. "I'm doing what Gran calls staggered planting, starting a few at a time, so we can harvest for a while, rather than have it all come in at the same time."

"Makes sense." He watched as she folded the first packet closed and opened a second one. "What's that?"

"Cucumbers." She planted eight seeds in a mound of dirt.

"You didn't do a row."

"Cukes are grown in a hill. The plants develop vines, so you start them in what amounts to a clump. It makes it easier to water them."

"Oh. What's next?" he asked as she closed that packet.

"Corn." She opened the packet and held a few out for his inspection. "I'm doing short rows, and I'll do two plantings, not as many as I'm using for the green beans. Corn should be planted in two rows so they pollinate each other."

"Wow – you really have a handle on this," he said, impressed. "Your gran would be proud."

"I hope so," she said, standing up and brushing her hands together.

"What's left?"

"Spinach, radishes, a lettuce mix, and kohlrabi. I'm going to do the spinach and radishes first. These are the long shots – they are generally cool weather plants, and this may not work. But if it does, we'll get fresh spinach and radishes for salads. You need the iron." She shook some tiny seeds out onto her palm. "There they are."

She planted two rows at the edge of the garden, one for spinach and one for radishes, where it might not be as hot. "I'm counting on the idea that the nights get cool. I'm not using all the seeds, as I may be able to plant more in late August." Cathy opened the lettuce mix seeds and did a row next to the spinach. "Same thing," she said, anticipating his question.

"Okay, what's kohlrabi?"

"It's a root-looking bulb vegetable that sort of tastes like cabbage," she said. "It can be eaten raw or cooked. It's one of Gran's favorites. She cuts them up and dips the pieces in salad dressing." Cathy got the seeds into the ground.

"What about the Brussel sprouts?"

"You don't like them."

"Plant them anyway."

"Okay." Cathy ran back to the cabin, returning in a minute with another seed packet. She checked her chart and put a short row of seeds in. "There. That's it for now. I want to make a small trench by each row so I can water without risking washing the seeds out, and I'll be finished for the day."

"I think I'll try using the sink." He grinned. "If I do that, you won't have to clean out the chamber pot."

"Thank heavens. Doing it reminded me of the days I worked at the hospital as an aide the summer before I went to college." Cathy watched his progress to the sink. She started her trenching, wishing she had a hoe and was finished with the corn trench when she realized he was going to need a cloth.

"Catie?"

"Coming right up," she answered. She dashed into the cabin and returned by way of the stream. "Here," she said, thrusting the wet cloth into the enclosed sink. "I'll put a short stack of cloths under a rock in there, now that you're using it."

"Good idea," John said as he emerged with a sheepish grin. "It's dumb, but I can tell you that I feel tons better now that I can do more things for myself."

"Understandable. Please remember that it will take you time to get out here," she commented as she walked with him back to the cabin. "You can't rush it. In an 'uh-oh, I have to go fast' moment, use the pot."

"Yeah, that makes sense."

"Why don't you lie down for a bit while I finish this?"

"I think I will," he said, disappearing inside.

Cathy made her trenches and used the bucket to pour water into them. Gathering up her seed packets and chart, she took a look at her garden. *It's a good start - hope it works.* She headed back in.

John was napping, so she didn't disturb him by changing clothes. She got the clothesline Mary had given her and took it outside to create her drying line.

At the edge of the clearing, she found two trees about ten feet apart, and each one had a perfect branch going almost straight up onto which she tied the ends. Mary, generous as usual, had also given her a handful of clothespins. Cathy went back into the cabin and got a stack of the cloth squares she had been using as surgery sponges and put them on a log inside the privy canvas, anchoring them with a small rock. She scooped a small hole to use as the receptacle for used squares and lined it with a square, hoping he'd spot it and figure it out.

Back inside, Cathy made herself a cup of tea, and sat at the table, contemplating that they really had what was necessary for a prolonged stay. Shelter, water, food, a potential food source, and some wonderful friends – life was quiet, and she felt oddly relaxed. It was constant work, but she knew that John was going to be okay and as he got better, he'd help. The big question was still the 'why' of their situation.

"Catie?" John called from the bedroom.

"Hi," she said, going in. She handed him a cup of water. "How are you doing?"

"Fine. I didn't mean to nap."

"I told you – you're going to get tired easily and you still need naps. No big deal."

"Yeah, but it feels so good to be able to do something again."

Cathy had to laugh at the little boy expression on his face. "Johnny, you are going to have to be patient. We're in good shape here, and just think: no commuter traffic, no publish or perish pressure, and no kids asking if this part of your lecture will be on the exam."

John laughed and shook his head. "You are absolutely right."

"I've been wondering if there is a way I can rinse out your uniform pants. They're wool, correct?"

"Yeah, and normally I have them dry cleaned, but it's not around yet."

"The next time I go into town, I'll see if Miss Martha has any ideas for them. Meanwhile, I guess I can sew the seam I cut."

"Catie, you mentioned you might put a cast on my leg. Are you still going to do that?"

"Probably, but not immediately. Let me guess: you want to walk into Gettysburg and take a look around."

"Damn, you really do know me," he stated wryly. "I confess: yes. We are living in the middle of what we know as history, and I want to take advantage of it."

"I would like to point out that you were severely injured less than a week ago – it will only be a full week tomorrow. Can you give it a few more days?"

"I suppose so," he said, looking downcast. "If I have to."

"You have to." Cathy regarded him and relented. "Tell you what. After lunch, let's take a walk and see how you do. It's going to take you about twice as long to walk into town, and you need to work up to it."

"Okay," he brightened a bit. "I guess I do need to build up to it."

"In the meantime, if you think you can manage it, later I'll put a chair outside. If I bring you logs, can you get enough leverage to swing the ax to chop wood? We've got logs, but some are too big for the stove."

"I can try," he said, thinking about it. "Maybe I can work out a system for doing it where I won't hurt myself."

"While you ponder that, can we play a game of cribbage? We didn't play yesterday, and it felt sort of strange."

"Sure, get the board," he said with a grin. "Can we play on the table?"

"All you have to do is get there," she said, laughing as she went ahead of him.

Cathy had the board set up by the time John got to the table. She also had a sturdy log placed by his chair so he could put his leg up.

"I'm not going to let you win this one," John said, dealing.

Cathy did, however not by much. John won the second and third games, again not by much.

"Let me know when you want me to teach you how to play poker," he commented as he replaced the pegs in the board's compartment. "You're ready. Your thinking process is getting more devious."

"Praise from a master of the art," Cathy said with a toss of her head. "I've made it to the big-time."

John laughed with her and asked about lunch.

"Coming up."

She served bread, hard sausage, and food bars, and chuckled when he wrinkled his nose. "Don't worry – supper will be real food."

Placated, he ate the food bar first and savored the sausage and bread. Then he picked up his crutches.

"Got to take a short trip."

"I'll meet you outside by the woodpile after I wash and put these things away," she said as she nodded. "I did put some cloth squares out there, by the way."

Cathy got outside in time to see John work his way to the chair she had at the woodshed. He sat. She handed him the ax and put a log on the ground in front of him.

"Put it end up. Can you brace it with a couple of logs so it doesn't fall over when I hit it?"

Cathy did as he requested and stood back. He swung the ax and it stuck in the log.

"Hmmm. I need to change angles. When I stand up offset the chair just to the side of the log – it will give me more room to swing."

Once she had done that, John freed the ax and tried again. This time, the log split.

"Bravo!" Cathy clapped. She put the larger piece between the stabilizing logs and told him to do it again.

Twenty minutes later, Cathy had a pile of split wood that would easily go into the stove and John felt as if he was finally contributing to their survival.

"Back inside – you should rest, in bed," she ordered, picking up the pieces. She noted that John didn't argue – for once – and that his arms seemed a bit tired as he lifted the crutches. It would pass, she knew, and she also knew he was pleased with his efforts. It took her two trips to take the wood inside and stacked next to the stove.

Once she had it all in, she took a cup of water into the bedroom. John was sitting on the edge of the bed, slowly rotating his right shoulder.

"It's a bit sore."

"You're doing the right thing. Keep it limber. Between the crutches and the ax, it got more exercise than normal."

"That's what I figured." He swiveled and lifted his bandaged leg onto the bed. "I tried doing that yesterday without lifting it by hand, so to speak. And it hurt like hell."

"As I said, pain is one of the great clues of life. You used the injured muscle, and it let you know. It will improve with time."

"I think I'll close my eyes."

"I think I'll read," she said, picking up the Stout volume. "Yell if you need something."

*****

An hour and a half later, Cathy was deep into the plotline when John called out, "Ready or not, here I come." She put the book down and waited by the open door, having a good guess as to what he was going to do. She chuckled as he went by her with "Thanks!"

John was on his way back to the cabin from the privy when she joined him outside.

"Ready for your walk?"

John's grin was her answer.

They strolled along the pathway towards town and John kept insisting he wanted to keep going. Cathy, who now knew the route well, stopped about half-way. There was a fallen log, and she suggested he sit for a few minutes.

"This is about the half-way point," she said. "I timed it yesterday, and I used the log when I was juggling everything on the way back."

"Dead-on spot for it," John agreed. "Do we have to go back?"

"I think so, don't you? This is pushing things quite a bit, you know." Cathy sat next to him. "It's work."

"No arguments."

"You'll probably be able to make town by the end of the week," she encouraged. "Remember that however far you walk out, you have to walk an equal distance back. That's the tricky part to bear in mind."

"Yeah, there are no cars or cabs to call."

"Nope, not even 911."

"Okay," John said, getting to his feet. "Back to the cabin."

By the time they reached it, John was tired. He made it but admitted that he had probably overdone it.

"Please don't say 'I told you so'," he asked.

"Johnny, you had to find your own limits, and this won't be the last time," Cathy told him gently. "Get changed, and back into bed. I'll bring you water and acetaminophen."

"Thanks." He trudged off to the bedroom and was lying down when she came in. Obediently, he took the pill, drank the water, and was asleep almost before she left the room.

John woke up to see it was dusk and realized he had slept for two hours. He reached for the crutches and got out of bed. He knew he had pushed way too hard during the day, but he wanted to make sure he could still get around. He got to the main room and sat down under Cathy's watchful eye.

"Do you want to go outside and use the privy or shall I get you the jar?"

"Is it okay for me to go outside?"

"As long as you can see what you are doing, yes, but I would plan on making this the last trip. It's going to be dark shortly." Cathy smiled as John took a deep breath and stood up. "If you're not back inside in, say, fifteen minutes, I'll come looking for you," she teased.

"Fair enough."

Cathy was working on supper when he came back in and sat down again.

"You look beat – would you like supper on the tray?"

"Yeah – I think so." He thumped his way back to the bedroom, and yelled, "Made it!"

"Good," she yelled back. "I'll be in shortly."

True to her word, Cathy brought the tray within twenty minutes and did her "Ta-da" with the towel. John saw real food – meat, vegetables, and bread.

"Looks good," he said, and a moment or two later added, "Tastes good, too."

After supper, Cathy cleared up and suggested reading.

"You're going to fall asleep early, but you probably should try to stay awake for at least another hour," she pointed out, "So you can sleep through the night."

"I'd rather play cards. Speaking of sleep, where are you going to do it? You can come back to the bed, you know."

"I think I'll move to the floor on the other side from where I have been until I'm sure it will be okay to move back to the bed. This way, if you want to get up you won't step on me, and I won't bother you. Can you handle a game of gin?"

Cathy let him deal the cards, and he won. Second game was hers, and so was the third one. Putting the cards away, she took the Christie anthology and opened it to a new story. As predicted, John started nodding off early, around eight-thirty but forced himself to stay awake until nine.

"Pills, jar, and sleep," she said, helping him as little as possible. "You'll be ready to do more tomorrow."

"Promise? I was afraid I set myself back."

"Probably not," she replied. "I think you simply wore your-self out, and you'll rebound nicely. The fact that you regularly exercise and take care of yourself, in general, is going to weigh in your favor. I would, however, like to check the bandages."

"Dressing change?" he asked warily.

"Nope – I want to take the elastic bandage off and make sure the suture line isn't oozing too badly. You don't have to do a thing."

Cathy was pleased to see the outer bandages were clean, so no damage had been done other than his fatigue. She rewrapped his leg and told him he was fine.

"Is there some way to tell if I'm bleeding?"

"It would probably feel like a burning, itchy sensation. Plain old itching will show up – it's one of the signs of healing – but a burning sensation or burning itch is not a good thing."

"Gotcha." John yawned. "I know I pushed, but I've got to say it felt great to get out of here for a while."

"I understand, I really do. I'm going to sit and read before I come in, but I'll set the bedroll out now so I don't disturb you."

"Frankly, Catie, I don't think anything short of a cannon bar-rage would disturb me," he mumbled as he snuggled down in the covers. "And maybe not even that…"

When she came in for the night, John was sleeping as soundly as he had predicted. She smiled as she got ready for her night's rest. John Buford had been saved, Johnny had survived the battle, and they had what they needed to wait out John's recovery. She slept soundly, confident that when the time was right – and John was healed completely – they would come full circle.

Epilogue:

One: They complement each other amazingly well.

Two: The teaming is wonderfully matched.

Three: They have done remarkably well for a first outing.

Two: Then this task is complete.

Three: We could pull them into Time and let his wounds heal before restoring them to their places.

One: There is another task of this period for which they may be suited.

Two: Yes.

Three: It will be an excellent final test for them.

One: We leave them in place. Are we agreed?

One, Two, and Three, in unison: Yes.

ABOUT THE AUTHORS

Aubrey Stephens is a retired teacher from Mississippi. He has Masters degrees in both theater and history, with certification in English, science, and special education. He is also a marine veteran and former military officer. The rumor that he has attempted to blow up the earth is just that a rumor, though he was on combat missile crew alert when the NORAD mistakes that caused a false report to believed that there were Soviet inbound missiles headed for the U.S. He is a trained martial artist with a second-degree black belt in karate, brown belt in judo, and brown belt in Kendo. He also studied and taught European fencing for over 45 years. His hobbies include recreating the Middle Ages and the American Civil War. He is squired to one of the S.C.A.'s most well-known knights and at this time holds the rank of Captain in Co. A – 2nd Mississippi Cavalry (Union and Confederate.) He has acted, written, directed, and done set design and construction for over 200 theatrical shows. He has written several articles on the history of the War Between the States for regional magazines. Since his retirement from teaching he has edited for Pro Se Productions and is now its Executive Editor. He has had published several stories and books. An anthology he created and edited, *Tales of the Interstellar Bartenders Guild*, won the 2019 Pulp Factory Award for Best Anthology. He is currently working on two alternate history novels, one a different WWII ending and the other a terrifying day in the cold war of 1968.

A native of Manhattan, New York, Dale Kesterson is a writer, editor, actress, singer, and character voice artist who has been creating stories and putting them on paper since the age of seven; she wrote, produced, and acted in her first play at age twelve. Life, however, kept her busy majoring in science in college, teaching math and science, studying nursing, and managing a small home business with her husband. Her first s/f short story appeared in the award-winning anthology, *Tales of the Interstellar Bartenders Guild,* edited by her Time Guards co-author Aubrey Stephens. An avid Star Trek fan, she founded a Trek club and a convention, one highlight of which was performing onstage with the late Grace Lee Whitney (Janice Rand, ST:TOS). Besides writing and editing, Dale performs in community theater productions, everything from singing as Cinderella's Stepmother in *Into the Woods* to a variety of character roles most of which required accents. A seasoned traveler and professional photographer who has lived in six widely diverse locations, Dale settled down with her husband, their hairless cats, and box turtle in the middle of nowhere in a town so small it doesn't even have a red-yellow-green traffic light. If she's not busy writing, editing, or performing, she does handcrafts – she hates being bored!